PARTISAN

Recent Titles by Alan Savage from Severn House

THE COMMANDO SERIES

COMMANDO
THE CAUSE
THE TIGER

THE SWORD SERIES

THE SWORD AND THE SCALPEL
THE SWORD AND THE JUNGLE
THE SWORD AND THE PRISON
STOP ROMMEL!
THE AFRIKA KORPS

PARTISAN

Alan Savage

This first world edition published in Great Britain 2001 by
SEVERN HOUSE PUBLISHERS LTD of
9–15 High Street, Sutton, Surrey SM1 1DF.
This first world edition published in the USA 2002 by
SEVERN HOUSE PUBLISHERS INC of
595 Madison Avenue, New York, N.Y. 10022.

British Library Cataloguing in Publication Data

Savage, Alan
  Partisan
  1. War stories
  I. Title
  823.9'14 [F]

ISBN 0-7278-5755-X

Typeset by Palimpsest Book Production Ltd.,
Polmont, Stirlingshire, Scotland.
Printed and bound in Great Britain by
MPG Books Ltd., Bodmin, Cornwall.

For the Angel of Death spread his wings on the blast . . .

Lord Byron

PART ONE

BLITZKRIEG

There is no trusting appearances.
Richard Brinsley Sheridan

Chapter One

Crisis

'It is perfectly true,' Colonel Brooke-Walters said. 'There has been a *coup d'état*. The government of Prince Paul has fallen, and King Peter is now head of state. Obviously no one can expect a seventeen-year-old boy actually to rule, but we may take it as read that Yugoslavia is now in the Allied camp.'

He paused to survey the three young men standing before his desk. They looked excited and enthusiastic, as he would have expected; for too long the British embassy in Belgrade, with all its attendant attachés and secretaries, had had to suffer an inferior status with regard to the power of Nazi Germany. Over the previous year of 1940 things had only got worse – the Wehrmacht had bundled the British Expeditionary Force out of Europe and driven the French armies, and indeed the French nation, to surrender. The dismissal of the pro-German regent of Yugoslavia had to be a good thing, but . . .

'Will Yugoslavia now come into the war, sir? On our side?' asked Major Leighton.

'That is certainly a possibility.'

'Will Hitler accept that, sir?' Captain Johnstone asked.

'The ambassador considers that he will not. In fact, that he dare not. The Italian army is in a mess after the drubbing they have just got from the Greeks. If Yugoslavia were to move into Albania, and take them in the rear, Mussolini

3

might well have a catastrophe on his hands. So it looks like a Nazi takeover is on the cards.'

'The Yugoslavs will fight,' Captain Davis said.

And you should know, the colonel thought, surveying his most junior attaché. Tony Davis had only been in Yugoslavia six months, having spent the previous three months recuperating from a wound suffered in Flanders during the disastrous retreat to Dunkirk. Technically an officer in the Buffs, he had been seconded to staff duties because of doubts as to how fit he was for combat; he had been shot in the leg and, although fully recovered, still walked with a slight limp. That he was an asset to the embassy could not be doubted, however. Tall and dark with somewhat saturnine good looks, he had a wicked sense of humour, but also a considerable knowledge of military matters, whether historical or current. He was also one of the few officers to have made himself proficient in Serbo-Croat, and thus had easily found several friends amongst the local population. At least one of these friendships was not regarded with too much favour by either the ambassador or Brooke-Walters himself, but that he had his finger on the local pulse could not be argued.

'Are you thinking of the Serbs, or the Croats?' the colonel asked.

'I would say both, sir.'

'Well, I hope you're right. However, we need to look facts in the face, Tony. The Yugoslav army, even supposing it will pull together, cannot under any circumstances face up to the Wehrmacht.'

Johnstone frowned. 'You think Jerry may actually invade, sir?'

'I would say it is very likely.'

'But . . . with all his other commitments—' Leighton said.

'He has no other commitments, at the moment. Europe is entirely his, save for places like Spain, which is benevolently neutral, and the Soviet Union, which is virtually an ally.'

'Well,' Tony Davis said, 'if Yugoslavia is going to fight, presumably we shall be helping her.'

'There is not the slightest chance of that,' Brooke-Walters said.

Tony was dismayed. 'But . . . we already have troops in Greece—'

'Which could ill be spared. Every other man, every other gun, every other tank we possess is committed, either to the defence of Egypt or the defence of Great Britain itself. But even if we had the men, there is no way we could get them here. Italy controls the Adriatic and Albania and is already at war with the Greeks, and Bulgaria is pro-Axis. No, I'm afraid the Yugoslavs are going to have to do what they can on their own.'

'That is outrageous,' Tony declared.

'It is one of those unfortunate concomitants of warfare,' Brooke-Walters reminded him. 'Now, we have two things to do. The first is prepare to close down the embassy and evacuate at the first sign of a German invasion.'

'Evacuate?' Tony was even more outraged.

'I'm afraid so. It's not going to be easy. We will ask for diplomatic passports from both the Yugoslav government and the German embassy, but the way out will still lie through Bulgaria, which, as I have said, is an Axis satellite. It is assumed that we have some time; there is certain to be a good deal of diplomatic activity before anything happens. So it's not yet a matter of burning files in the courtyard. But we must be prepared. We also need to find out as much as possible about what is going to happen. I'm making this your province, Tony. See what you can learn from your friends. Especially that German chap. What we need more than anything else is some kind of timescale. We also need to know some more about the possible Yugoslav reaction to any German aggression. You will not, of course, let on as to anything we have discussed here today, or may discuss in the future. Thank you, gentlemen. You have a lot to do.'

5

The three officers saluted and left the office.

'Now there's a turn-up for the book,' Leighton said. Shorter than his two companions, and inclined to rotundity, he was invariably ebullient. 'I have to say, it'll be a treat to see some action.'

'What action?' Tony asked bitterly. 'All we are going to do is scuttle away with our tails between our legs.'

'With the idea of coming back one day,' Johnstone suggested. A heavily built Scot, with bushy eyebrows, he was the closest thing to a friend Tony possessed amongst the embassy staff. But even he would admit that he did not know the newcomer very well.

'One day.' Tony commented. 'After the Nazis have had a go at them.'

'I understand how you feel,' Leighton said. 'But . . . it's not as if you're married to the girl. Or even engaged.'

Tony shot him a look.

'Good lord!' Leighton said. 'You're not, are you?'

'I have had it in mind.'

'Good lord!' Leighton said again and looked at Johnstone, who waggled his eyebrows. If his brother officers might envy Tony Davis for having so rapidly acquired a Yugoslav mistress, they were all well aware that Elena Kostic – the name was pronounced Kostich – was not really the sort of young woman with whom a British officer should have been associating in the first place. 'Does the old man know about this?'

'I haven't discussed it with him, if that's what you mean. Now I don't expect I'll have the opportunity. I don't suppose we could take her with us, when we go?' Tony asked.

'Well . . . that you *would* have to take up with the old man. But I very much doubt he'll agree. We're obviously going to have enough trouble getting ourselves out.'

'She'll survive,' Johnstone said. 'Won't she?'

'I've just been told to find that out,' Tony said.

6

Partisan

* * *

Belgrade was cock-a-hoop. The Yugoslavs had for a long time been technical allies of the French, and since the beginning of the War – now some eighteen months ago – they had, at least verbally, supported the British as well. Yet economically and physically they were firmly in the German orbit. Germany was their principal trading partner, and since the advent of Hitler not yet ten years ago they had lain beneath the shadow of the growing German military might. Thus far the Germans had shown no territorial ambitions south of the Danube, but it was certainly unlikely that the Nazi regime would tolerate a potential enemy in their very own backyard. The signing by Prince Paul of the Tri-Partite Pact with Germany and Italy, granting the Axis powers the right to use Yugoslav territory for the movement of their troops, had been a logical extension of the political situation. Certainly, Tony supposed, no one in Berlin or Rome, or in the corridors of power here in Belgrade itself, could possibly have anticipated such a violent reaction.

Which, if Brooke-Walters was right, was going to provoke an even more violent reaction from the Germans. Yet no one seemed to be worrying much about that. If just about everyone knew and understood the situation, they still did not enjoy having it rammed down their throats, as the government of Prince Paul had been doing for the last couple of years. Would they then fight, Tony wondered, as he had so confidently predicted to Colonel Brooke-Walters?

The street beyond the embassy gates was crowded with people waving flags and blowing bugles, cars blaring their horns. Tony's uniform was instantly recognised, and he was surrounded by people eager to shake his hand or slap him on the back. It was as if they had just won a war, rather than being on the brink of risking one. On the other hand, they reminded him of photographs of the crowds in London, and Paris and Berlin, when war had been declared in 1914 – the year in which he had been born.

7

None of those people had had any idea what they were letting themselves in for; no one had cheered, in either London or Berlin, much less Paris, when war had been declared in 1939. But surely the Yugoslavs, born out of that earlier conflict, could still remember the horrors of the Austrian onslaught?

Tony laughed with the crowd as he made his way through narrow streets towards the bar where he was sure he would find the company he sought. Belgrade had fascinated him from the moment he had arrived, and he thought it always would. Principally this was due to his sense of history. As a soldier he had understood at first sight the White City's – as it had been known to the ancients – strategical significance. Built at the confluence of the Danube with the Sava, it straddled the three routes which would be of enormous importance to any army on the move: from Vienna along the valley of the Danube to the Black Sea, from Belgrade itself along the valley of the Sava to the northern Adriatic, and – possibly the most important of the three – from north-west to south-east, along the valleys of the smaller Morava and Vardar Rivers to the Aegean Sea.

There had been a bridge – built by the Celts – across the Sava ever since the fourth century AD. Since then it had been fought over as often as any city in the world, from its destruction by the Huns in 442 to its initial period as capital of Serbia in 1402. A generation later it had been seized by the Turks, to remain in Muslim hands until the beginning of the nineteenth century, when the Serbs had regained their independence. The generations of Turkish occupation remained evident in the narrow streets and walled houses.

Predictably the bar was more crowded than the streets; even the outside tables were packed, for all that it was only early April and still quite chilly. Elena was not to be seen, but Sandrine was there – with Bernhard. The most unlikely couple in all Belgrade, Tony supposed, and even more so now. Yet, as they appeared to be genuinely fond of each other, it was equally natural that they should seek each other out at such a time.

'Tony!' Sandrine spoke French, as the group usually did amongst themselves, but in her case it was her mother tongue. She was very blonde, as befitted the girlfriend of an Aryan officer, with straight yellow hair which she wore unfashionably long enough to rest on her shoulders. Short and slender, she yet had a full figure, and with her symmetrically clipped features she was a most attractive young woman. Tony considered Bernhard to be a very lucky man. 'You have heard the news!'

Tony nodded, and shook hands with Bernhard. 'What do you make of it?'

'I think it is madness,' the German officer said. And then grinned. 'But I would say that, wouldn't I?'

Equally blond, Bernhard Klostermann was every bit as handsome as Sandrine. Were they ever able to spare the time to have children, Tony supposed they would undoubtedly be beautiful. But over and above his handsome face and his splendid uniform – the blue and silver tunic and breeches, the black boots and the high-peaked cap making such a strong contrast to Tony's somewhat drab khaki, even if Tony wore combat medal ribbons and Bernhard did not as yet even possess an Iron Cross – he had a self-deprecating sense of humour. It was reassuring to think that he could not be the only officer in the German army so blessed.

Now his face was again serious. 'It is a bad business.'

Sandrine Fouquet clung to his arm. 'He is leaving.'

'You've been transferred?' Tony asked.

'I have been recalled. We all have. The entire embassy staff,' Bernhard said.

'So you're breaking off diplomatic relations. Just because of a change in government here?'

'Ah . . . I really have no idea,' Bernhard said, embarrassed at having to lie to his friend.

'And he won't take me with him,' Sandrine complained.

'Well, of course I cannot take you with me,' Bernhard said. 'The moment you set foot on German soil you are an enemy alien. You'd be interned.'

'That is nonsense,' Sandrine said. 'I have a Vichy passport. I am a neutral.'

'Officially. But it could be very bad. You have to leave Yugoslavia. As quickly as you can.'

'Why should I leave Yugoslavia? How can I? I can't give up my job, just like that.'

'Stay here a moment. I need to speak to Tony.' Bernhard grasped Tony's arm and drew him against the wall. 'Can I trust you?'

'I'm not sure you should, old man. We're enemies, remember?'

'Bah! Our governments are enemies. And I suppose if we were ever to meet in battle I would try to kill you, as you would try to kill me.'

'Absolutely.'

'But we can still be friends. Or is that no longer possible?'

'I suppose not,' Tony said doubtfully. In real terms, he and Bernhard had become enemies on 3 September 1939, even though they had not yet met. But he genuinely liked the man. He had thus far found no reason to dislike any German as an individual, and as a professional soldier he could not help but admire the tremendous efficiency and technique, not to mention the élan, of the Wehrmacht. Obviously they had brought death and destruction to a great many innocent people in their drive to conquer Europe, and he found the political ideals of their leaders abhorrent, but then, his parents had felt the same about the Kaiser's lot. In the bizarre situation of a neutral capital, where German and British, and Italian and French, military attachés used the same bars and attended the same cocktail and dinner parties, they were required to preserve the formalities of polite society, but he and Bernhard had taken to each other from the moment of their first meeting. He had dutifully kept his superiors informed, and had been encouraged to see more of the enemy captain, providing he relayed any information he might glean from their conversations. No doubt Bernhard had been operating under similar instructions. Yet Tony had always wondered if Bernhard, with his apparent total lack of political commitment and his French journalist girlfriend, could possibly be a true Nazi. Of course, it was possible that he was merely using Sandrine to obtain any information she might have, but that was difficult to accept unless he was a consummate actor in his obvious affection for the girl. But now . . .

'What are you going to do?' Bernhard asked.

'I would say that depends upon you chaps.'

'You will have to leave.'

'I'll mention it to the ambassador,' Tony said drily. 'I should point out that the mere fact of having changed governments does not mean that Yugoslavia is not still a neutral country.'

'I do not think there is any room for neutrality in this war, Tony.'

'You are saying that Germany intends to invade?'

Bernhard's mouth twisted. 'I am not saying anything. I am recommending that you get out, because you are my friend. But more important, I wish you to take care of Sandrine for me.'

'Me?'

'I can no longer do so. And I love her. You know that, Tony.'

'Well . . . of course I do. But . . . can't you marry her? Then you could take her with you.'

Bernhard's face stiffened. 'That is not possible.'

'Because she's French?'

'Because she is not a German. My superiors have made that quite clear to me.'

'She doesn't seem to understand this.'

'Well, it is not something we have wished to discuss.'

11

'But you knew of it. Don't you think you've been a little dishonest with her?'

'Do you intend to marry Elena?'

'Well, of course I wish to.'

'But your superiors will not let you.'

'Well . . .' Tony flushed, hoist with his own petard. 'I haven't discussed it with them yet. I mean to.'

'I will wish you good fortune. But listen, you must get Sandrine out of the country.'

'How am I supposed to do that? Even supposing she wishes to go? She's a grown woman, Bernhard. And she has a responsible job. As long as *Paris Temps* maintains an office in Belgrade, she will stay.'

'I am asking for your help as a friend. Listen, it is going to be very bad.'

'Should you have told me this?'

'No. But I *am* telling you this. Because we are friends, and because of Sandrine. I do not know what I would do if anything happened to her.'

'Well—'

There was a shout. 'Tony!'

Elena Kostic elbowed her way through the throng towards the two officers, Sandrine following her – it was because of her close friendship with Sandrine that he had met Bernhard in the first place. The two women made the strongest contrast, for where Sandrine was all petite femininity, Elena was very nearly six feet tall, a big, strong young woman with long legs and a full figure. Her face was strong rather than pretty, and was shrouded in a mass of curling black hair. With Elena you got what you saw – good-humoured earthiness glowed from her dark eyes. Tony had liked what he saw from the moment they had been introduced, despite the fact that her earthiness had almost certainly embraced others before him. To his utter delight, she had reciprocated.

Now she threw her arms round him and held him close. 'Isn't it marvellous?'

He kissed her. 'Bernhard doesn't think so.'

'Ha!' she snorted, but she released Tony to kiss the German officer in turn. 'What are you going to do about it?'

'He's been ordered back to Germany,' Sandrine muttered.

Elena raised her eyebrows. 'You are that important? I never knew.'

'I am not the least important,' Bernhard said. 'We are all going. The entire embassy.'

'I see. You no longer wish to know us. Well . . . let us have a last drink together.'

Tony and Bernhard elbowed their way into the crowd round the bar to procure four beers. The German uniform called for some derogatory comment, but they both ignored it, and the fact that Bernhard was both well known to the barman and in the company of a British officer removed any risk of a crisis.

'So tell us, what is going to happen?' Elena asked when they returned. The women had managed to secure a table.

'I wish we knew,' Tony confessed. 'Bernhard is going. I may have to go—'

'You? Why should you go?' Elena's voice was sharp. 'We will need you here.'

'I am staying,' Sandrine said.

'No, Sandrine,' Bernhard said.

'So you will know where to find me when this crisis is over.'

Bernhard had taken off his cap and placed it on the table. Now he scratched his head and looked at Tony.

'I think we're all probably a little hysterical,' Tony said. 'In a day or two things will have settled down.'

'But Bernhard will not be here,' Sandrine pointed out.

'When things have settled down, he will come back.'

Bernhard had been looking more and more embarrassed. Now he finished his drink, stood up and put on his cap. 'I must get back to the embassy.'

'Already?' Sandrine demanded.

'There is a great deal to be done. I would hope to see you all again, in happier times.' He brought his right hand against his shoulder. 'Heil Hitler!'

'Bernhard!' Sandrine wailed.

He checked, bent over her, and kissed her mouth. Then he was gone into the crowd.

'Just like that,' Sandrine said.

'He has a lot on his mind,' Tony suggested.

'I am yesterday's woman to him,' Sandrine muttered. 'When I think—'

Elena squeezed her hand. 'He is a brute.' She glanced at Tony. 'Will you leave me like that?'

'I need to talk to you.'

'Oh. Right.' She looked at Sandrine. 'Will you be all right?'

'I am going to get drunk,' Sandrine announced.

'Oh, shit!' Elena remarked. 'You had better come with us.'

'Ah—' Tony wasn't sure that was what he wanted.

'She won't mind.'

Tony hadn't actually been thinking of sex, at that moment. 'We really need to talk.'

'So? She's my best friend. I'm not leaving her here to get pissed and tossed off by some lout. Or louts.'

'I am never going to get tossed off by any man, ever again,' Sandrine declared.

Looking at her, Tony found it difficult to imagine someone so beautiful, so composed, always so perfectly groomed – unlike Elena, Sandrine's dress was neat, her shoes polished, and there was not a ladder in her stockings – ever being tossed off by anyone, even Bernhard.

'That's because you're not drunk yet,' Elena pointed out. 'Come along. We'll go home. Don't worry, they're probably all out celebrating.'

Elena's parents operated a boarding house some distance

14

away from the city centre. It was an eminently respectable place of overstuffed furniture, chintz curtains and
antimacassars. They had always welcomed Tony – he suspected that they regarded him as a possible future son-in-law,
which was why they permitted him to take liberties with their
daughter – but he was rather glad that Elena was right about
their being out.

He was even more relieved at the absence of Svetovar,
her brother, a young man who always made Tony feel
uncomfortable. This was purely psychological, he knew;
Svetovar gave every indication of the deepest admiration
and respect for a man who had actually been in battle.

But the Kostics were Croats. Tony had only discovered
this after he had met and fallen for Elena. Then he had not
wanted to do anything about it, however his superiors might
have disapproved of the relationship – and those of them that
knew of it disapproved of much more about Elena Kostic than
her nationality. But the fact was symptomatic of the problem
that was Yugoslavia.

The country was the brainchild of President Woodrow
Wilson, in complete disregard of his own often-stated belief
that national boundaries should be determined by national
majorities and desires. Thus Serbia, governed from Belgrade,
had been the hub of the new state, as a reward for her resolute
opposition to Austrian aggression – and again in complete
disregard of the fact that it had been Serbian-inspired plots
that had caused the Great War in the first place. But to
the Serbian heartland had been attached a host of other
nationalities: Croats, Bosnians, Slovenes, Montenegrins, even
Albanians who happened to be living in the province of
Kosovo, each of whom had their own identity and their own
aspirations – and each of whom heartily loathed the Serbs.

The imposition of western-style democracy with its so-
civilised rules was never going to work in a society where
every MP carried his gun with him to parliament – and was
not reluctant to draw it and start shooting at any opposition

member who offended him. The Croatians had always been the least willing to conform, and the reality of the situation had been starkly underlined thirteen years before when King Alexander, having grown weary of the perpetual wrangling in parliament, had abolished that institution and declared his intention of ruling as a dictator. Six years later he was shot and killed while on a visit to France . . . by a Croatian terrorist.

Tony did not suppose for a moment that the Kostics had been even remotely involved, but they were Croatians, and thus regarded with mistrust by the British embassy. And with reason, quite apart from the assassination of the king: it was well known that there was considerable support in Croatia for an Italian annexation of at least their province, with an Italian royal duke as their king. But as the Kostics had chosen to leave Zagreb and live in Belgrade they surely could not subscribe to such disloyalty. What Tony had to find out was how deeply that pro-Italian feeling had taken hold of the country as a whole.

'I will make coffee,' Elena announced, leading them into the kitchen.

'I would prefer to have beer,' Sandrine said, sitting at the kitchen table. 'Or whiskey. I would like a whiskey. Do you have a whiskey?'

'I do not have whiskey,' Elena said. 'Or beer. Coffee is better for you.'

'I have decided what I am going to do,' Sandrine announced. 'I am going to stand outside the German embassy, and when Bernhard comes out, I shall cut my throat before his eyes. That'll teach him.'

Tony gave her an anxious glance as he also sat down. Definitely hysterical, he decided.

But Elena could handle any situation. 'You cannot possibly do that until after lunch,' she said. 'No one commits suicide before lunch. I would have thought you, as a journalist, would know that.'

Sandrine thrust her hands into her hair, disarranging her immaculate coiffure.

Elena busied herself at the stove. 'Did you say something about leaving as well?'

'We've been ordered to prepare to move out,' Tony said, keeping a careful eye on the coffee she was ladling into the percolator; normally the most good-humoured of women, Elena possessed a formidable temper.

But she remained equable for the moment. 'Why?'

'Simply because if we remain here, and the Germans occupy the country, my comrades and I will become prisoners of war.'

'Occupy the country? Just like that? Do you not suppose we would have something to say about that?'

'You mean your army would fight?'

'All of us would fight.'

'Informed opinion holds that you would be destroyed.'

'Ha!' She set the steaming cups in front of them. 'We would make them suffer first. If you really want to die, Sandrine, why do you not wait until the Germans come, then get a gun and shoot a few of them before they shoot you.'

Sandrine slurped her coffee; her hands were shaking and tears were dribbling down her cheeks. Tony had never seen her in such a state – before today he would have found it impossible to *imagine* her in such a state.

'Listen,' he said. 'If I could swing it that you could come with us, would you?'

'Leave my home?' Elena sat beside him.

'My dearest girl, if the Germans come, you might not have a home.'

'I will shoot a few of them first.'

'Elena, I do not want you to die. I want you to live. I want . . . I want to marry you.'

She stroked his cheek. 'You say the sweetest things.'

'Don't you want to be my wife?'

17

'I would love to be your wife, Tony. But you know that is impossible. You are a British officer. One day you will be a general. Probably a sir. How can you be married to a Croatian boarding-house keeper?'

'Well . . .' Her accurate assessment of their situation had embarrassed him.

'So just let us make love. Let us make love now. I feel like it. When I am excited I always wish to make love.'

'In the middle of the morning?'

'What does the time have to do with it, if we feel like it? You English are so regimented. You sleep by the clock, you eat by the clock, you drink by the clock . . . and you make love by the clock. That is absurd.'

'The fact is, I should be getting back to the office.'

'You can go back to the office, afterwards.' She held out her hand, and he took it. Because he did want sex. Not because he was excited or had a sense of looming catastrophe, but because Elena always had this effect on him.

'You stay here,' Elena told Sandrine. 'Make yourself another cup of coffee. If you are hungry, there are biscuits in that tin. Just do not leave the house.'

'Do you not suppose I have an office to go to as well?' Sandrine asked. 'I have a story to write.'

'About contemplating suicide?'

'About the German embassy closing.'

'It can keep. It won't be a scoop. Everyone in Belgrade will know by now that the German embassy is closing. We won't be long.'

Still holding Tony's hand, Elena led him up the stairs and into her bedroom. He had been here before, of course, but always at night and after several glasses of wine. In the middle of the morning, with the curtains drawn back and the room filled with light, and with his every sense totally alert, he understood that this was going to be either the experience of his life or a total disaster. If only there weren't so many things preying on his mind.

'Will she be all right?'

'If you mean, will she stay here until we go down, yes she will. She does not really wish to do anything, at the moment. As for when she gets over the shock of Bernhard's running out on her, I should think she will be very angry. And I agree with her.'

Elena kicked off her shoes and lifted her skirt over her head. She wore a vest and knickers – which were rapidly thrown on the floor – but no brassiere. Her breasts were things to dream about, but then so were her legs, long and strong and powerful. No doubt one day she would become overweight and sagging, but at twenty-four years old she was serious competition for any statue of Venus.

She lay on the bed. 'Don't you want me?'

Tony undressed as quickly as he could, remembering that his uniform would have to be worn back to the office and could not be carelessly thrown on the floor. Then he was in her arms, and her hand went down to hold him. 'You are going to need re-training,' she said.

'And you are impatient,' he pointed out, nuzzling her breasts, which had the required effect.

'You will still have to come in the front door,' she said. 'You will not make the back.'

Which she preferred.

He was surprised, and relieved, that he had been able to make it at all. And the moment he had, thoughts crowded into his brain again.

'If the Germans invade, *will* your people fight?'

'Of course.' She was attending to him with a wash cloth.

'*Can* they?'

'Of course. We have a very powerful army. But you must know this.'

'I do. You have an army of twenty-eight divisions, six hundred and forty thousand men.'

'And you still think the Germans can beat us? Or would dare try?'

'Your army is not at this moment mobilised, and it is armed mainly with somewhat out-of-date rifles. The German army is counted in millions, with the most modern equipment.'

'You overestimate them,' she suggested, throwing the wash cloth into the basin and sitting at the foot of the bed with her legs drawn up – an unforgettable sight. 'Because they beat you in France.'

'It's a good reason.'

'Well, they cannot possibly bring all their millions down here,' she pointed out.

'I also believe you have a tank corps of just fifty machines. Do you know how many thousands of tanks the Germans have?'

'This is not good tank country.'

'Any country is good air-power country. You have two hundred and eighty-four combat aircraft. Again, the Germans talk in thousands.'

'But your Royal Air Force claims to have defeated them, last autumn.'

'Well . . .' He did not suppose it would be tactful to suggest that the RAF pilots were light years ahead of the Yugoslavs in training and tactical ability. 'They had Spitfires. And the odds were only about two to one, not ten to one.'

'I never thought to hear a British officer being so defeatist.'

'In war, my dearest girl, both optimism and pessimism are luxuries. Only realism works. And the reality is that if it comes to a fight you are going to be outnumbered in every aspect by at least ten to one. That just *isn't* going to work.'

'And do we not have allies? Will the British not help us? You are helping the Greeks.'

'We are helping the Greeks because we can reach them. We cannot reach you.'

'The Royal Navy cannot reach us?'

'At the moment, no. We do not have the ships to take on the Italian fleet in such narrow waters.'

'Then we will do it for you.'

'One old cruiser and four destroyers? Oh, and I forgot, four submarines. They wouldn't last five minutes against one Littorio-class battleship, and the Italians have at least three.'

'What are you trying to say? That we should just surrender?'

'I wish you to understand that it would be very grim. You can't even be sure that your people would fight beside the Serbs.'

'We are all one nation now.'

'Do you really believe that? What about the Ustase?'

She frowned at him. 'What do you know of the Ustase?'

'I know that they are a Croatian terrorist organisation, that they assassinated King Alexander, and that they support some sort of union with Italy. Which happens to be Germany's ally.'

'As you say, they are a terrorist group,' she said equably. 'Oh, hello.'

The bedroom door opened, and Sandrine came in. Tony hastily reached for the covers, but Elena was sitting on them. Sandrine regarded him with interest. 'Lucky for some,' she remarked.

'Did you want something?' Elena asked. 'You can't have him right now; he's incapable.'

'I bet he isn't,' the Frenchwoman remarked as Tony began to twitch. 'But I do not want sex. I am never going to have sex again.'

'Except with Bernhard, presumably. When he comes back.'

'He is not going to come back,' Sandrine said. 'They are all going. Every one of them. Every German in Belgrade.'

'Eh?' Tony rolled out of bed and ran to the window to look

down on the street. It was as packed as earlier, but now a large proportion of the crowd was composed of cars, heavily laden with both people and luggage, the suitcases strapped on the backs and roofs. The people surrounding the cars were jeering and whistling, but there was no violence.

'Those are all Germans,' Sandrine said, standing at his shoulder.

'Running for their lives,' Elena suggested.

'But . . .' Tony turned, and found himself against Sandrine. She gazed into his eyes for a long moment before stepping away. 'What is threatening their lives, here in Belgrade?'

'Oh, they are just afraid,' Elena said. 'If there is a war, they will all be rounded up and put in internment camps. They are afraid of that.'

Tony didn't agree with her, but decided not to say so. He started to get dressed. 'I must get back to the embassy.'

'When will I see you again?'

'As soon as I can make it.'

'Tonight?'

'I can't promise that. Elena,' – he took her in his arms – 'you understand that if I am ordered out I will have to go.'

'I know. You are a soldier.'

'I will try to obtain permission for you to come with me.'

She shook her head. 'I must stay here.'

'Even if there is a chance you might be killed?'

'I must stay,' she said again.

He sighed and glanced at Sandrine.

'I will stay too,' Sandrine said. 'As long as there is work to be done.'

Tony kissed her, then hugged Elena. 'I'll try to get back to you as soon as I can.'

'It's a wholesale evacuation,' Tony told the colonel. 'Just about every German in Belgrade is on the move. Presumably that means every German in Yugoslavia is getting out.'

'Strange,' Brooke-Walters commented. 'Talk about the herd instinct . . .'

'I don't think it is strange, sir. And I don't think it is the herd instinct. I think every German-occupied household has been warned by the embassy that they should leave, now.'

'In a flat spin? You say they're going by car, mostly. They can't possibly carry all their gear. What are they anticipating? A German invasion? If that were the case, wouldn't they be better off just to shut themselves in their houses and wait for their troops to arrive? If the Yugoslavs decide to fight at all, they'll hardly have the time to organise any internment camps. Anyway,' he mused, 'if all those cars and trucks are moving north to the border, they are going to clog the roads and make movement south by any military units next to impossible. If the evacuation has been ordered from Berlin, someone has dropped a clanger.'

Tony suppressed a sigh with difficulty. It seemed that since the beginning of this war, every British leader from Chamberlain down – with the honourable exception of Churchill himself – was anxious to discover German mistakes. He hadn't actually seen any of those so far.

'I would say that depends on just how Jerry intends to come, sir. Have we any orders as yet?'

'No we have not. Because nothing has happened yet. There has been no official diplomatic response from Berlin. But this evacuation presupposes that there will be one, soon enough. For the time being, proceed with your preparations for departure.'

'Ah . . . supposing we do leave, sir . . .'

Brooke-Walters had been looking down at his papers. Now he looked up, his expression indicating that this supposition was taken for granted.

Tony drew a deep breath. 'Will we be able to take anyone with us, sir?'

'We will take everyone who holds a British passport and wishes to come.'

'There's a Frenchwoman, Sandrine Fouquet, on the staff of *Paris Temps*. Well, she's sort of a friend of mine—'

'There is a French embassy in Belgrade, Tony. If she wishes to leave, they'll look after it. We have enough to worry about with our own people. You'll be asking me next if we can take the Kostics.'

'I'm not sure they wish to go, sir.'

Brooke-Walters nodded. 'That is very sensible, and very patriotic. Now get on with it.'

Tony saluted, and went to his room to wash and brush up before lunch. He was in a distinctly agitated state, compounded certainly by what was happening, but equally by what had just happened.

His previous sexual encounters with Elena had been anticipatory, exploratory, less memorable than they should have been because of their transience; each had borne no relation to anything previous, and had merely been a promise of the next time, of their slowly building relationship. This morning's encounter had been nothing like that. There had been no mental rapport. He had the feeling that he might as well have been a man Elena had picked up off the street, to satisfy the excitement she had admitted feeling.

There had also been an air of finality, not just in her admission that marriage between them was impossible, but in her acceptance that she would probably never see him again. He had been an incident in her life, nothing more. And now she was being called to sterner duties.

Oddly, he did not feel bitter, only hurt. And guilty that he could not stay to put things right.

The presence of Sandrine had not helped, either. Quite apart from the fact that he had never before been naked in the presence of two women at the same time, there was the fact that, entirely without wishing it, he had found himself attracted to the Frenchwoman. She was in every way better looking, better groomed, better mannered, better bred . . .

24

better suited to be the wife of an English officer. He had had these thoughts before, but had immediately rejected them, firstly because she belonged to a friend – even if he was also an enemy – and more importantly because Sandrine had never shown the slightest interest in him as anything other than a friend. Today had been different. Was that because it was the first time she had seen him naked? Or because she was angry and grief-stricken at being abandoned by Bernhard? Or simply that, like Elena, she had been excited by the sudden crisis?

As if it mattered. He was never going to see her again, either. He had not actually promised Bernhard anything, and as the colonel had said, if she wanted to get out, her best bet was the French embassy.

What a right royal fuck-up!

Pinder, his batman, had almost completed packing. 'Some do, sir,' the corporal commented.

Pinder was a Yorkshireman, an apple-cheeked, somewhat heavy young man, who viewed life with a pessimistic pragmatism. Tony had only acquired him after leaving hospital, and they were still on a mutual learning curve as regards each other, but the corporal maintained an earnestly respectful air, not only as due to an officer, but to a man who had actually seen action – Pinder had not got to France.

Now he asked, 'Will we be leaving then, sir?'

'It looks like it,' Tony acknowledged.

'The Jerries do get around,' Pinder commented.

'At the moment, yes.'

'By sea, will it be, sir?'

'I'm afraid not.'

'Air?' They had arrived in Belgrade by air, and the corporal had not enjoyed the journey.

'No. It's going to be by car and truck, across some pretty rugged – and hostile – terrain.'

'But we're a diplomatic mission, sir.'

'We may have to convince people of that,' Tony said. He washed his hands, checked his uniform – it was not as neat as it should be; he wondered if Brooke-Walters had noticed that – and went down to lunch.

Leighton and Johnstone, and indeed the entire embassy staff, were full of information and speculation.

'If you ask me,' Leighton remarked, 'I think the old man is overreacting. So the Germans are getting out. That's because they've been taken by surprise. They're not used to being defied like this. There's no need for us to do the same.'

'What does your German friend say about it?' Johnstone asked.

'He only knows that he and his people have been ordered out, and are getting out.'

'And Elena?'

'All martial ardour. If the Jerries come, the Yugoslavs will whop them.'

'What do you think?'

'I think it's a shitting awful mess,' Tony said.

By dusk the embassy was ready to go, but as they had as yet received no orders, it was a business of sitting around, or standing around, or walking in the garden.

Obviously a great deal was going on behind the scenes, and beyond the scope of the junior officers. The ambassador was attempting to arrange diplomatic passports to get his people out. He also felt that it was necessary to keep a continuing liaison with the Yugoslav military command. This was sufficiently important to be dealt with by Brooke-Walters personally, even though he could only convey to General Simovic the same bleak appraisal of the chances of British military help as he had to his three officers that morning.

But the waiting was tiresome. As was his personal situation. He was tempted to go looking for Elena when darkness fell, but he still could not get over the feeling that their morning get-together had been her way of saying goodbye.

The city appeared to have settled down somewhat from the frenzy of the breaking news. Presumably all the Germans had now left. Tony envisaged the roads to the north, only one or two of them even remotely qualified to be called highways, clogged with bumper-to-bumper traffic. What would they meet coming down? And what, indeed, would they meet at the border?

He played a couple of rubbers of bridge with Leighton and Johnstone and one of the secretaries, none of them concentrating very hard on the fall of the cards. In the middle of the evening Brooke-Walters came in, but went straight up to see the ambassador, his face like a looming thundercloud.

Tony said goodnight to Pinder, got into bed, switched off the light, and listened to the sounds of the night seeping through his closed window. After a few minutes he got up and stood at the glass, looking out at the lights. Belgrade was certainly a brilliant sight, far more so now than usual. But then, he doubted anyone was going to sleep tonight.

He closed the shutters, hoping to keep out both the light and the noise – the curtains were only thin, transparent material – and frowned as he heard the drone of aircraft. Aircraft, over Belgrade, in the middle of the night?

He turned back, opened both shutters and curtains, and looked out again as the first bombs fell.

Chapter Two

Panic

T he first explosion was not very far away, and the blast
sent Tony tumbling across the room in the middle of a
cloud of shattering glass. He fell across the bed, his hands
having instinctively come up to protect his face; even so, from
the stinging he guessed he had been cut in several places.

For a moment he lay still, his half-awake mind unable to
determine exactly where he was, even as waves of understanding swept through his brain. The Germans had never
intended diplomatic manoeuvring, or indeed anything so
mundane as a declaration of war. They had not even intended
an invasion until Yugoslavia, or at least Belgrade, had been
wiped off the map. Once again the rest of the world, including
the British, had been caught with their pants down because of
their continuing, outmoded belief that there were necessary
negotiations to be undergone, procedures to be followed,
before the fighting could begin.

He wondered if Bernhard had known what was going to
happen – or at least suspected would happen – following
the peremptory orders to evacuate the city, and, indeed, the
country.

Now the entire night was shrouded in the noise of the
explosions, and even lying on his bed Tony could see the sky
brightening with the first of the fires. Now too the continuous
rumble was being penetrated by other sounds: the wail of
sirens, the shrieks of terrified people, and even one or two

gunshots, as if someone were attempting to bring down one of the planes with a rifle.

There were shouts of alarm within the embassy itself, and a good deal of noise. Tony dragged on his clothes, and added his revolver holster and cartridge pouch. He did not suppose there was going to be anyone to shoot at, at least for a while, but it made him feel better.

He had just finished dressing when Pinder appeared, panting and looking distraught, still buttoning his tunic. 'What a rum do, sir.'

'Yes. Are you ready to move out?'

'Just give the word, sir.'

'The word will need to come from someone else. Just stand by.'

'Excuse me, sir, but your face is cut. Would you like me—'

The lights went out; either a German bomb had struck the electricity plant or someone in authority had realised that the fully lit city was too simple a target. But the sudden plunging of Belgrade into pitch darkness – apart from the fires – caused a fresh outbreak of screams and shrieks.

'Where are you, sir?' Pinder inquired.

'Follow me,' Tony told him, and felt his way along the corridor to the stairs. On his way he encountered several other people, emerging from their rooms and bumping into one another, but he reached the ground floor without actually being knocked over.

In the dining room someone had managed to light several candles, which sent light guttering into the corners as the building continued to shake to the blast of explosions; Tony supposed it was a miracle it hadn't yet received a direct hit. Brooke-Walters was in command here, surveying the motley crowd of dressed and half-dressed men and women gathering in front of him.

'You will carry out your drill,' he said. 'Proceed down to the cellars in an orderly fashion. There is no need to panic.'

'Are we going to move out, sir?' someone asked.

'We are awaiting orders,' the colonel said. 'The ambassador is trying to get through now. There has been no declaration of war.'

'You wouldn't describe dropping a few tons of bombs on a capital city a declaration of war, sir?' asked someone else.

The building shook again as there were some more explosions close at hand.

'Get down to the cellars,' Brooke-Walters repeated, no doubt thankful he did not have to answer the awkward question. 'All of you. We'll be told what to do come daylight.'

Daylight! Tony looked at his watch. Three thirty. Daylight was at least two hours away.

He stepped back against the wall as people started to file past him.

'Aren't you coming down?' Johnstone asked.

'I'm going out. Cover for me, if you have to. I'll be back by first light.'

'You're taking a bit of a risk, old man.'

'I need to know,' Tony said.

He stepped into the corridor, and was instantly plunged into darkness. But the explosions had ceased. The raid was over.

The sentries still stood at the front door, although inside the building rather than out in the open.

'Captain Davis,' Tony said, as they couldn't possibly identify him in the gloom.

'Sir.' They stood to attention. 'You're not going out?'

'Orders,' Tony explained.

'It's a bit tricky out there, sir. There are people inside the gates. They've been banging on the door.'

'Didn't you send them off?'

'We received no orders, sir. Just to refuse admittance.'

It occurred to Tony that they were all suffering from a considerable lack of orders.

'I'll manage,' he said.

They opened the doors, and he stepped out into the morning

'I also have orders I must obey.'

She nodded. 'I understand this. Listen. Fuck me, and then I will get dressed, and we will go together.'

'You mean you'll come with me?' He could not believe his ears.

'I will come with you to find Sandrine.'

'Sandrine? But—'

'Are you not worried about her too?'

'Ah . . .' Tony realised that he had not actually thought about the Frenchwoman at all.

'She is my best friend,' Elena reminded him. 'We must make sure she is all right.'

'She will have gone to the French embassy.'

Elena shook her head. 'No, no. She will be at her place. She will not wish to leave. We will have to make her.'

'And you will come too?'

She made a moue. 'Give me a good fuck, and I may.'

It was incredible how people's reactions to a certain situation could be so completely different. Tony knew it would be wrong to attribute Elena's overactive sexuality to the German attack; Elena had always been overactive, sexually. It had been one of the aspects of her personality that Tony, brought up in the cosy gentility of an English country village where none of the girls would allow a kiss from someone they had not known for at least a month and for whom the concept of losing one's virginity before marriage was on a par with making a pact with the devil, had found most compelling from the moment of their first meeting. But that she should allow nothing – not even the outbreak of a war – to interfere with her desires was startling.

And he was happy to go along with her. He was the male, the soldier, the officer, but she was the dominant character, he knew, simply because he could not resist her invitation to lose himself in the splendid contours of her body, stroke that velvet flesh, sink into the emotional discharge which accompanied her climaxes, when she would gasp and grunt and shout, 'Again! Again!' until he was himself spent.

How he wanted to spend his life right where he was, or at least have the right to return there whenever he could. Of course he understood that everything she had said yesterday was true – that the impact of Elena Kostic on his parents and friends would be every bit as traumatic as the threatened Nazi invasion. But it was still something he wanted to do. And if she was now willing . . . Besides, he was having an idea. If she were to accompany Sandrine to the French embassy – where, from what he had heard, there was far less red tape than at the British – they might be able to get out together, and he would be able to find them afterwards.

'We must hurry,' he said. It was starting to get light.

'I understand.' She poured water into the basin. 'Where will we go?'

He needed to proceed methodically. 'To find Sandrine, first.'

She nodded, splashed vigorously, and then dressed with equal energy, putting on stockings and a deep green dress, and finding herself a matching floppy hat, which made her look something like a femme fatale. Tony put on his uniform and watched her, his jaw dropping as she opened a drawer and took out a Luger automatic pistol, which made her look even more like a woman of mystery.

'Where did you get that?'

'I have had it for years.' She slapped the magazine into the butt, reached into the drawer and took out two more; these she placed in her satchel, beside the gun. 'Let's go.'

'Who are you meaning to shoot?'

'Any Germans we may come across.'

Tony reflected thankfully that there wouldn't be any around at the moment. 'Just keep it out of sight.'

'Yours is not out of sight.'

'I am a soldier, in uniform. I'm supposed to be armed. Does your mother know you have that thing?'

'Of course.'

'And you understand that your mother's idea is to surrender to the Germans rather than shoot them?'

'The only thing Mummy and I have ever agreed on is that you are the right man for me. You said we should hurry.'

'Aren't you taking anything else?'

She shook her head. 'There is no time for that.' She pushed past him and went down the stairs. He could do nothing but follow her. 'I am going out with Tony,' she told Martina, who was standing in the street doorway looking out at the fires and the people.

'When will you be back?'

'Soon.'

Tony followed her down the steps and into the crowd. 'Should you lie to your mother like that?' He spoke French so as not to be understood by any family friend who might be within earshot.

'Everyone lies to their mother.'

Tony couldn't remember ever doing so. 'You didn't even kiss her goodbye.'

'I told you. We never have got on. To kiss her would have made her suspicious.'

They reached a main street, and were pushed back by several policemen. It was now close to dawn, but the promise of day was darkened by the clouds of smoke hanging above the city.

'We need to go across the river,' Elena explained.

'Listen,' the police sergeant said.

A police car was coming down the street, a voice blaring from its megaphone.

'Attention! Attention!' the voice said. 'We are at war with Nazi Germany. German forces have crossed the frontier and are advancing on Belgrade. They will be here today. All reservists must report at once to their units. I repeat, all reservists report at once, with weapons and equipment, to their units. All civilians should return to their homes and stay indoors. I repeat, go home and stay indoors. Put up your shutters. You must not clutter the streets by attempting to leave the city. I repeat . . .'

The car drew level with them and then passed on.

'You are a British soldier,' the sergeant said. 'You should report to your embassy.'

'He must see me home first,' Elena said. 'You say we must all go home. My fiancé is seeing me home.'

'You are this woman's betrothed?' the sergeant asked.

'Yes, I am,' Tony said.

'And I live across the river,' Elena pointed out.

'I do not think you can cross the river. The bridge is down. It was struck by a bomb. Maybe more than one.'

'It is destroyed?'

'Not entirely. But it is down. To cross it will be very dangerous.'

'We will manage it. Come along, Tony.'

They crossed the street. The sergeant scratched his head, but did not attempt to prevent them. Only one or two people seemed to be obeying the police command; they had to push their way through quite a throng to reach the river. And the bridge. Here there was an even bigger crowd, staring at the collapsed stonework, through and around which the fast-flowing water tumbled. But the bridge, if impassable to motor or horse-drawn traffic, was still crossable; as they watched, several people made their way from block to block of masonry, shouting and occasionally screaming.

'We can do that,' Elena said.

'Then let's do it,' Tony said. It was now a quarter to five and he would need to be back at the embassy by half past.

Elena climbed down the embankment and on to the first stones, her satchel slung on her shoulder. A dawn breeze had sprung up and she had no time to attend to her skirt; several people cheered as her legs came into view. She ignored them, and made her way to the next stone.

Tony clambered behind her. It was slow going, as the river was quite wide at this point and there was a constant stream of people coming the other way. Passing them was a matter of carefully selecting the right place. But at last they reached the other side.

'Ugh!' Elena commented. 'To think that we have to do that again, going back. Shit!' She had straightened her skirt, and only then discovered that her hands were covered in mud and slime.

'Where now?' Tony asked. He had never been to Sandrine's apartment. As for going back . . . He just could not see the chic Frenchwoman coping with crawling across those muddy stones. And his leg was starting to hurt.

'Down here.'

On the river the air had been reasonably clear. Now they plunged once again into smoke and flames, heat and distraught people.

'There!' Elena pointed. 'It is still standing.'

They hurried up to the small block of flats and ran up the steps. The street door was open, swinging on its hinges.

'Number six,' Elena said. 'It is a walk-up.'

A man stood in the doorway of one of the downstairs apartments; he carried a shotgun and looked aggressive. 'If you are here to loot I will shoot you,' he announced.

'We have come to see Mademoiselle Fouquet,' Elena said.

'She is not here. She went out when the bombing started.'

'Where did she go?' Tony asked.

'I do not know.'

'She will have gone to the newspaper office,' Elena said. 'It is a story, yes? The bombing of Belgrade. She will be telephoning it to Paris.'

The *Paris Temps* office was on the other side of the river. At least this time they would be travelling in the right direction.

*　　*　　*

At last the crowds were thinning. They were largely replaced by men in uniform, striding purposefully towards the north; none of them seemed to have linked up with their units as yet. Then a solitary tank rumbled down the street, cheered by the people. Tony wondered what one tank was going to do, apart from raising civilian morale, when it could not even get across the river.

But then the tank was made irrelevant by the wail of a siren.

The air-raid warning signal had not been activated before the first raid; everyone had been taken too much by surprise. Even now its warning was only just in time; the aircraft were already in sight, lethal black objects gleaming in the first rays of the sun – these had not yet reached the city.

Anti-aircraft guns opened fire. There was no sign of any Yugoslav aircraft; Tony presumed these had either all been destroyed on the ground or were needed further north.

Most people had stopped to stare at the approaching enemy, but now the Stukas switched on their own sirens as they began their dives towards the defenceless houses. People screamed and scattered in search of shelter. Tony forced Elena off the road and into a ditch, and they crouched together while the explosions started.

'Bastards!' Elena shouted. 'You have seen this before?'

'Yes.'

'You were in London during the Blitz?'

'Actually, I wasn't. My blitz was earlier.'

But it hadn't been like this at all, he realised as he gazed at collapsing buildings, listened to shrieking, terrified people. He buried his head in his arm – his other was round Elena – as waves of dust and debris scattered across them. He had never seen a city being systematically destroyed before. In Flanders the Stukas he had seen were seeking only military objectives, the men on the ground. As such they could be respected; however much one wanted to hit back at them and hated them when a comrade was hit, they were carrying out a necessary business in time of war. Of course he had heard stories of how they had bombed and strafed refugee columns, but he had not actually seen it happen, and had no idea if the stories were true or just propaganda.

As a military attaché he knew there were no military targets in the centre of Belgrade. He supposed it could be said that knocking out the bridges across the Danube was a necessary part of any German invasion plan – although this would hamper the Wehrmacht even more than the Yugoslavs – but the repeated assaults on the useless heart of a great city was both senseless and criminal. He could not imagine Bernhard condoning that.

But in real terms, Bernhard's opinions no longer mattered.

The raid lasted some fifteen minutes, and at the end of it the city was once again engulfed in flame and smoke. And the time was five fifteen. If the embassy had received any orders they would have them by now.

'We have to hurry.' He dragged Elena to her feet. Her hat had come off, and her hair was scattered and covered in dust, as was her face and dress. He presumed he must look the same.

'It is just down here,' she gasped, and led him round the next corner. There they stopped on the pavement, suddenly oppressed by the heat; the entire street in front of them was ablaze. Halfway down the street had been the newspaper office.

'Sandrine!' Elena screamed.

Tony had to grasp her round the waist to stop her from running into the holocaust. He wondered just how close she was to the Frenchwoman to feel such a sense of loss.

'Elena? Tony?'

They both turned. Sandrine was as immaculately dressed as they could ever remember her, in a white frock which seemed singularly inappropriate on a day like this. She was hatless, but not a single golden hair was out of place; a white

41

shoulder bag bumped on her hip. She had clearly not been sheltering in a ditch.

'Sandrine!' Elena screamed, leaping at her friend to hug and kiss her. 'We thought you were dead!'

'I had stepped outside to take photographs when the building was hit,' Sandrine explained. 'They are all dead. All my colleagues, all my friends.'

'*We* are alive,' Elena pointed out.

'Yes.' Sandrine gave her a perfunctory hug. 'I am so glad about that.'

'Let's go,' Tony said.

'Where?'

'Well . . . to the French embassy, in the first instance.'

'Why?'

'To get you out of Belgrade.'

'Why?'

'Well . . . when the Germans come—'

'I keep telling you,' Sandrine said, 'I have a Vichy passport. I am a neutral.'

'Did all the people in your office have Vichy passports?'

'Of course they did.'

'And they are now all dead.'

Sandrine bit her lip. 'The bombing has been indiscriminate. We reported this. As to whether they will print it—'

'I still don't think your having a neutral passport is going to do you the least bit of good,' Tony interrupted. 'Anyway, you no longer have a job.'

She made a moue. 'I hadn't thought of that.' She peered at him. 'Your face is cut. Do you know you have cuts on your face?'

'He was blown up,' Elena explained. 'I have put iodine on them.'

'He is going to have a scar,' Sandrine pointed out. 'More than one.'

'Forget about my scars,' Tony said. 'You have to go home to France. If we can get you there.'

'I will come with you,' Elena said.

'You? Why?'

'Tony thinks I should leave Yugoslavia until this is over.'

'But . . . do you have a passport?'

'No.' Elena looked at Tony. 'Do I have to have a passport?'

'I suppose you do, in normal circumstances. But you will be a refugee. No one expects refugees to have passports.'

'I think you want to think about this,' Sandrine said. 'I am going back to my apartment. Come with me, and we will talk about it.'

Tony was growing both irritated and anxious; time was rushing by while they argued about what to do. The raid was now over, and people were returning to the streets. Things would be happening at the embassy. 'You won't find it easy to get home,' he pointed out. 'The bridge is down.'

Sandrine looked at Elena.

'This is true,' Elena said. 'But the wreckage can be crossed. We have done this, just now.'

'Why?'

'We were looking for you.'

'Oh, you sweetheart.' Sandrine gave her a hug. 'Was the building still standing?'

'Oh, yes.'

'Then let us go there, and have a coffee, and decide what is best for us to do.'

'Sandrine,' Tony said, as unemotionally as he could. 'The Germans are going to be here in a couple of hours.'

'That is nonsense,' Elena declared. 'Our army will fight them. It is fighting them now.'

'Your army is not going to hold up the panzers,' Tony said. 'If you do not leave now, you will not be able to leave at all.'

'Then we will stay.'

'You are going to surrender?'

'No, no, I am going to fight.'

43

'Now that *is* nonsense,' Sandrine declared. 'The Germans do not harm women. If you do not fight them, they will leave you alone.'

'I wouldn't bet on it,' Tony said.

'They have not harmed our women in France. Unless they were actively resisting.'

Tony sighed, overtaken by a wave of desperation. 'Sandrine . . . Elena . . . for God's sake be real. The Germans regard the French as acceptable human beings; they regard the Slavs as subhuman.'

'Are you saying I am a Slav?' Elena demanded.

'Aren't you?'

'I am a Croatian,' she said proudly.

'A Croatian?' someone asked. They had been surrounded by people trying to understand what they were arguing about. But French was a fairly common language in Belgrade.

'What's it to you?' Elena demanded aggressively, answering in Serbo-Croat.

The man waved his arm. 'These people are Croats!' he shouted. 'They are Fascists, supporters of Mussolini. They will betray us to the Germans.'

The crowd uttered a roar and surged forward. Sandrine gave a little shriek, torn between identifying herself as French and thus abandoning her friend, and by saying nothing and risking what was beginning to look like mob violence.

Tony had no such scruples. 'Hold it!' he shouted. 'I am a British officer. I am taking these women to the French embassy.'

'Why?' demanded the self-appointed spokesman.

'This woman is French.' He indicated Sandrine.

'I know this,' said a woman in the crowd. 'I have seen her. She works in that building . . .' She pointed down the burning street. 'She *did*. Down there.'

'Then you may go with the officer, Frenchwoman,' the spokesman said. 'But you—'

'She is my fiancée,' Tony said.

'She is a Croat.'

'What has that got to do with it?'

'She is a traitor to Serbia. All Croats are traitors to Serbia.'

'I will fight for Yugoslavia.' Elena jerked her arm free.

'Grab her,' the man said.

Elena had already put her hand into her satchel. Now she withdrew it, her pistol levelled. 'Take one step forward and I'll blow your fucking brains out.'

She spoke at large, but the gun was pointing at the spokesman.

'Oh, shit,' Tony muttered. 'You'd better get out of here, Sandrine.'

'No,' Sandrine said. 'She is my friend.'

'She defies us,' the spokesman said, keeping very still. 'Will you let her do this?'

'Help me, Tony,' Elena said. It was more a command than an appeal. 'If you let them take me, they will lynch me.'

Tony sighed, but he suspected she could be right; they would certainly beat her up. They were both angry and frightened, the ultimate lynch-mob characteristic.

'I am taking this woman to the French embassy,' he said. 'If you wish to bring charges against her, you may do so there.'

'The French embassy is closed,' someone said. 'I saw this. They have all gone, and the gates are locked.'

'Oh, *shit!*' Tony said. He supposed he had to be classified as a deserter. Unless they assumed he was dead. But that was something he would have to sort out later. 'I am still taking this woman,' he said.

The crowd surged forward. Sandrine gave another of her little shrieks. Elena fired. Tony suspected she had intended to shoot into the ground in front of them, but she was overexcited and her hand jerked; the bullet ploughed into the leg of one of the men. He gave a shout of pain and fell down.

The forward movement ceased, and Tony, realising that

they had burned their bridges, drew his own revolver. 'Just stay put,' he snapped. 'Let's get the hell out of here,' he told the women.

'Where?' Sandrine asked.

Tony gave a hasty glance left and right. People were accumulating from either side, and every street not blocked by fire was crowded. Even had they wanted to, they lacked the ammunition to shoot their way through, and if they tried that and failed they would certainly be lynched.

There could be only one escape! 'There!' he pointed.

Sandrine looked at the flames swirling across the street behind them. 'We'll burn.'

'It's better than hanging. Go.'

Cautiously Sandrine moved down the street. Elena went behind her, walking backwards, pistol still pointing at the crowd. Tony followed.

'Fetch a policeman,' someone shouted.

But the police had already arrived. 'You there!' a constable shouted. 'Are you mad?'

'Run,' Tony commanded.

He turned to set an example, holstering his revolver as he did so. Sandrine had stopped at the wall of heat and smoke confronting her. Tony grasped her arm and urged her forward; she began to choke and fell to her knees. He wrenched off his belts and tunic and wrapped the heavy material round her head, making sure there was enough left over to use himself; then he scooped her from the ground and ran. A glance over his shoulder told him that Elena was behind him; she had followed his example and scooped her skirt up to wrap round her own head. He dug his face into his share of the tunic and stumbled forward.

The heat was so intense it was almost a physical force, and more than once he nearly fell. He could feel his arms and hair burning, but it was a surprisingly short distance to the other side. He stumbled into open air – and more people, but these were on his side, at least for the moment.

'He's on fire,' someone shouted.

'The baths! Quick!' shouted someone else.

Eager hands grasped his arms and hurried him forward. He gathered that others were doing the same for Elena. The tunic slipped from Sandrine's head and she stared at him. 'My legs are burning,' she said.

Tony couldn't speak, and a moment later they were being hurried up the steps of the municipal baths. This building had been struck by a bomb, and the façade had crumbled. But the large pool inside remained. Tony and Sandrine were half carried across the rubble to the edge and thrown into the water, which brought forth another of Sandrine's little shrieks.

Then they were in the mercifully cool water, going down, down . . . Tony's feet touched the bottom and he kicked to send himself up again, only then wondering if Sandrine could swim. Apparently she could not. She was beating the water and gasping for breath. Tony held her shoulders and towed her to the side, where other hands lifted her out. She lay on the coronation, panting and spitting water. The chic was all gone. She had lost her shoes and her bag, her stockings were in tatters, her dress was torn and clinging soddenly to her body, and her hair was plastered to her head.

But she was alive.

Tony was helped out of the water next, and he looked round for Elena. She was also being pulled to safety, a soaking mass. But she retained her satchel.

'I thought we were dead,' she said.

'You should have been,' said a heavily built, somewhat elderly man who was crouching between them. 'Where did you come from?'

Elena and Tony exchanged glances, and she got the message: it was safest to leave the talking to him for the time being.

'We were in the *Paris Temps* office,' he explained. 'This lady' – he indicated Sandrine – 'is an editor there. When the raid started, we went down to the cellars. We had meant to stay there, but the heat grew too intense, so we made a run for it.'

'You were lucky,' the man said. 'But you are wearing a uniform,' he said to Tony.

Tony had lost his cap, and his tunic, lying on the coronation, was scorched beyond recognition. But his khaki trousers and heavy brown shoes indicated that he was not a civilian.

'I am a British officer. We were going to go to the French embassy. But I understand it is closed.'

'I believe so. Now we must get you some dry clothes.'

'No,' Elena said.

'But mademoiselle—'

'We will let them dry on us. I am still burning.'

'And you are burned,' the man pointed out. 'At least let me look at you.'

'Are you a doctor?'

'I am the bath-keeper,' the man said. 'I am Ivkov.'

'Can you not send these people away?'

There were still quite a few people in the building, staring at them, discussing them.

Ivkov stood up and clapped his hands. 'All right,' he said. 'You have seen enough. Get out. Go and see who else you can rescue.'

Reluctantly they withdrew.

'I have an office,' Ivkov said. 'Come in there.' He helped Elena to her feet.

Tony scooped Sandrine into his arms. She snuggled against him; water continued to dribble from her hair. 'My legs—'

'Mr Ivkov is going to help us,' he told her.

At the far end of the baths there was a doorway, which gave access to a surprisingly large and even more surprisingly undamaged office. Ivkov let them in, and then closed the door behind them.

'Her first,' Elena said.

Tony laid Sandrine on the desk, and she moaned. Ivkov

bent over her, then carefully lifted the tattered dress to her waist. Her stockings were in threads, dangling from her suspender belt; predictably she wore spotless white knickers. A good deal of the flesh on her legs was very red, but it did not appear that the skin was broken. Tony realised with a guilty start that she had the most splendid legs. Because of both Bernhard and Elena he had never allowed himself to look too closely before. But then, he had never had an opportunity like this before.

'Getting her into the water saved her,' Ivkov said. 'I have some cream.' He opened a cupboard, and returned with a jar.

'I will do it,' Elena said.

'I should look at you also,' Ivkov said.

'Very well. You do it.' She took the jar from Ivkov's hands and gave it to Tony, then turned back to the bath-keeper. 'Where do you want to look?'

Tony let them get on with it; he palmed some of the cream, hesitated a moment and then slowly and carefully began to rub it on Sandrine's legs; he had never done this to a woman before, and was terribly aware of the white silk only inches away from his fingers.

At his first touch she gave one of her little screams; these subsided into a series of groans, accentuated when he had to tear away strips of torn stockings. He would have liked to take them right off, but her suspender belt was beneath her knickers, and that would have been a shade too intimate – certainly with Elena only a couple of feet away.

She stood at his elbow. 'Let me.'

She took over the massaging.

'Are you all right?'

'Just a few slight burns. Let Ivkov look at you.'

'You are all right,' Ivkov said. 'Your hair is singed. You have no eyebrows, eh? And your face is cut.'

'I'll survive. But thank you, friend. You saved our lives.'

'You did that for yourselves. You say you are going to the French embassy? But—'

'I know. It's been evacuated. Well, we'll have to try the British one instead.'

'I think it has been bombed.'

'Shit.'

'I am so thirsty,' Sandrine said.

She had at least stopped moaning.

'I have water.' Ivkov produced a bottle. 'Or would you prefer schnapps?'

'A bit of both,' Tony said. 'I don't suppose you have anything to eat?'

'There is some bread and cheese – what is left of my dinner.'

'That would be very nice,' Elena said.

Ivkov bustled off.

'He is a good man,' she said in a low voice.

'I still wouldn't tell him who or what you are,' Tony said.

She made a face.

'Did he say your embassy has been bombed?' Sandrine asked. She was sitting up now and had straightened her skirt, but she was shivering as shock set in. Tony reckoned she should be in bed.

'He didn't say it had been destroyed. I still think we should get along there, then you can be seen by a doctor.'

'I am all right,' Sandrine said. 'I will be all right.'

Tony looked at Elena.

'Let us have breakfast,' she said. 'Then we will decide what to do.'

Ivkov had returned with the food. They ate hungrily.

'Were your homes hit?' the bath-keeper asked.

'I don't think so,' Elena said.

'You should return there, before the Germans come. It is not good to be on the street when the enemies come. I remember 1914, when the Austrians came. I was only

a boy then, but what they did, and two handsome women . . .'
He shook his head. 'You should be at home, behind locked doors.'

'He is right,' Elena decided. 'If we cannot leave the city, then we should go home. You will come home with me, Sandrine, and I will look after you. You too, Tony.'

'Oh, he will be all right,' Ivkov said. 'He is wearing a uniform. They will take him prisoner.'

'Do you think he wants to be taken prisoner?'

Ivkov scratched his head.

'Suppose we run into those dreadful people again?' Sandrine asked.

'We will shoot our way through,' Elena decided.

'With one pistol?' Tony asked.

She grinned at him. 'I have your gun as well.' She took the belt out of her satchel. 'I picked it up when you dropped it.'

'You are a genius.' He holstered it.

'What dreadful people?' Ivkov asked.

'Croatians,' Elena replied without hesitation. 'Traitors who were declaring for Mussolini.'

'They are swine,' Ivkov said. 'All Croatians are swine.'

'I am sure you are right,' Elena said. 'Well . . .'

Ivkov opened the door.

Elena kissed him and hugged him against her. 'I will never forget you.'

'Nor I you,' he agreed, going very red in the face.

Tony helped Sandrine off the table. Her legs gave way, and he had to catch her round the waist. 'Can you make it?'

'I will make it,' she said through gritted teeth

'Let me help.' Elena came back to hold her other arm.

The two women looked like a pair of the most pitiful scarecrows, their hair hanging in streaks around their faces, their dresses torn and smoke-stained, their legs bare except for the tattered remnants of their stockings, and neither of them had shoes. Compared with them, Tony realised he was relatively well dressed, and if his tunic was beyond repair, he still had the rest of his clothes – and his shoes.

On the other hand, he reflected, once they gained Elena's house she would be able to fit them out, somehow. But first they had to get there.

He shook hands with Ivkov. 'As Elena said, we shall be eternally grateful for your help.'

'It was nothing,' Ivkov said. 'It has been an adventure.' He grinned. 'If ever you feel like another bath, come back.'

'We may just do that,' Tony promised. He put his arm back round Sandrine's waist and eased her away from the desk. His fingers touched Elena's, and she smiled at him over Sandrine's head. Between them they half carried the Frenchwoman to the door, and stopped as they heard the sound of rippling gunfire, the shouts of men and women.

The Germans had made good time.

Chapter Three

Escape

'You cannot go out there,' Ivkov said. 'You'll be killed.'
'We cannot stay here,' Elena said.

'Well . . .' He looked from one to the other. No matter how bruised and dirty and untidy they might be, they were still two very pretty girls.

'You go home to your wife,' Elena told him. 'We will go home to my mother.'

She nodded to Tony, and he cautiously stepped out of the shattered main doors. The crowd had entirely disappeared, with good reason. Aircraft were again circling overhead, but now they were altogether larger planes, and they were dropping men rather than bombs. He thought he could count hundreds of the small figures drifting downwards, and from the firing he assumed there was a considerable number already on the ground.

Once again the unexpected. If he knew that the Germans had used paratroopers in Belgium and Holland at the very start of the War, he had never personally seen them in action. But the strategy was simple: seize Belgrade long before the main body could reach it, but equally before the Yugoslav resistance could be organised.

Fortunately this street, at any rate, was for the moment empty, of either soldiers or civilians.

'Let's go,' he said.

Elena helped Sandrine down the steps.

53

'I am a hindrance,' Sandrine said. 'You should leave me.'

'What, with Ivkov? He may have helped us, but he'd still have your pants off in a moment. He was virtually drooling when he looked at your legs.'

'Come *on*,' Tony said, holding Sandrine's other arm and remembering how affected he had also been by the sight of Sandrine's legs. But war and obscene thoughts went together, because war was itself an obscene thought.

'That way.' Elena pointed, and, still clinging together, the three of them hobbled their way towards the corner, the women grunting as they barked their bare toes and insteps on the cobbles.

There was firing all around them. Tony reckoned they had been very lucky not to be involved so far, but as they reached the corner they encountered a hastily erected barricade, behind which there crouched half a dozen soldiers and three civilians, also armed. They were peering down the street, which had obviously been on fire a few minutes earlier, but turned sharply at the sound behind them, weapons thrust forward.

'Who are you?' the sergeant asked.

'Who do we look like?' Elena countered.

'Where are you going?'

'Home.'

The sergeant pointed. 'You are in uniform.'

'I am a British officer,' Tony told him.

'An officer!' The sergeant was obviously considering handing over his command, but was distracted by a shout from one of his men.

'Germans!'

As he spoke there was a chatter of automatic fire. Tony forced the women to the ground as bullets thudded into the barricade and whined overhead. One of the Yugoslav soldiers gave a grunt and slumped against the piled rubbish, blood oozing from his tunic.

'Return fire!' the sergeant snapped, and looked at Tony almost apologetically.

'That seems a good idea,' Tony said, and crawled to the stricken man.

He was gasping for breath, each pant accompanied by a froth of blood from his open mouth.

Elena joined him, also on her hands and knees. 'He is dying.'

'I'm afraid he is.' Cautiously Tony peered past the barricade. Beside him the Yugoslavs were firing fiercely, but at no visible target, the Germans having taken cover. 'I would save your ammunition,' he suggested. 'How much have you got.'

'Not enough.' The sergeant showed him one spare clip for his rifle.

'And then what?'

'We will have to retreat.'

'Don't you think it might be a good idea to do that before you run out?'

The sergeant scratched his head.

'What are *we* going to do?' Elena asked.

'I don't think we are going to make it to your house. The Germans are between us and it.'

'We can go to my apartment,' Sandrine suggested. 'We will be safe there. I am a neutral.'

'I imagine the Germans are in strength along the river,' Tony said, not wishing to resume the discussion regarding the improbable value of her neutrality in these circumstances. 'I think our best bet is to pull out with these chaps, and consider our next move later.'

'Well—' Elena began, and was checked by another sound from behind them.

'You are surrounded,' someone called in Serbo-Croat, but with a pronounced foreign accent. 'Throw down your weapons and raise your hands.'

'Shit!' Tony muttered. While they had been discussing the

55

situation the Germans had used another street and got round behind them.

One of the Yugoslav soldiers started to climb over the barricade to get to the other side. This was a sound idea, but unfortunately the Germans were still manning the other end of the street. There was a burst of fire, a cascade of blood, and the soldier was dead before he hit the cobbles.

'Oh!' Sandrine cried.

The sergeant came to a decision. 'Hold your fire!' he shouted. 'We surrender!'

He threw down his rifle and stood up. Slowly his men followed his example. Tony looked at Elena. 'I think we've been scuppered.' He too laid his revolver on the cobbles and stood up, hands held high. The two women did likewise.

'I will protect us,' Sandrine said. 'I am a neutral.'

The Germans emerged and advanced, rifles thrust forward. They wore grey-green uniforms with masses of equipment, and the smaller than usual leather caps of parachutists. Tony recalled that these were elite troops.

Their officer was in front, armed with a tommy-gun, although a pistol holster hung from his belt. 'What is your unit?' he demanded.

'The Fourth Regiment of Foot,' the sergeant said.

The officer spoke in German, and the man beside him slung his own tommy-gun to take out a notebook and write the information down.

'You.' The officer pointed at Tony. 'You are not a Yugoslav.'

'I am a British officer,' Tony said.

'Serving with the Yugoslavs?'

'Not actually. I was with the embassy.'

'The embassy has been evacuated.'

'I know. Unfortunately I was not there at the time, and so was left behind.'

'You are a prisoner of war.'

Tony nodded. 'That does seem to be the case.'

The officer looked at the three civilians, and at the weapons lying at their feet. 'You are guerillas.'

'We are patriots, comrade,' one of the men said.

The captain gave a cold smile. 'One man's patriot is another man's guerilla.' He gave an order in German, and four of his men moved forward; they seized the three civilians by the arms, pulled them from the barricade, and forced them across the street.

'What is going to happen to us?' one of the men shouted.

'You are going to be shot. All civilians found in arms against the Reich are to be shot on sight. Those are my orders.'

'You cannot do this,' Tony protested. 'It is against the rules of war.'

'I obey the rules of the Reich,' the captain informed him. 'Not the rules of war.'

Tony swung round to look at the civilians at the same time as the executioners opened fire. The men had been thrust against a wall, and were being shot at a range of only a few feet. They collapsed in a welter of blood, and Sandrine gave another of her shrieks.

'I will report this to your senior officer,' Tony said.

'You are welcome.'

His sergeant asked a question, gazing at the two women and pointing at the Luger which lay at Elena's feet.

'Is that your weapon?' the captain asked. 'My sergeant says he saw you drop it when you surrendered.'

'Yes, it is my weapon,' Elena said.

'You are a civilian.' Another order, and some more of his men moved forward.

'Now, hold on,' Tony said, and a rifle butt was swung into his stomach, which had him gasping.

The sergeant asked another question, and the captain shrugged. The men gave a whoop of anticipated delight and surrounded Elena, beginning to tear the dress from her shoulders. Elena endeavoured to resist them, but two of them held her arms and she could only kick, albeit ineffectively.

Two more men held Sandrine and began tearing at her clothing as well.

'You cannot do this,' Sandrine shouted. 'I am a French citizen. I have a Vichy passport.'

'Wait,' the captain commanded. 'Show me this passport.'

'Well, I do not have it with me,' Sandrine panted. 'It is at my apartment.'

'And where is that?'

'It is north of the river.'

'I do not believe you, Fräulein.'

'I can prove I am French. Listen. I am French, born and bred,' she said in French.

'I do not know what you are saying,' the captain said. 'I do not speak French.'

'Help me,' Sandrine begged Tony.

'She is French,' Tony said. 'I can vouch for her.'

'I do not believe you either, Englander. She is a civilian, in arms against the Reich.'

'I have never fired a gun in my life!' Sandrine shouted. 'I have never *touched* a gun.'

'However,' the captain said, ignoring her protests, 'as they are going to die anyway, I have told my men they may have them first. They will enjoy that.'

'Bastard!' Tony shouted, and received another blow in the belly, which had him on his knees.

Elena reacted. Her dress had been torn from her shoulders and hung from the belt round her waist, but the men stripping her had stopped for the moment, distracted by the discussion about Sandrine. Now she slid through their arms to kneel on the cobbles and pick up the Luger; it had only been fired once and contained a virtually full magazine. She brought it up and in the same movement shot the captain through the chest. He half turned as he fell, landing at Tony's feet. He had still been holding his tommy-gun, and this rolled away from him. Tony grabbed it and sprayed the men around him, then turned towards Elena. One of the Germans had struck her on the back of the head, and she had slumped forward. Now he was straightening up and at the same time unslinging his rifle to hit her again. Tony cut him down with a single burst and then turned his attention to his companion.

Realising what was happening, the remaining Yugoslav soldiers also seized their weapons and began firing. The men holding Sandrine released her to reach for their own. Sandrine fell flat on the road with one of her shrieks while the men above her died.

The remaining Germans ran for shelter, but they were firing as they did so, if for the moment wildly. Tony grabbed Sandrine's shoulders and dragged her up. To his surprise – and, he thought, hers – she was holding a discarded tommy-gun.

'Run!' he shouted at Elena, who was just recovering from the blow on her head. She scrambled to her feet while Tony threw Sandrine over his shoulder and ran for the next corner. He was surrounded by firing but neither of them was hit. He reached the shelter of the buildings, set her down, leaned against a wall and panted. Elena joined them, along with the Yugoslav sergeant and two of his men; the other two had fallen. Although they did not appear to be dead, yet, as they were on the exposed street there was nothing to be done about them.

Sandrine was sitting on the ground, fondling her newly acquired tommy-gun. 'I want to shoot this thing,' she said. 'Tell me how to shoot this thing.'

'You squeeze the trigger,' Elena told her. 'After pointing it at the enemy,' she added hastily as Sandrine's fingers curled round the trigger guard.

'Where are we?' Tony asked.

'In hell,' the sergeant said.

Sandrine fired a burst round the corner, and then said, 'Shit! Nothing is happening.'

'Your magazine is empty,' Elena told her.

'Then give me another magazine.'

'Where am I supposed to get that?'

'Shit!' the Frenchwoman said again. 'Do you think I hit anyone?'

'Just let's assume you did.' Elena was trying to do something about her dress; her vest did not leave a great deal to the imagination.

'Where is your headquarters?' Tony asked the sergeant.

'Over there.' He gestured vaguely at the city. 'But it has been overrun. That is why we left.'

'So what are you going to do now?'

'I don't know. Will you command us?'

Tony hesitated, but there did not seem to be any alternative.

'Is there any movement?' he asked the soldier who was peering round the building.

'They are talking. I think they are waiting for a new officer to come.'

'We need to be out of here before that happens. We need to get out of the city. It is no longer defensible.'

'In the open they will pick us off like flies,' Elena objected.

Tony looked at his watch. It was only eleven o'clock. 'Let's get back to the baths. We'll shelter there until it's dark.'

'Don't you think the Germans will look there?'

'Only in passing. Ivkov will have to hide us.'

They hurried down several side streets, seeing no one, although the sound of firing continued to hang over the city.

'I am so hungry,' Sandrine said. 'Do you have no rations?' She still carried her empty tommy-gun; Tony reckoned it gave her a sense of security.

'Only a few biscuits,' the sergeant said.

'I would love a biscuit,' Sandrine said.

'Well . . .' The sergeant unslung his haversack.

'Over there,' Elena said suddenly.

They looked across the road at a charcuterie. It had been struck by a bomb blast and the windows were shattered.

'There will be food inside,' she said.

'Looting is a criminal offence,' the sergeant said. 'Punishable by death.'

'So is starvation,' Elena told him, and crossed the street.

The rest hesitated only a few minutes, then followed her. Beyond the broken glass was a treasure chest of cold meats and bowls of coleslaw. The men, and the women, crammed some of the food into their mouths, then filled their haversacks.

Ten minutes later they were at the back of the baths. Tony banged on the door, and it was cautiously opened by Ivkov.

'You!'

'Spot on.'

'There were soldiers here, only a few minutes ago. They were looking for . . .' He gaped at the six people, all armed, all looking very desperate. 'You!'

'That's reasonable. But if they were here and did not find us, they are unlikely to come back. We wish to stay here until dark.'

'Here?' Ivkov's eyes rolled.

'We won't be any trouble. We have our own food. But we will require water.' He pushed the bath-keeper aside and entered the building. The women and the soldiers followed.

'They will shoot me,' Ivkov protested.

'Only if you tell them we were here,' Tony pointed out.

Sandrine stood on the edge of the pool. 'My legs are so painful. I would like to bathe them.'

'Why not? Now,' – Tony turned to the sergeant – 'we will mount a guard, two hours on and six off, eh? He will situate himself just inside those broken doors, and he will watch the road and alert us if there is any movement towards this building. Understood?'

'Yes, sir,' the sergeant said enthusiastically, deputing one of his men. He had no intention of taking the first watch himself, now that Sandrine was sitting on the edge of the bath, her skirt pulled to her thighs and her legs dangling in the water.

'That feels so good.'

'I am going to wash all over,' Elena announced, and commenced removing her tattered clothing.

'Do you think that's a good idea?' Tony asked, realising that he might be going to have problems which had never been visualised at Sandhurst.

'I do not like being dirty,' she pointed out, now completely naked.

Tony did not suppose anyone actually made a sound, but it seemed as if a collective sigh seeped through the building, reaching from Ivkov to the man who was supposed to be watching the street.

Elena dived into the water, swam beneath the surface for some yards, and then emerged, tossing wet hair from her eyes.

'I wish permission to bathe, sir,' the second soldier said. 'I am also very dirty.'

Tony and the sergeant gazed at one another.

'Why don't you come in, Sandrine?' Elena said. 'You will feel much better.'

'I cannot undress in front of these men,' Sandrine said.

Elena blew a raspberry.

'Sandrine is right,' Tony decided. 'We will go outside while you bathe. That includes you, Ivkov.' He turned to the private. 'You can bathe when the women are finished. They will not be long.'

He shepherded the reluctant men out of the pool area into the lobby.

'Do you know them well?' the sergeant asked wistfully.

'Yes,' Tony said, and joined the sentry at the doors, trying not to listen to Sandrine's squeals as she entered the water. There were definitely going to be problems ahead, he thought

– and perhaps not only with the other men. The only saving factor was that Sandrine seemed to be off sex, at least for the moment.

He stood beside the sentry and gazed at the rubbled street. He wondered if Belgrade would ever recover. And there was still fighting going on, although the continuous gunfire had slackened. But the city continued to burn; the morning sky was almost obliterated by the clouds of smoke.

'What are we going to do, sir?' asked the sergeant.

'Do you think your army is still intact?'

'I do not know, sir.'

'If it is, our best bet would be to link up with it.'

'They will have retreated to the hill country,' the sergeant said. 'We should go there.'

'How far?'

'Thirty miles.'

Tony pulled his nose. Thirty miles, and the women were shoeless. He supposed Elena, big and strong and essentially coarse – however attractively so – could make it. But Sandrine . . . She was a creature of the Champs Élysées, not the mountains.

'Listen!' the sentry said.

The sound crept across the morning, a steady grind.

'Tanks,' the sergeant said unnecessarily. 'That means the German army is here on the ground. They will have taken over the entire city by tonight.'

'It's a big city,' Tony said, more optimistically than he felt.

'Soldiers,' the sentry said.

A patrol had appeared at the top of the street.

'Inside,' Tony snapped. 'You stay here, Ivkov.'

'They will shoot me,' the bath-keeper wailed.

'Of course they will not. Just don't tell them we are here.'

'And when they wish to come inside?'

'Tell us where to go.'

Ivkov chewed his lip. 'The pump room. Go in there and hide behind the pump. . It is a very small area. They should not wish to look in there.'

'When you say small . . .?'

'You will fit in. If you squeeze. But you must take all your weapons. And the women.'

The sergeant rolled his eyes.

The four men ran back into the pool room.

'Gather everything up,' Tony said. 'Don't forget the food.'

'Have you come to join us?' Elena asked, bouncing up and down in an unforgettable manner. Sandrine had sunk into the water until only her eyes were showing.

'Germans,' Tony said. 'Come out.'

Elena scrambled out, dripping water, and the sighs began again.

'And you, Sandrine.'

'I cannot come out,' Sandrine said. 'I have nothing on.'

'You'll have even less on if the Germans find you in there.'

She approached the side; Tony reached down, grasped her wrist, and plucked her out of the water to the accompaniment of one of her shrieks.

'Go, go, go,' he snapped, holding her in his arms and carrying her round the pool to the door at the back. 'Bring those clothes,' he told the sergeant.

Elena ran in front of him and opened the door; the soldiers crowded into the pump room, the sergeant bringing up the rear with the women's discarded clothes.

'To the back,' Tony said. 'Behind the pump.'

This was a large machine, which filled the centre of the already small room. The men and women squeezed in there, Sandrine still in Tony's arms.

'I think you could put her down now,' Elena suggested in French.

Tony relaxed his grip and Sandrine's wet body slid down

his front. But she remained standing against him, preferring to conceal her front rather than her back. Elena pressed against her back, and the men pressed against *her* back. She looked at Tony above Sandrine's head. 'I think she's growing on you,' she remarked.

Sandrine made a stifled sound against the middle of his chest, and he put his arms round her to encompass Elena as well, preferring not to reply.

'Listen!' the sergeant whispered.

They heard the tramp of booted feet, the rasp of harsh voices. The Germans had come into the building after all. Ivkov was protesting, asking what they were looking for. But they did not even try the pump room door, and the noise quickly receded again.

'I would like to get dressed now,' Sandrine said.

'Just let's wait for Ivkov, first,' Tony suggested.

It was ten minutes before Ivkov opened the door. 'You see my hair?' he asked. 'It has turned white.'

'At least you know they will hardly be back a third time,' Tony told him.

The bath-keeper stared at the women. 'I should receive a reward.'

'We'll talk about it.' He ushered the men outside to allow the women to dress. 'We'll continue as before.'

The guard was re-mounted, and they settled down to wait, listening to the sound of the German army moving in. Now there was only sporadic gunfire.

Tony knew he needed to concentrate very hard, but it was intensely difficult – he could still feel Sandrine's naked body pressed against him. In addition, so much had happened during the day that he had not had the time really to consider the overall situation, or his own.

From a personal point of view his duty was to regain the embassy staff as rapidly as he could, regardless of the risk of a court martial for being absent without leave. The problem there was that he had no idea where they were, or how to get to them.

That was caught up in the general problem of what had happened to the country as a whole, and what was likely to happen in the immediate future. Were the Germans carrying out a punitive expedition just to inform the world that they would not be defied by any nation in Europe, however small it might be? He had thought so during the initial surprise bombing raid, and even when they sent in the paratroops. But the logistical cost in deploying panzers and ground forces strongly suggested they were here to stay.

That made no sense in cold terms. Yugoslavia had nothing to offer Nazi ambitions, save the necessity to devote a large number of troops to keep the country in subjugation.

On the other hand, the mountain passes did provide a corridor to Albania and thus Greece. It would therefore be possible to send aid to Mussolini, who certainly seemed unable to deal with the Greeks on his own. And a campaign in Greece would provide occupation for the German army, stagnating since its dramatic victory in France.

It occurred to Tony that he might accomplish some good if he could find out just what the Germans had in mind. Which indicated remaining in Yugoslavia for a while. Which was going to require survival. But that . . .

Elena sat beside him. If her tattered clothing made her look like a scarecrow, she was at least clean now.

'How do you feel?' he asked.

'I am fine.'

'Those bastards—'

'Forget them,' she said. 'We killed them before they could get to me.'

'Is Sandrine all right?'

'I don't know.'

'I know she was very shaken by what happened.'

Elena nodded. 'It began with Bernhard's abandonment of

her. And then . . . She is not accustomed to physical violence. To being manhandled.'

'Where is she?'

'She is in the pump room.'

'Still?'

'She is ashamed to come out. She is not used to being naked in front of a lot of men, either.'

'Shit,' he commented.

'I think you should go to her.'

'Me?'

'She needs reassuring.'

'Surely you're the one to do that.'

'She needs the reassurance of a man. She is very complex.'

'You can say that again. I must confess I've always felt that she was, well—'

'She is, I think, basically.'

'You're not going to tell me she's ever made advances to you?'

Elena gave a throaty laugh. 'No, no. I made advances to her.'

'You . . .' He was speechless.

'Well, she is a lovely woman, don't you think? I love lovely things.'

Tony scratched his head.

'So, do you still want to marry me?'

'Of course I do.' He spoke without thinking.

'Good. If we get out of this we will get married. I do not think even your superiors will object, if we survive a war together. But listen, go and cheer Sandrine up. If you want to fuck her, you have my permission.'

'But you have just said—'

'That she is a very complex character.'

'I don't even think she likes me,' Tony said. 'Anyway, the whole idea is obscene. Especially in our circumstances.'

'But you would like to do it. Admit it.'

'Oh, for God's sake, Elena. As you say, she's a lovely woman. But really, I have too much else on my mind right now. Apart from the fact that I am engaged to you.'

Could he really be engaged to a lesbian, even if she was only a part-time lesbian? Not for the first time he was realising that he had plunged into a world of human relationships that could not possibly be recognised, much less accepted, in a Somerset village. He wasn't at all sure that he could accept it himself.

'I have given you my permission. Just so long as you remember you belong to me. And what else do you have on your mind? We can do nothing until it is dark. That is still several hours away.'

'I still have to work out what we do then.'

'Well, we get out of the city.'

'And then?'

'We must try to get down to Montenegro.'

'Do you not think the Germans are going to move into Montenegro as well?'

'It will take them some time. We will get to Montenegro first, and you will requisition a boat in the name of the British army, and we will go—'

'Yes? The Adriatic is an Italian lake.'

'Shit! But you will think of something.'

'That is what I am trying to do. But the first thing I am trying to think about is how we get to Montenegro. Or anywhere else.'

'We will walk.'

'Maybe a hundred miles. You have no shoes.'

She looked at her feet, seeming to realise that for the first time.

'And neither does Sandrine,' he added.

Elena giggled. 'You will have to carry her.'

He went down to the pump room, as Elena insisted. The door was closed, and he knocked.

'Who is it?' Sandrine asked. 'Is it you, Elena?'

'It's Tony.'

'Oh. What do you want?'

'To speak with you. I'm coming in.'

He opened the door. She had retreated behind the pump.

'For God's sake,' he said. 'I am not going to harm you.'

'You think that saving my life gives you the right to me.'

'Listen. I'm engaged to Elena. And what about Bernhard?'

'I shall never see Bernhard again. I shall never speak to Bernhard again. I shall never even *think* of Bernhard again. And the next time I see him, I shall kill him.'

Tony deduced that she was not in a logical frame of mind.

'That seems to be a sound idea,' he agreed. 'Now listen. You have to come out of here and join the others.'

'Those men saw me with nothing on.'

'Do you really think you're the first naked woman they've seen? Okay, so it's a good bet they've never seen anyone quite as beautiful as you, but I do promise that none of them is going to trouble you in any way. I will see to that. We are a team. We survive together, or we die. Remember this.'

'Do you really think I am beautiful? Or are you just saying this?'

'I really think you are beautiful.'

'Do you think I am more beautiful than Elena?'

Tony hesitated. But Elena had given him carte blanche as to how to handle the situation. Besides, it was the truth. 'Yes.'

'Does that mean you wish to fuck me?'

'Yes. But now is not the time. The first thing we have to do is get out of Belgrade and link up with the Yugoslav army.'

'All I need to do is reach my apartment and get my passport.'

'Sandrine,' Tony said as patiently as he could, 'by now your apartment has been destroyed, or occupied by the Germans. And even if you could get your passport, it wouldn't do you any good. We didn't kill all of those German soldiers.

Those who survived will have circulated our descriptions, and they will certainly remember you. If the German army lays hands on you again, it is going to execute you, probably after considerable unpleasantness first. Do you want that to happen?'

She bit her lip. 'You are trying to make me into some kind of outlaw.'

'You already *are* an outlaw, in German eyes. I am trying to make you understand that your only hope of survival is to come with us.'

'So that you – and those others – can have sex with me.'

'I give you my word that neither I nor any of those soldiers is going to lay a finger on you unless invited to do so. All I am trying to do is save your life.'

'You want to link up with the Yugoslav army. Where will you do that?'

'There's the point. It may take a little while, and involve a bit of walking.'

She looked down at her legs and feet; both were red, and her feet were cut.

'Yes,' he said. 'Now, obviously, if we see an opportunity, we will find you some shoes. But for the time being, we will have to wrap some of our clothes round your feet. I can't promise it'll be comfortable, but it should give you some protection. Now, will you please come out and remember that everyone here only wants to help you.'

Sandrine sighed, but followed him into the pool room.

The soldiers were enthusiastic about helping the two women, but Ivkov was the most useful. Several of his regular clients apparently left their swimming costumes in his changing rooms, and these were very useful for wrapping round the women's feet, to be secured with lengths of string. When Elena looked down at herself she burst out laughing, and even Sandrine smiled; when they walked they flapped like penguins.

'I would like to come with you, when you go,' Ivkov said.

'It will be dangerous,' Tony pointed out.

'I do not think it will be as dangerous as staying here.'

'What about your family?'

The bath-keeper shrugged. 'My children have all gone away from Belgrade. I cannot help them by staying here.'

'You have a wife, haven't you?'

'I have had a wife for thirty years. The same wife. Now she has a moustache. And now . . .' He looked at the women, sitting together, whispering.

'I think you need to be certain of one thing, Ivkov,' Tony said. 'If you lay a finger on those girls, or if you harass them in any way, I will shoot you.'

Ivkov snorted. 'You think you have the right to do that?'

'I am assuming the right, now. I have been asked to take command by the sergeant, and I have done so. If you really wish to come with us you are welcome, but you will then be placing yourself under my command, and will obey my orders at all times.'

Ivkov considered. 'I saved your lives.'

'And we are grateful. But now it is up to us to save our own lives. And we can only do that by acting as a unit, with one commander.'

Ivkov nodded. 'I will come with you. It will be better than staying here.'

'Then, welcome.'

But the conversation had raised other considerations. He sat beside Elena. 'What are you going to do about your family?'

'What *can* I do about my family?'

'Not a lot, I'm afraid. But—'

'My mother wishes to make peace with the Germans. If she manages to do this before they shoot her, she will be all right. My father always does what my mother tells him to, so he will be all right. Svetovar is with the army. If he

71

has not been killed, he will have withdrawn with them and
be somewhere in the hills. Maybe I will see him again. But
I can do nothing about him at this moment.'

Tony wondered if, in similar circumstances, he would be
capable of such pragmatism. But at least her courage and
determination were not in doubt. He hoped Sandrine would
turn out as well.

He joined the sergeant.

'What is your plan, sir?'

'Firstly, to have you tell me your name.'

'It is Matanovic, sir.'

'Right. Well, Sergeant Matanovic, as soon as it is dark we
are going to get out of the city, and then we are going to try
to link up with your people. I am relying on you to help me
in this.'

Matanovic nodded. 'They will have retreated to the south.'

'That makes sense. Will we find them?'

'I should think so, sir. Or they will find us.'

'Well, then, that is our plan.'

It was Tony's idea to reach Dubrovnik, although he had no
positive plan as to what he could do after that; the Adriatic
was an Italian lake. But if he could get to a radio and send
a message, it might be possible for him to be taken out by
submarine, or even by aircraft. If anyone in Athens or Cairo
would be sufficiently interested in an itinerant captain, that
is. Especially if he intended to get the women out as well.
He did not feel he could just abandon them.

But his first business was to get them out of Belgrade.

The sounds of conflict dwindled throughout the afternoon; the
sounds of conquest grew. The rumble of tanks and transport
filled the air, and aircraft continued to zoom overhead. An
occasional shot rang out, but this was just the Germans
flushing out any final resistance. An armoured car rumbled
past the baths, a voice in good Serbo-Croat issuing orders
through a loudspeaker: as the city had surrendered it was the

duty of its citizens to welcome their new masters. Instructions were added as to where people should go to apply for their ration cards.

Tony and his group continued to be on the lookout for a return visit from an enemy patrol, but although they saw the occasional group of soldiers, none approached the baths. In fact this area of the city was very quiet, with apparently all resistance stamped out.

'This is a sad day for Yugoslavia,' Matanovic observed. 'For all Serbia.'

'You are Serbian?' Tony asked.

'Of course, sir.'

'But there are other nationalities in your army, are there not? Croats, Slovenes, Montenegrins . . .'

'Bah,' Matanovic said. 'The only good soldiers are Serbs. The rest are useless. They are cowards, and cannot be trusted. The Croats are worst of all. They are Fascists at heart.'

Tony looked at Elena, willing her to be silent; she accepted his unspoken command, even as she looked daggers.

Fortunately the sergeant had made no inquiries as to her nationality, but Tony was beginning to realise that this six-person unit was going to be far more difficult to command than a company of the Buffs.

They ate part of their looted food, and as dusk approached – it was still only early April – carefully packed the rest away in the soldiers' haversacks, Elena's satchel, and a shoulder bag Ivkov produced.

'My handbag!' Sandrine exclaimed, apparently realising for the first time that she no longer had it.

'I'm afraid it got lost in that fire we ran through,' Tony said.

'It will have been burned to a cinder,' Elena said.

'But . . . my make-up was in there.'

'You look fine,' Tony assured her, hoping she was not going to get to a mirror in the near future.

'But . . . the key to my apartment!'

'When we get back to your apartment, we'll break the door down,' Tony promised.

'If someone else hasn't done it first,' Elena said, receiving a glance from Sandrine which could, Tony suspected, indicate the end of a close relationship.

'I should have a weapon,' Ivkov said. 'I cannot escape without a weapon.'

'There are none to spare.'

Ivkov looked at Sandrine, who still clutched her tommy-gun. '*She* has a weapon.'

'There is no ammunition for it. There is very little ammunition left for any of our weapons,' Tony told him. His service revolver and Elena's Luger, which she had reloaded, were the only fully functional guns they had left, and there was only one magazine left for Elena and a handful of bullets for him.

'Then what will we do when we meet the Germans?'

'Our objective must be to not meet any Germans.'

It was now quite dark, partly because of the heavy pall of smoke which hung above the city. An eerie red half-light rose from the many burning buildings. There was a great deal of noise as the invaders, no doubt helped by the local constabulary and fire brigades, attempted to control the various blazes. Occasionally there was a rumbling explosion as they blew up ruined houses, or a rumbling crash as something fell down. There was also an occasional gunshot, and even burst of automatic fire; it was impossible to say whether this meant that there was continuing resistance or that the Germans were shooting people they did not like the look of.

'Time to go,' he said.

They retreated to the rear of the bath-house, and used the back door.

'I have been here fifteen years,' Ivkov said sadly. 'Will I ever see it again?'

'Of course, if you wish to,' Tony said, more certainly than he actually felt. 'You will come back after the war.'

'After the war,' Elena muttered.

'Do you think my apartment will still be there?' Sandrine asked.

'Of course,' Tony said again. 'The Germans will not bomb Belgrade again. If your apartment is there now, it will be there when you come back.'

He wondered if he had chosen his words correctly, especially as he should have added, *if* you come back.

But Sandrine was thinking of other things. 'All my good clothes are there,' she said. 'All of my books. My photo albums . . .'

That such personal treasures might survive really was a pipe dream. Tony hurried on. 'There must be no noise,' he told them. 'No talking. Just follow the person in front of you. I will lead with you, Ivkov, as this is your part of town. You will come next, Elena, and then you, Sandrine. You two privates will follow, and you, Sergeant Matanovic, will bring up the rear. There can be no straggling. Anyone who drops out will have to be on his own. Equally, there must be no shooting. Understood?'

They nodded, their faces, now indistinct in the gloom, looking suitably determined.

'Then let's go.'

Tony stepped out into the open air and inhaled; his nostrils were instantly assailed by a variety of odours, ranging from the smell of scorching wood and billowing smoke to the stench of death. It was now some eighteen hours since Belgrade had suffered its first casualty, and very few had as yet been buried or even moved from where they lay.

He crept forward cautiously, keeping to one side of the street to stay in the shade of the shops and houses, but every so often having to move out as he came upon a fire. He did not look back, but he could hear Ivkov panting behind him, and from time to time the bath-keeper would touch him on the shoulder to indicate the direction he should follow. Certainly the fat old man, however lecherous he might be, was proving invaluable.

Tony kept them going for over an hour before he held up his hand to signal a rest. Instantly the two women sank to the ground with various grunts. They were still surrounded by heat, flame and noise, but thus far they had seen no Germans.

'How much further?' Tony whispered to Ivkov.

'We are already in the suburbs. Another hour will see us out of the city.'

'Another hour,' Sandrine groaned. 'I cannot go another hour.'

'We may have to walk all night,' Elena told her.

'I cannot do that. My feet are in agony. You will have to leave me.'

'I will carry you,' Tony said.

'Would you?' Her face lit up.

'You are going to carry her all night?' Elena asked.

'We will all carry her,' Matanovic said. 'We will take turns.'

He looked at his men, who nodded eagerly.

'Oh,' Sandrine said.

'I will carry her too,' Ivkov volunteered. 'I will carry her first.'

'Oh!' Sandrine remarked again.

'I will carry her first,' Tony said. 'And for as long as possible.'

'How are you going to do that?' Elena asked.

'You'll have to get on my back,' Tony decided, as Sandrine also looked uncertain. 'Put your legs round my waist and your arms round my neck.'

He half stooped as Sandrine climbed on to him, watched with great interest by the other men as she hitched her skirt up to her thighs and as Tony put his hands behind himself to hold her buttocks and get her into the best possible position. Each man was obviously anticipating his turn.

'Let's go.'

Her face nuzzled his neck. 'You are a good man,' she said, this being apparently the first time she had considered the matter. 'I will never forget the way you are taking care of me.'

'We are all taking care of you,' he pointed out.

'Those others,' – she gave an interesting shudder against his back – 'they only want to get their hands on me.' Then she gave a little giggle. 'I forgot. You would like to get your hands on me too.'

'I already have my hands on you,' he reminded her, reaching behind him to give her another squeeze. 'Now concentrate.'

As Ivkov had promised, after another forty-five minutes the houses began to thin. By then Tony was feeling the strain. Sandrine was a small woman, and he did not suppose she weighed much more than eight stones, but that was eight stones more than he was used to carrying.

He gave a sigh of relief as he set her down. 'Next donkey.'

'Me,' Ivkov answered before anyone else could get in.

'Oh, lord,' Sandrine muttered, but she climbed on to the big man's back.

'You are making him very happy,' Elena pointed out, and moved up to be beside Tony. 'Did she not make you very happy?'

'She made me very tired,' Tony said.

Elena snorted. 'Well,' she said, 'the way *my* feet are feeling, I may soon be making you more tired yet.'

Now they saw people, peering at them from round corners. Some were even still in their homes, looking out of the windows. Here in the suburbs there was less damage. Most of the people hurried off when they saw them, as at least three of them were identifiable as soldiers.

But the fact that this area appeared virtually undamaged gave Tony an idea. 'Cover me,' he told Matanovic, and went up the front path of one of the houses in a terrace, which had recently been repainted to suggest some prosperity on the part of its owner. More importantly, he had caught the glimmer of a candle behind the window overlooking the street.

He knocked. There was no immediate response, but the candle went out. He knocked again. 'Open up,' he said, 'or I shall break the door.'

He heard movement, and then the bolt was drawn. The door opened a few inches and a woman peered at him. She was small, well-dressed, quite good-looking, and not very old, he estimated, although fear and anxiety made her appear older than she probably was.

'We are Yugoslav soldiers,' Tony said. 'Will you let us in?'

'The Germans will shoot me. They were here this afternoon, and they told me that harbouring fugitives is a capital offence. You must go away.'

Matanovic had joined him while the others waited on the path; Ivkov reluctantly set Sandrine on the ground, where she promptly sat. 'The Germans can only shoot you, madame, if they know we were here,' the sergeant pointed out.

'Do you not suppose my neighbours have seen you?'

'Are your neighbours not your friends?'

She made a moue. 'Some of them.'

'We will not be long, but we need your help.'

'How can I help you?'

'Just let us in,' Tony said. 'Five minutes.'

She hesitated, looking past him in an attempt to determine how many of her neighbours *might* be watching, but with all the houses opposite in darkness it was impossible to tell. Then she stood back and opened the door.

They entered the house, Elena putting her arm round Sandrine's waist to help her up the steps.

'Are you alone?' Matanovic asked.

Tony was content to allow him to do the talking, as these were his people.

'I have my children.'

'Where?'

'We are here,' said a boy.

Tony peered into the gloom, identified two small bodies. Elena had identified a settee, and on this she laid Sandrine, who gave a sigh of relief.

'You have a candle,' Matanovic said. 'We saw it from outside. Light it, Maric,' he told one of his soldiers, 'and draw the blinds.'

Maric obeyed. A match scraped, and a moment later the candle was lit.

'Hold it up,' Tony said to the woman.

She did so, and he was able to look around. It was a cultivated room, with masses of photographs, a few prints on the walls, overstuffed furniture, and good carpets. The two children, a boy and a girl, were hardly teenagers, he estimated. 'Where is your husband?'

'I do not know. He went out, and did not come back. Now I do not know if he will be able to. The Germans have announced a curfew. Anyone seen on the streets after dark will be shot. You will be shot.'

'It's becoming a habit,' Tony agreed. 'We need shoes.'

'Shoes?' She looked down at his feet.

'For the ladies.'

She looked at Elena and Sandrine in turn, obviously wondering if the word lady could possibly be applied to two such bedraggled and tattered creatures.

'You see they have none,' Tony explained. 'Have you anything that might fit?'

The woman moved closer to look at Sandrine. 'Is she wounded?'

'No. It is her feet. From being barefoot.'

The woman bent over the Frenchwoman, holding the

candle close. Sandrine instinctively drew up her legs, away from the flame. 'This is very bad. There are open cuts.'

'That is why she must have shoes,' Elena said.

'She needs medication,' the woman said. 'I will fetch some.'

'You have medication?' Elena asked.

'My husband has. He is a doctor.'

'And you know how to use it?'

'Before I married Josef, I was a nurse.'

'Well, glory be,' Tony commented. 'Seems we have fallen on our feet. Go with her, Elena, and see what you can find in the way of shoes.'

'Take the candle,' the woman said. 'I have another.'

The two women left the room and from the creaks appeared to be climbing some stairs. Tony sat on the settee beside Sandrine. 'How do you feel?'

'I am in agony. But I am sorry to be such a nuisance.'

'We're just glad to have you with us. I know I am speaking for all of us.'

She made a face, and he looked at her feet, gently pulling away the remaining pieces of bathing costume. She winced, but did not speak. Like the woman, he did not like what he saw. Apart from being bruised and cut, as well as singed, both feet were starting to swell. It was going to be a few days before she would be able to walk again. But my God, he thought, if infection sets in, or perhaps gangrene . . . The thought of having to cut off Sandrine's feet was not acceptable, even if he could find a surgeon to do it for him.

'She will have food,' Matanovic said, kneeling beside Tony. 'Shall we not take some of it?'

'Did you not say that looting is punishable by death?'

'We would requisition it. We would give her a receipt. We could even pay her for it, now. I have money.'

'And she and her two children would probably starve,' Tony pointed out. 'We don't know how soon they'll be able to obtain any more food.'

'And will we not starve, sir? That food we brought with us will only do for one more meal.'

'We are soldiers, Sergeant Matanovic. Being hungry goes with the job.'

'I am not a soldier,' Sandrine remarked softly.

He grinned at her. 'You have been conscripted.'

She stuck out her tongue at him.

Elena and the woman returned. 'Look what I found,' Elena said, displaying the lace-up walking boots she was wearing.

'Brilliant! You're the best shod of us all, now.' But Tony could not stop himself from looking at the woman; she was half the size of Elena, and had tiny feet.

'They belong to my husband,' the woman said. 'I have a pair of my own which will fit this lady. When she can put them on. Now let me see . . .' She began working on Sandrine's feet. She had bottles of antiseptic and various ointments. But she also had a bowl of water, with which she carefully washed the savaged flesh. Sandrine moaned a bit and did some weeping, but on the whole she bore up very well. Finally the woman bandaged both feet, and when that was done, inserted them carefully into the boots and laced them in turn. 'That is the best I can do. But she will not be able to walk very far.'

'We will carry her,' Ivkov said, anxious to resume his duties.

The woman nodded. 'But when next you stop, you must take off the boots and the bandages, and let the flesh breathe. Then' – she gave Tony a tube of ointment – 'apply some more of this on her feet, and re-bandage them.'

Tony pocketed the tube, and then led the woman into the corner. 'You have been very helpful,' he said.

'Are you going to fight the Nazis?'

'If we can.'

'Then I am glad to be helpful.'

'And we will always be grateful. Will you answer a question, truthfully?'

'If I can.'

'Will the mademoiselle be all right?'

'If you do as I say, I think so. She is your woman?'

'Ah . . . no. She is a good friend.'

'She should be your woman,' the doctor's wife said. 'She is very pretty. Now you must go.'

Tony nodded.

'You have food?'

'Enough.'

She regarded him for some seconds, then she said, 'Come.'

She led him into the pantry and opened a walk-in larder, in which there hung several huge smoked hams. 'Take one of these.'

'I could not possibly do that,' Tony protested. 'What about you, and your children?'

'There is enough here for us, for a long time.'

'We will be eternally grateful. One day we will repay you.'

'There is something you can do for me. My husband's name is Dukic. Dr Josef Dukic. If you happen to meet up with him, will you tell him we are all right, and that the house was not bombed.'

'I will do that, Madame Dukic.'

Tony went back to his people; Sandrine stood up, and then sat down again. 'It is too painful.'

'Then it's the same drill as before. Private Maric, you're up next. Let's go.' He gave the ham to Elena.

An hour later they were clear of the houses and in open country. They made slow progress, both because they had to stop and rest at regular intervals, and because the terrain was very uneven and it was utterly dark. But they could soon tell they were on rising ground, and shortly after that stumbled into a fast-rushing stream, from which they were able to slake their thirst. Matanovic, who was carrying Sandrine, stumbled and fell to his knees, dislodging the woman so that she fell

82

off him and into the water with a gigantic splash and one of her shrieks.

Tony dragged her up and carried her to the bank.

'My God,' she said. 'I am soaked through.'

'Don't tell me you want to strip off again,' Elena said. 'It's becoming a habit.'

'I have no intention of stripping off,' Sandrine snapped. 'But I shall certainly catch cold. On top of everything else.' She was close to tears.

'We're all pretty wet,' Tony told her. 'At least you chaps can fill your canteens.' He watched them as they did so, then stood up to look back down the slope and across the fields at the burning city.

Matanovic stood beside him. 'It makes the blood boil.'

'Is Belgrade your home?'

'*Was* Belgrade my home, sir. Yes. I was born there and have lived there all my life, save when on army duties.'

'Are you married?'

'No, sir. Thank God. But my parents are in there. If they are still alive.'

'We must hope they are. Let's move.'

'Can we not stay here, sir? We are all very tired . . .'

'We are too close to the city, Sergeant. Come daybreak the Germans will commence their cleaning-up operation all over again. We've been lucky so far. Let's ride that luck for as long as it holds.'

By the first light they had covered a further five miles, Tony estimated. Now they really were exhausted, and when Tony led them into a gully in the hillside, they collapsed where they stood. He felt like doing the same, but he laid Sandrine – it was his fourth turn to carry her – on the ground, and then surveyed his command.

'Is anyone hungry?'

No one even responded.

'Right,' he said. 'Now, we are going to stay here until we

see what the day brings. We may have to stay here all day. But
we should be quite comfortable. We have food, and we have
sufficient water, if we don't drink it all at once. However,
we do need to mount a lookout. I will take the first watch,
for two hours, and then I will wake you, Sergeant.'

'Sir,' Matanovic muttered; his eyes were half shut.

'So get on with it.'

Tony moved to the front of the gully and stationed himself
behind a bush; from there he could look down the sloping
hillside. Belgrade was now just a distant cloud of smoke, and
there was no evidence of any German activity outside of the
town, save for a column of tanks rumbling along a road some
five miles away. But the road led south rather than south-west,
towards them. This seemed to indicate that the Germans were
more intent upon consolidating their hold on the country than
in rounding up stragglers from the Yugoslav army. But soon
he saw aircraft flying low over the plain and sweeping over
the hills as well. So they were still looking. What Tony and
his group were going to do if they were spotted was difficult
to determine. He had to believe they would not be, as long
as they did not attempt to move themselves in daylight.

As to what the Yugoslav army might be doing, if it even
still existed, it was impossible to say; there was no evidence
of any fighting close at hand, or around Belgrade.

He heard movement behind him, and looked over his
shoulder at Elena. She sat beside him.

'Are you not tired?' he asked.

'I would rather be tired with you.'

He hoped she wasn't going to suggest sex. He was far
too tired, and he didn't know how many of the others
were asleep.

'I want to tell you that I love you,' she said. 'And that I
think you have been magnificent.'

'I think we have all been pretty magnificent.'

She snorted. 'Even Sandrine?'

'Sandrine more than anyone else. She couldn't help her

feet being so badly hurt. She has been in great pain, but she has borne up very well.'

'She has complained a lot.'

'She was entitled to. I thought she was your best friend. I thought she was your lover.'

'You are my lover. Nobody else. And for you, too.'

He put his arm round her shoulders. 'Relax. She's not my type.'

How unethical can you get? he wondered. Lying to your prospective wife before you are even married to her.

When he was relieved by Matanovic he slept with Elena in his arms, which seemed to reassure her. But when he awoke at another changing of the guards and looked over at Sandrine, he saw that her eyes were also open, gazing at him. When she saw him looking at her over Elena's head, she gave a quick, nervous smile, and turned away.

They lunched off the ham, slept again, and made ready to move that evening. Although aircraft activity had continued all day, and from time to time they even heard firing in the distance, they had still seen no Germans close at hand, and by dusk they were rested and full of energy.

As instructed by Madame Dukic, Tony and Elena had removed Sandrine's boots and bandages as soon as they had awakened. The Frenchwoman had gasped with relief, and Tony could guess why: her feet were still swelling. And . . .

'My legs are peeling,' Sandrine said.

'It is only one layer,' Elena said. 'You should be glad to be rid of it, all brown and crinkled. You have better skin underneath.' She put her lips to Tony's ear. 'We'll never get her feet back into those boots.'

'Well, it does not matter, as she is going to have to be carried anyway,' Tony said. 'So we'll let them air. That's probably the best thing.'

'I am a nuisance,' Sandrine said. 'Why do you not just leave me?'

'I'd be obliged if you'd stop making that inane suggestion,' Tony told her. 'Where we go, you go.'

'And where are we going?' Ivkov asked.

'Nothing has changed, except in our favour. We are going to make for Dubrovnik.'

'I have been to Dubrovnik,' Matanovic said. 'It is a very long way. We went by truck, as part of an army manoeuvre, and it still took us two days from Belgrade.'

'So it'll take us a while longer on foot,' Tony said. 'We have the time.'

'But what do we eat?'

'Madame Dukic's ham will last another couple of days. Then there must be farms in these mountains, from which we can obtain food.'

Matanovic scratched his nose.

'There is a village, not far from here,' Ivkov said. 'We could obtain shelter there.'

'Well, glory be. You know this area, Ivkov?'

'I have been here,' Ivkov said cautiously.

'And you have been to this village before?'

'My brother lives there. I have visited my brother.'

'This gets better and better. I'm jolly glad you decided to come. Right. Point us in the right direction. How far?'

'It is to the north-west. Perhaps forty miles.'

'Forty . . .' Tony gulped. But it seemed their only hope. 'Right. Let's move out. I'll carry you first time around, Sandrine.'

'I am glad of that,' she said.

'Well, then . . .' He stooped, helped her climb on to his back, and checked – from all round them they heard the click of rifle bolts.

PART TWO

CHAOS

With women, the heart argues, not the mind.
Matthew Arnold

Chapter Four

Serbs

S andrine gave one of her little shrieks. Tony checked the
instinctive movement of his hand towards his holster. The
others merely looked frightened; in their packing up they had
forgotten to leave anyone on guard.

Now they were surrounded by men who stood on the slopes
above them; Tony reckoned they might have been there for
some time, watching them. But they were not Germans:
they wore the uniforms of Yugoslav soldiers. Now one
of them, from his insignia a lieutenant, asked, 'Where are
you from?'

He also had identified the uniforms of Matanovic and the
two privates.

'We are from Belgrade,' Tony said. 'We escaped last
night.'

The lieutenant frowned at the unfamiliar accent. 'What is
your unit?'

'I am Captain Anthony Davis, from the British embassy.'

'The embassy was evacuated two days ago.'

Tony nodded. 'I was not there. I linked up with these
people.'

The lieutenant studied him for several seconds, then looked
at Matanovic. 'And you?'

'Sergeant Anton Matanovic, Fourth Foot, sir. My platoon
was destroyed by the Germans, and I placed my remaining
men and myself under the command of the English officer.'

'And you?' the lieutenant looked at Ivkov.

'I am Ivkov, the bath-keeper.'

'Why are you with these people?'

'I did not wish to stay under the Germans.'

The lieutenant looked sceptical. 'And two women,' he remarked.

'I am Elena Kostic,' Elena said. 'I am Captain Davis's fiancée.'

The lieutenant raised his eyebrows.

'That is true,' Tony said.

'She is not wearing a ring.'

'We haven't had time to buy one.'

'And you?' he asked Sandrine.

'I am Sandrine Fouquet. I am – was – an editor with *Paris Temps*, but the building was blown up.'

'You are Vichy?'

'Yes, I am Vichy.'

'Then you are a neutral.'

'I do not wish to be a neutral.'

The lieutenant looked more sceptical than ever, but Tony couldn't blame him for being suspicious: Sandrine's abrupt changes of mood were confusing to him as well. 'And what is the matter with you?' the officer asked, regarding her bandaged feet.

'My feet are cut.'

'They are also burned,' Elena said.

'So she cannot walk. Well, then—'

'She will be carried,' Tony said.

'Do you wish to join forces with General Mihailovic?'

'Mihailovic has escaped the city?'

Tony had met the chief of the Yugoslav General Staff at various official functions during his short stay in Belgrade, and had formed the opinion that he was a good soldier but an intensely orthodox one; no one could have been further from his concept of a commander who might be capable of coping with a situation like this.

'General Mihailovic left the city before the Germans occupied it,' the lieutenant said carefully. 'He has assumed command of all our forces which have refused to surrender to the enemy.'

'What sort of forces would that be?'

'Enough. You are aware that our army was ordered to lay down its arms by the traitors who now command in Belgrade?'

'No, I was not aware of that. So your country has effectively been destroyed.'

'Yugoslavia can never be destroyed. Our country has been occupied, temporarily, by the Germans.'

'But if you no longer have an army—'

'We still have an army: those of us who have refused to surrender and now fight for General Mihailovic. Now, do you wish to join his command?'

'My wish,' Tony said, 'and my duty, is to rejoin my embassy people as quickly as possible.'

'I do not think that is at all possible,' the lieutenant said. 'Your embassy has left Yugoslavia, to travel through Bulgaria to Greece. They are probably there by now. You cannot follow.'

Tony nodded. He had accepted that some time ago. 'Well, then, I shall try to make Dubrovnik, and leave from there. With the women. But I have no doubt these soldiers will wish to go with you.'

'Dubrovnik is in German hands,' the lieutenant said. 'They came down the Adriatic by ship. There is no place for you to go, Englishman, save with us.'

Tony shrugged. 'Then I will come with you, at least to speak with your general.'

'It is a march of several hours,' the lieutenant said. 'The sick woman will have to remain.'

Sandrine gave one of her shrieks.

'She says she is Vichy French,' the lieutenant pointed out. 'All she has to do is tell the Germans this.'

'And prove it?' Tony asked.

'Does she not have a passport?'

'She has lost her passport.'

'Well, I am sure that if she is who she claims to be, an editor with *Paris Temps*, there will be several people in Belgrade who will vouch for her.'

'There will be even more people who can vouch for the fact that they saw her as part of a group – us – killing Germans in order to get out of the city. No, lieutenant, she is coming with us.'

'We have no means for carrying wounded. It is accepted that they must be abandoned.'

'We have the means: our backs. We have brought Mademoiselle Fouquet this far. We are not going to abandon her now.'

'You will slow us up.'

'So leave us behind. Just tell us where to go, and we will get there.'

The lieutenant snorted. 'And when you are captured by the Germans, you will tell them where General Mihailovic is to be found.'

'Good point. It looks as if you will have to travel slowly.'

The lieutenant glared at him, and then looked at the others. Tony could tell exactly what he was thinking, what he was tempted to do; they had become nuisances. But that would be undertaking an enormous responsibility, and Tony was technically his superior officer. Additionally, if he did decide that they would have to be eliminated, he had no idea what sort of resistance might be encountered; Tony's group appeared to be very well armed. The lieutenant could not know that they had only about a dozen rounds between the seven of them; he could only be sure that a shoot-out might involve him in unacceptably heavy casualties. Fighting his own people.

'You will answer to the general,' he said. 'Let's go.'

*   *   *

Tony took Sandrine on his back, and they followed the soldiers.

'He does not like me,' Sandrine muttered into his ear. 'He disliked me on sight.'

'Any man who can dislike you on sight has the wrong idea about women,' Tony told her.

'He is a Serb,' said Elena, walking on his other side. 'All Serbs are swine.'

'For God's sake, keep that opinion to yourself,' Tony begged. 'Mihailovic is a Serb, isn't he?'

'Yes,' she said, loading her voice with sinister inflection.

Tony reflected that life was not getting any easier, and the future was becoming increasingly difficult. He had no fears for himself. As a soldier who had already been wounded he accepted that he was living on borrowed time. But to his fears for Sandrine's health were now added his fears for Elena's safety, if – as was becoming increasingly likely, from what he had seen over the preceding twenty-four hours – this so carelessly cobbled-together nation disintegrated into separate, and mutually antagonistic, ethnic groups under the impact of defeat.

At least he could for the moment concentrate on the physically demanding but mentally simple task of getting his motley band to safety. It was a long night, and as they penetrated various valleys and mountain passes he lost all sense of direction or awareness of his whereabouts. To make matters more obscure, this night there was a low cloud cover, and it was impossible to see the stars. The cloud brought with it several rain squalls, which soaked them to the skin and left them chilled, but at least willing to keep moving in an attempt to get warm.

As before, Sandrine was passed from man to man throughout the night. In the beginning the other soldiers merely watched the proceedings with amused contempt, but as the night wore on they began to consider what might be in it for them, and soon several volunteered to take their turn. Tony did not feel that he could refuse them without antagonising them, but unlike Matanovic and his two men, or even Ivkov, they had not agreed to accept his command, and therefore his discipline; several times he heard Sandrine complain about an uninvited intimacy, and once he heard the sound of a slap.

'To be felt up by a dozen men in the course of one night,' Elena remarked. 'There is an achievement.'

'I think you mean, an experience,' Tony suggested.

Lieutenant Vidmar was unhappy about the whole thing. 'This is very bad for discipline,' he said, dropping back to walk beside Tony. 'I will be very relieved when we reach the camp.'

'Amen,' Tony agreed. 'But your men volunteered.'

'They are men,' Vidmar pointed out. 'And she is a pretty woman, who is also a foreigner. Is she something special to you?'

'Just a friend. She had a boyfriend in Belgrade, but we do not know what happened to him.'

Save that he is probably back in the city by now, Tony reflected. Lord of all he surveys. He wondered if Bernhard would waste any time looking for Sandrine.

'Ah,' Vidmar commented. 'You mean she is, how do you English say, footloose and fancy-free.'

'That's very clever of you,' Tony said. 'However, you should know that I promised her boyfriend that I would see her to safety, and that is what I intend to do. So you had better tell your people that I will shoot dead any man who assaults her, much less attempts to rape her.'

'You think you can make threats like that? Are you not my prisoner?'

'On the contrary,' Tony said. 'I am your ally. An ally without whom you have no hope of surviving this war. The sooner you realise this, the better.'

Vidmar stamped off to resume his place at the head of his men.

'I suppose one of the things I most admire about the

English,' Elena said, 'is their quite insufferable arrogance. Do you really suppose you can shoot a Yugoslav soldier?'

'Probably not. Although as an officer I do have the right to execute any man found guilty of rape.'

'After a court martial,' she argued. 'That would not be practical, here.'

'I don't think Lieutenant Vidmar is quite sure of that,' Tony said. 'Just remember that you're on our side.'

Tony was glad when it was his turn to carry Sandrine again.

'I really am sorry about all this,' he said to her.

'Bah,' she commented. 'They are only men. And they are afraid of you, eh?'

He was also very relieved when, soon after dawn, they were challenged by a lookout, and a few minutes later staggered into the guerilla encampment. Situated in a deep valley between two mountains, it could be overlooked only from the air. Because of its size, however, it was certainly vulnerable to discovery by aircraft; Tony estimated there were well over a thousand men camped here, and quite a few women and children as well, not to mention animals of every variety from horses, donkeys and sheep to dogs and chickens. The encampment, which consisted of various tents and makeshift dwellings, most of them still under construction, stretched for half a mile on either side of a fast-running mountain stream.

'A bath!' Sandrine said. 'Oh, how I would love a bath.'

'You have water on the brain,' Elena remarked. 'You had a bath . . . when was it?'

'Two days ago,' Tony suggested.

Elena gave a shriek of laughter. 'When she got dunked in that stream.'

'I was actually thinking of the baths in town.' Was that two days ago, or three?

'I feel filthy,' Sandrine said.

'Well, I think you had better wait until we find out what the local custom is,' Tony said as Vidmar came up to him.

'Tell your people to wait here,' Vidmar said. 'You will come with me to General Mihailovic.'

Draza Mihailovic was a thin man with a prominent nose and chin, both reasonably concealed by his heavy beard and moustache. Wire-rimmed glasses gave him a studious, thoughtful air; Tony felt this was a fairly accurate indication of his personality. Once again he reflected that the general, spic and span in his uniform, was an unlikely leader of a guerilla army. His headquarters were situated in a large tent, in the centre of which there was a trestle table covered in maps and sheets of paper. Two senior officers stood to either side, and two orderlies waited at the back. All the officers were smoking, and the air in the confined space was heavy.

But Mihailovic looked pleased to see him. 'Captain . . . Davis, is it not?'

'Sir.'

Mihailovic shook his hand. 'I hardly recognised you, out of uniform and with that growth of beard.'

Tony stroked his chin in surprise. It hadn't occurred to him that he would have sprouted a beard by now. 'I apologise, sir. I haven't actually had an opportunity to look in a mirror for a few days. And I lost my tunic getting out of Belgrade.'

Mihailovic waved his hand. 'No matter, Captain. You have brought word from the embassy? About British aid?'

'Ah . . . no, sir. I became separated from the embassy staff when they evacuated.'

'But still, you know about the aid, eh?'

'There will be no aid, sir.'

Mihailovic frowned.

'At least in the immediate future,' Tony added.

'But we are all on the same side now.'

'I know that, sir. And so does London, I am sure. It's a matter of logistics. Our people cannot get to yours.'

'But you, and the Greeks, have beaten the Italians. You will soon have regained Albania. Or enough of it to reach our border.'

'I think the Germans may have something to say about that, sir.'

Mihailovic wagged his finger at the young officer. 'You will never beat the Germans while you are afraid of them.'

Tony sighed. These people were positively medieval in their thinking. They still thought that warfare was a matter of courage and waving a sword, of a single Horatio holding the bridge against a thousand Tarquins.

'Sadly, sir,' he said, 'it is again a matter of logistics. The Germans have more and better-equipped men, more tanks, more guns and more aircraft than us – at least here in the Balkans.'

Mihailovic gazed at Tony for several seconds. Then he said, 'Then what are you doing here, Captain?'

'Escaping the Germans, sir. We were attempting to reach Dubrovnik when we encountered your patrol.'

'Dubrovnik is occupied by the Germans.'

'So Lieutenant Vidmar told us, sir.'

The lieutenant had remained in the tent, standing to attention.

'So what is your intention now?' the general asked.

'As I cannot leave, sir, it is to serve under your command.' He attempted to lighten the atmosphere. 'In the absence of any other British aid.'

'You have combat experience?'

'I was with the BEF in Flanders, sir.'

'You were at Dunkirk?' asked one of the other officers.

'No, sir. I was wounded during the retreat from the Dyle, and evacuated from Calais before it fell.'

Mihailovic stroked his chin. 'I am sure you will be useful. I will put you on our ration strength, and find something for you to do.'

'If you have a radio, sir, I could perhaps make contact with Athens. Or even Alexandria.'

'To what purpose, if you say they cannot send us help?'

'Well, sir—'

'To let them know you are alive? I do not think that is of sufficient importance to give away our position to the Germans by using our radios. In any event, before they could think of coming to get you, you may well be dead, eh?' He gave a thin smile. 'As you are here, Captain, you will have to get used to our company.'

'Ahem!' Lieutenant Vidmar remarked.

'Yes, Lieutenant?'

'The people Captain Davis brought with him, sir.'

'Yes?'

'Three of them are regulars, sir. Fourth Foot.'

Mihailovic nodded. 'Some of their regiment are with us. Have them join those. The others?'

'One is the bath-keeper from Belgrade.'

Mihailovic looked at Tony. 'Can he fight?'

'He must have been a conscript once, sir.'

'How old is he?'

'Early fifties, I imagine.'

'That is too old. Send him on his way.'

'I must protest, sir. Ivkov is a good man. He helped us get out of Belgrade. And he may be over fifty, but he is as strong as an ox.'

'I can have no useless mouths on my strength, Captain.'

'At least give him a chance to prove himself, sir.'

Mihailovic considered. 'Very well. He can be your servant. And your responsibility.'

'There are also the two women, sir,' Vidmar said.

Mihailovic looked at Tony.

'One is my fiancée, sir. The other is her friend. She is French.'

'Vichy French?'

'Yes.'

'Then she is a neutral.'

'I'm afraid she cannot prove that, sir; she has lost her passport. She also assisted us in getting out of Belgrade, and this involved shooting Germans. She is also suffering from severe burns.'

'She appears to be quite a problem,' the general remarked. 'And they are more useless mouths.'

'They are both very capable of fighting, sir.'

Mihailovic looked as sceptical as Vidmar had done. But he took a different approach. 'Who are they going to fight?'

'Well, whoever we fight,' Tony said. 'The Germans.'

'That is something we shall have to consider,' the general said. 'I make the women, and the bath-keeper, your responsibility, Captain. You may draw rations for four people.'

'Thank you, sir. And my duties?'

'You said you had field experience?'

'Yes, sir. In Flanders, last year.'

'Ah. That was as part of the British Expeditionary Force. Yes. I have never been to Flanders, but my understanding is that it is very flat, very wet terrain.'

'That's pretty accurate, sir.'

'It is not the same thing as fighting in mountains. Equally, when you were defeated, you were evacuated back to England. We cannot be evacuated if we are defeated; there is nowhere for us to go.'

Tony decided against pointing out that they had already been defeated. 'Except further into the mountains, sir.'

'Yes,' Mihailovic said drily. 'We will show you how to fight in the mountains, Captain. For the time being, get yourself and your, ah, women, billeted. Captain Matovic will come with you.'

'Thank you, sir.' Tony saluted, but Mihailovic had already turned back to his maps.

Tony followed the captain outside, accompanied by Lieutenant Vidmar.

'How soon do you think we will move against the Germans?' Tony asked.

Matovic frowned. He was a short, thick-set man with bushy eyebrows. Like the general, his uniform was immaculate, and he wore a holster on his belt. 'Move against them?' he asked.

'Fight them, Captain.'

'Ah. That is for the general to decide. His first business is to reconstitute the army.'

'Can he do that, here? He gave me the impression that he was short of food.'

'We are short of everything. We left Belgrade in a great hurry. As soon as it was determined by the traitors in command that we should lay down our arms, we moved out.'

Tony nodded. 'I know it was grim. I was there. It's a miracle you brought so many men with you.'

'They are coming in all the time. Like you, eh? But it is a considerable logistical problem.'

Tony followed him and Vidmar between the huts and the people and the animals. 'You will have to split up.'

'We will do whatever the general tells us to do.'

Tony didn't suppose he could argue with that; he just wished Mihailovic had revealed a more positive attitude.

'You!' They had stopped in front of a hut near the stream, and the captain was addressing a woman who stood outside it. She was quite a young woman, with straight black hair, a strong face and a matching body beneath a somewhat shapeless dress; her feet were bare. A small child clung to her skirt. 'I am requisitioning this hut for this officer,' Matovic said.

The woman moved her gaze, slowly, from the captain to Tony. 'My husband built this hut,' she said.

'And it is of good construction. He can build you another.'

'Hold on a moment,' Tony said. 'Where is your husband?'

'He is on patrol. He is a soldier.'

'Well, I'm sure there is room for us all.'

'You cannot share your house with a soldier,' Matovic said.

'And three women,' Vidmar added. 'What about the bath-keeper?'

'We'll manage. If that will suit you, madame?'

The woman continued to regard him for several seconds, then she nodded, with the slow deliberateness that seemed to be her chief characteristic.

Matovic snorted, and opened the door to peer inside. A goat came out. 'I wish you joy of the fleas,' he commented. 'Where are your people?'

Tony pointed. 'At the stream.'

Which was about fifty yards away, down the slope. Elena and Sandrine were seated at the water's edge, bathing their feet; they had removed Sandrine's bandages. Ivkov was sitting a little higher up the slope, watching them. So were several other men, on both sides of the water.

'You are fortunate,' Matovic remarked. 'Will you introduce me?'

'Certainly.' Tony led him down the slope.

'There, you see.' Matovic pointed. 'The latrine trench is over there. I am afraid there is no privacy. And the commissariat is that large hut over there. Rations are issued at twelve noon.' He looked at his watch. 'That is just over one hour from now. Officers form a separate line.' He grinned. 'It is shorter, eh? You may have your women in that line, and your servant.'

'Thank you,' Tony said. 'What about clothes?'

'Eh?'

'Both my women need clothes,' Tony explained.

'It may be possible to buy some from the other women,' Matovic said.

That didn't sound too promising; as far as Tony knew, none of them had any money. But now they had reached the water. The women heard them coming and looked up, while Ivkov scrambled to his feet.

'Tony!' Elena cried. 'We thought you had got lost.'

'I've been getting us organised,' Tony explained. 'We even have somewhere to live. Come along.'

Elena got up, and helped Sandrine to her feet.

'This is Captain Matovic, from General Mihailovic's staff,' Tony explained.

Elena smiled at the captain, who was staring at her.

'I know this woman,' he announced. 'She is Elena Kostic.'

'Why, that's quite right,' Tony said.

'She is Croatian.'

'Ah . . . well, yes, she is.'

Matovic turned to Vidmar. 'Arrest this woman,' he said.

Chapter Five

Enemies

E lena's hand instinctively dropped to the catch for her satchel. But Tony caught her wrist; for her to shoot somebody at this juncture would be disastrous. 'Are you out of your mind?' he demanded of the Yugoslav captain.

'Croatians are enemies of the state,' Matovic declared.

'You *are* out of your mind,' Tony said. 'This woman has stood beside me, shooting at Germans, while you were running for your life.'

Matovic, whose hand had also dropped to his holster, glared at him. More practically, Vidmar had blown a whistle, and soldiers were hurrying up.

'Do not let them take me,' Elena muttered.

Tony bit his lip. If there was a way out of this, it had to be by negotiation: they were simply too outnumbered.

Sandrine was clinging to Ivkov's arm; the bath-keeper was looking totally bewildered.

'I will vouch for this woman,' Tony said.

'You cannot vouch for an enemy of the state,' Matovic insisted.

Tony concluded that he must have been a lawyer before joining the army.

'So what do you intend to do with her?' he inquired.

Elena shot him a glance, and he squeezed her arm as reassuringly as he could.

'She will be placed under guard, until she can be tried.'

103

'On what charge? Of being a citizen of Yugoslavia? You are starting to sound like a German.'

'Take this woman,' Matovic commanded. 'Secure her.'

Two of the soldiers moved forward.

Now Tony followed fashion, abandoning his previous reasoned approach. He dropped his hand to his holster and unbuttoned the flap. 'I will shoot the first man who lays a hand on her,' he said.

Matovic looked close to having a fit; his face reddened and his eyes bulged – even his moustache seemed to bristle. 'You think you can defy the Yugoslav army?'

'I will defy any man who seeks to take the law into his own hands. I am a British army officer. I will yield this woman to no one save a superior with a warrant.'

Matovic was clearly coming to the same conclusion about him. But this was a situation the Serbian officer had not previously encountered. 'Fetch Colonel Zardov,' he told Vidmar.

The lieutenant hurried off.

'I thought these people were our friends,' Sandrine remarked in French. Ivkov had put a presumably protective arm round her shoulders, but she didn't seem to notice.

'I have no friends,' Elena muttered. 'Not here. What is going to happen, Tony?'

'Just keep calm,' he told her as he watched the colonel approaching.

Colonel Zardov had also been in Mihailovic's tent, but was an altogether better-looking specimen than Matovic. His moustache was white and the wings beneath his cap were grey, but his aquiline features were gravely distinguished, and he moved with the energy of a much younger man.

'What is the problem?' he inquired. 'You were told to billet Captain Davis, Matovic. And his people.'

'This woman is a Croatian, sir.'

Zardov frowned at Elena. 'How do you know?'

Matovic's cheeks, starting to fade, brightened again. 'I

have seen her, in Belgrade. Her name is Kostic. Her father runs a brothel.'

'That is a lie,' Elena snapped.

'What is a lie?' Zardov asked.

'That my parents run a brothel. It is a respectable boarding house.'

Zardov looked at Tony.

'I can vouch for that, sir,' Tony said. He only hoped he was telling the truth. A brothel? And yet . . .

'But you do not deny that she is a Croatian.'

'I do not deny that she is a Yugoslav, who has fought against the Germans and wishes to go on doing so.'

'Our information is that most people of Croatian origin are Fascist sympathisers, and that large numbers have actively cooperated with the enemy,' Zardov said, continuing to speak very reasonably.

'I can only answer for this woman,' Tony said. 'Who also happens to be my fiancée.'

'She is your fiancée?' Zardov looked astonished, and glanced at Sandrine.

'And are you going to tell me, sir, that there are no other Croatians in this camp?' Tony asked.

'Not to my knowledge.'

'But . . . that is absurd. Are you saying there are no Croatians in your entire army? This woman's brother is a serving soldier.'

'There are Croatians in the Yugoslav army, Captain. Or there were. But as I have said, they have proved to be unreliable, even when they have not actually collaborated with the enemy. The decision to exclude them from this concentration was made by General Mihailovic himself.'

'Then I had better see the general again,' Tony said.

'He is coming,' Vidmar said.

By now a considerable crowd had gathered, and the hubbub had attracted the general's attention. Mihailovic strode down the slope towards them, his people parting before him.

'What is the problem?' he demanded.

Several people spoke at once, but Mihailovic had been addressing Colonel Zardov.

'This woman is a Croatian, sir.'

'A spy,' Vidmar suggested.

'This woman happens to be my fiancée, General,' Tony said. His mind was still reeling with what Matovic had suggested.

Mihailovic looked from Tony to Elena and then back again. 'I have given orders that no Croatians are to be admitted to this camp. This was for security reasons, you understand, Captain.'

'I appreciate your reasons, sir. However, Miss Kostic and I were unaware of those orders when we came here. I should also point out that we were brought here, by your people.'

Mihailovic looked at Vidmar.

'They told us they were refugees from Belgrade, sir,' the lieutenant said. 'Who wished to join us in fighting against the Germans.'

'And you did not inquire into their antecedents?'

'Well . . . as they were led by a British officer—'

'Yes,' Mihailovic said.

'If you do not wish Miss Kostic in your camp, General,' Tony said, 'then she will leave. But you will understand that I must go with her.'

'Leave?' Mihailovic snapped. 'How can she leave? She knows where we are, she knows our numbers, she knows that I am in command.'

'And do you suppose that she is going to rush off and locate the nearest German unit to tell them these things? Like Mademoiselle Fouquet, she was standing beside me when we were killing Germans, only a few days ago. She was seen to be doing this.'

'I cannot take that risk, Captain. There are more than a thousand lives involved here. More – there is the life of the nation.'

'Very well, General,' Tony said. 'These are your people and your command. You are quite entitled to make the rules. As I have said, if we are not welcome here, we shall leave. I will take responsibility for Miss Kostic's loyalty. You have my word that she will not divulge your whereabouts to anyone.'

'You cannot leave,' Mihailovic said again.

'I beg your pardon? I am not under your command, sir. Unless I choose to be.'

Mihailovic pointed. 'You, Captain, can go to the devil, if you choose. You have already explained to me that we can expect no help from the British. Well, we can manage without you. But I am now military commander of all Yugoslav resistance forces, and as such of any civilians who find themselves in the resistance category. It is my decision that the Croatian part of the Yugoslav population is untrustworthy at best and openly Fascist at worst. This woman knows the whereabouts of my position and can estimate the strength of my command, information which would be of great value to the Nazis.'

'I have given you my word, as a British officer—'

'Your word, Captain Davis, is meaningless.'

'Sir?'

Mihailovic waved his hand. 'Oh, I do not mean you are not to be trusted. In normal circumstances I would be happy to accept the word of a British officer. But these are not normal circumstances. If you leave this camp with your women and are captured by the enemy, what then? You may well be able to withstand torture. They might even respect your uniform and rank. But what of the women? They are not trained for such things. When a Gestapo agent shoves an electrode up their ass and switches on the current, they will tell him anything he wishes to know.'

Tony gulped. The concept of such a thing happening to Elena, much less Sandrine, was impossible. So was the concept of Bernhard doing, or permitting, such a thing.

But Bernhard, he remembered, had not been a member of
the Gestapo.

Mihailovic watched Tony's expression, and gave a thin
smile. 'You are an English officer and a gentleman, Captain.
That means you are also an innocent when it comes to how
men will act, when given unlimited power over those they
regard as inferior beings. I cannot risk your fiancée falling
into German hands, either for her sake or for ours. Therefore,
as she is here, she will have to stay.'

'That is all she wishes to do,' Tony pointed out.

'But we have no facility for keeping prisoners. It is not
our intention to take any.'

Elena gasped, and again she tried to open her satchel.
But Tony caught her wrist again. 'Just what are you saying,
sir?'

'It is regrettable,' Mihailovic said. 'But in our circumstances . . .'

'Sir, if you execute this woman, a loyal and faithful
Yugoslav citizen, without any evidence of treachery or even
opposition on her part, I shall be obliged to make a full report
of the incident to my government.'

'Is that my concern, Captain? You have just told me that
your government is not interested in what is happening here
in Yugoslavia.'

'My government will undoubtedly convey the facts to your
superiors.'

'I have no superiors,' Mihailovic pointed out.

'You do, you know. There will be a Yugoslav government-
in-exile, situated in London. This is what has happened with
the governments of Czechoslovakia, Norway, Holland and
Belgium, all the countries that have been overrun by the
Nazis. There is even an alternative French government to
Vichy. In London.'

'Governments-in-exile,' Mihailovic sneered. 'I am the
government of Yugoslavia, here on the ground, where it
matters.'

Sandrine decided to join the fight. 'I will report it in *Paris Temps,*' she announced. 'We have correspondents with every newspaper in the world.'

Mihailovic glowered at her. 'If you are ever in a position to submit a story to your newspaper again, mademoiselle,' he pointed out. Clearly he was wondering whether it might not be a good idea to shoot all three of them. But there were too many witnesses. 'I will consider the matter,' he said. 'But for the moment, this woman is under arrest. Put her in the punishment cell.'

'There are three men in there already, sir,' Zardov said.

'I am sure there is room for one more.'

'If they put me in there I will be raped,' Elena muttered.

Tony hesitated. But he reckoned he had gained an initial victory, in that she was to be locked up instead of summarily executed. 'I'll get you out,' he said. 'You have my word. Just give me a little time.'

She gazed into his eyes. 'Do you believe what this man said? About my parents? About me?'

'Of course I do not.'

He had never been able to lie convincingly.

'Do you love me, Tony?'

'Yes, I do.'

'Will we still be married?'

'Just as soon as we can find a priest.'

Another long stare. Then she gave him her satchel. 'I will leave this with you,' she said meaningfully, making sure he remembered that the Luger was still inside, 'and wait for you to come and get me.'

'Lieutenant,' Mihailovic said.

Vidmar stepped forward to take Elena's arm.

'I am holding you personally responsible for this lady's safety,' Tony said.

Vidmar gulped, and looked at the general.

'The responsibility is mine, Captain,' Mihailovic said. 'However, in view of everything that has happened, I think it would be best if you were to hand over your sidearm. It will be returned to you when you next have need of it.'

Tony unbuckled his belt and handed it to Matovic.

'Thank you,' Mihailovic said, and turned to face the crowd. 'This incident is now closed,' he shouted. 'Return to your duties.'

Reluctantly they melted away; Elena had already disappeared.

'What a fuck-up,' Sandrine remarked in French. 'What are we going to do?'

'We need to think about that,' Tony said, then realised that Colonel Zardov was still standing beside him.

'I am most terribly sorry about this, Captain.'

'But?'

'General Mihailovic is my commanding officer. Yours too, as long as you remain with us. We must accept his orders.'

'Even if we know they are unjust?'

'It is not our business to consider whether they are just or not. It is our business to obey orders. I would beg you, Captain, not to make it harder on yourself, or the young lady, by attempting to oppose him. Now, get settled in. I will arrange for you to be placed in command of one of our patrols as soon as possible.'

'But you do not intend to undertake any offensive action against the Germans.'

'That again is for the general to decide. But I should tell you that the Germans have issued a proclamation over the radio, warning us – warning all groups which have not yet surrendered – that any attempts to resist their forces, by word or deed, will bring the most severe retaliation upon the civilian population.'

'So you will not fight.'

'It is a grave responsibility. One which your own government may have to face when the Germans land in England.'

'The word is *if*, Colonel. And I will tell you this: in England we will fight, regardless of retaliation.'

'That remains to be seen. I will send for you when I have something for you to do.'

'Like I said, a right royal fuck-up,' Sandrine observed. She peered through the door into the little hut. The goat had resumed residence, as had the woman and child. All three of them stared at her with wide eyes. 'You mean this is it?'

'For the time being,' Tony said.

'Shit! Where is the toilet?'

'That ditch up the hill.'

Sandrine looked up the hill; there were several bare backsides to be seen. 'Shit!' she commented again.

'Never was a truer word spoken in jest,' Tony agreed.

She glanced at him. 'You think this is a joke? What about Elena?'

'I do not think Elena's situation is a joke, and I intend to do something about it. But it cannot involve taking on what remains of the Yugoslav army. It may involve getting out of here, though. Do you intend to stay behind?'

'No way.'

'Well, we are going to have to walk. So the first thing we have to do is get your feet into shape. Oh, come in, Ivkov, do.'

The big man had been hovering in the doorway. Now he sidled into the hut, nodding his head towards the woman and child.

Sandrine sat on the ground and drew up her feet to peer at them. 'The swelling is going down.'

'Great. I'll put on some more of this ointment.' He knelt beside her.

'I need some clothes,' she said. 'Look, my dress is torn . . . here, and here. I think even my underwear is torn. It is certainly filthy.'

'Maybe this woman has something to spare.'

Sandrine looked at the woman, and then at the goat; her expression said it all. 'I am also very hungry,' she said.

'And there is the lunch bugle,' he said. 'Perfect timing. I'll just bandage you up, and then we'll go eat. Ivkov, you can carry mademoiselle.'

'Oh, yes,' Ivkov said. 'I will carry mademoiselle.'

Sandrine pulled a face. 'I would rather you carried me. I think he has designs.'

'We all have designs,' Tony assured her.

They took their places and secured their food, which consisted of thick soup with various pieces of vegetable floating in it, and some very hard bread.

'Is there no meat?' Sandrine inquired. 'I am starving.'

The man ladling out the soup merely looked at her. Everyone else was looking at them too, including the other officers and various women who were attached to them. Tony reckoned it was not merely because they were obviously foreigners or because Sandrine was an intensely attractive woman; everyone knew of the fracas earlier.

Following the meal, he carried Sandrine on his back – again to the vociferous interest of the spectators – to the prison cell, where after some argument he was allowed in.

Elena sat on the floor against one wall; her three companions sat against the opposite wall.

'Trouble?' Tony asked.

'Not yet. I have told them that if they touch me you will kill them all. They believe me.'

'I would go on doing that,' Tony told them. 'This woman is my betrothed. I will cut out the heart of any man who molests her.'

The three men attempted to grin, but did not succeed. Tony supposed that with his three-day growth of beard he looked far fiercer than he probably was, although he was feeling pretty fierce at that moment.

'When are you going to get me out?' Elena asked, speaking French.

'The moment Sandrine can walk properly.'

112

Elena looked at her friend.

'Only a day or two, now,' Sandrine said. 'The swelling is going down.'

'Well, I hope they won't shoot me before then.'

'They won't,' Tony said as confidently as he could. 'How do you feel?'

'That I'd like to shoot the whole fucking lot of them.'

'Have they fed you?'

'Was that food?'

'I'll come back this evening,' Tony said, and switched back to Serbo-Croat. 'Just to make sure these fellows are behaving themselves.'

'She is not in a good mood,' Sandrine remarked as he carried her back to their hut.

'Would you be?'

'I am not in a good mood either,' Sandrine pointed out. 'My feet hurt, and I stink. I would like a hot bath.'

'Keep dreaming,' Tony recommended.

Ivkov was sitting outside the hut.

'Where are the others?' Tony asked.

'Her husband came back from patrol. He was very angry to find that his house had been given away.'

'Oh, Christ! You didn't fight with him?'

'No, no. He had been told this, by his sergeant. But he said his wife would not sleep in the same house as a lot of strange men, and took her, and the child. And the goat.'

'Thank God for that,' Sandrine said.

'But I think the goat left quite a lot behind,' Ivkov said, scratching. 'Apart from droppings.'

'Well, let's get this place cleaned up as much as possible,' Tony decided. He sat Sandrine outside the door while he and Ivkov got rid of as many of the goat droppings as they could.

'Typhus,' Sandrine remarked, now also scratching. 'We will get typhus, and die.'

'It's not my intention to hang around here long enough for

that,' Tony said. 'Now, Ivkov, I have to know: are you with us or with them?'

'Them?'

'These people.'

'They are my people. You never told me that woman was a Croat.'

'I didn't think it mattered. You are both Yugoslavs.'

Ivkov shook his head. 'Croats are bad people.'

'They don't have too high an opinion of you, either. But you're all in this together. And now you're in this with me, and Miss Kostic . . . and Mademoiselle Fouquet . . .' he said, adding a slice of quite unreal carrot. 'I have to know if you can be trusted.'

'You are asking me to go against my own people?'

'I am asking you to go against the Germans, which is more than these people seem prepared to do at the moment. And I don't think they are quite as much your own people as you think. The general would have sent you off to try to survive on your own, had I not protested.'

Ivkov gulped.

'So if you hang about when I leave, you might not have it so good,' Tony pointed out.

'You are going to leave?'

'Just as soon as it is possible.'

Ivkov scratched his head.

'You said you have a brother who lives in a village in these mountains.'

'I believe so.'

'You believe? He is your brother.'

'We do not see each other very often.'

'Surely he comes to Belgrade?'

'Not very often.'

'What is the name of this village where he lives?' Sandrine asked.

'Divitsar.'

'Ah,' Sandrine said.

Tony looked from one to the other. 'One of you is going to have to explain all this.'

'I think his brother is a Communist,' Sandrine said.

Tony turned back to Ivkov. 'And you are opposed to him?'

'No, no,' Ivkov said. 'Well,' he added hastily, 'I am not a Communist. But you see—'

'Communism is outlawed in Yugoslavia,' Sandrine said.

'Ah,' Tony said.

'And this village, Divitsar, is well known to be a Communist centre. One of our feature writers did a piece on it last year.'

'Does the government know this?'

'They must.' Sandrine smiled. 'If they read our paper.'

'But they have done nothing about it.'

'I think they were considering the matter. But to arrest a whole village is a difficult business. Certainly publicity-wise. And now—'

'Now the government is discredited, no matter how you look at it. Will your brother help us, Ivkov?'

'Perhaps. If I ask him to.'

'Will he have a hot bath?' Sandrine asked.

'Perhaps.'

Sandrine and Tony slept next to each other, retiring as soon as they had eaten their evening meal. Neither of them undressed. They were both exhausted, emotionally and physically, and were also, Tony suspected, too confused to think about sex.

Sandrine was an intelligent woman, and had to know that he found her attractive. But then, so did just about every man she met. The question was, did she find any man attractive? Apparently not, according to Elena. Even Bernhard? Tony had often wondered at their relationship. But until Elena's revelation – if it was true – he had always supposed that Sandrine's somewhat cold approach to life was because she was intensely feminine. Although he had watched that reserve begin to break down during the disasters of the past few days, he could still believe that her concern had less to do with being in a situation in which mere survival was the key issue, and more to do with the fact that she was filthy, smelt filthy, that her hair was unwashed, and that her dress was in rags.

Tony was utterly confounded by the events of the day, and hardly less so by their current situation. Quite apart from any danger to Elena – which he felt could be combated by continuing to act the stiff-necked Englishman – there was the camp itself, and the absence, so far as he could see, of any great determination to oppose the invaders. He allowed that he might be misjudging the general, that Mihailovic might be waiting to see just how big an army he could command before undertaking any sort of counter-attack. Nonetheless, Tony would have supposed that the sooner such action was begun the better, before the Germans got a stranglehold on the country. But even more disturbing was the absence of any real discipline or cohesion in this camp, as typified by the lack of any blackout precautions. The valley was a line of fires, which, however necessary for cooking and warmth, was also a beacon waiting to beckon the Luftwaffe.

Another reason for getting out just as soon as possible.

Sandrine's breathing and restless movements indicated that she might still be awake, unlike Ivkov, who was snoring loudly on the far side of the hut. 'What are you thinking about?' he asked.

Her answer was predictable. 'A hot bath. I think of sinking beneath the suds, of feeling the water everywhere. Oooh . . .! Do you trust Ivkov?'

'I think he needs us as much as we need him.'

'What would you have done if he had refused to cooperate? Had said he was going to tell Mihailovic we were planning to leave?'

'Well . . .'

'Would you have killed him? Are you that ruthless a man?'

'We're fighting a war,' Tony said, not at all sure that he *was* that ruthless a man. But he had something even more important on his mind. 'How well do you know Elena?'

'How well does one know anyone?'

'All right. How long have you been friends?'

'We became friends soon after I came to Belgrade. That was two years ago.'

'How did you meet?'

'When I first arrived, I had no place to live, so I put up at her father's boarding house until I found my apartment.'

'Ah.'

She rolled on her side to face him, only just distinguishable in the gloom. 'You are concerned about what that stupid officer said?'

'Well . . .'

'You English,' she said. 'You think the world revolves around sex, but you are afraid to come into the open about it. You are a prurient people.'

'I won't deny that. Are you saying that the boarding house *is* a brothel?'

'Are *you* saying that you think Elena is a whore? The woman you are going to marry?'

'No, I am not saying that,' he snapped. 'It's just that . . . well . . .'

'She gave herself to you too easily? That is her way. Has she ever charged you for sleeping with her?'

'Of course not.'

'There, you see.'

'But—'

'She was not a virgin when she went to you. She has a relaxed approach to life. A continental approach. I was not a virgin when I went to Bernhard.'

'You?'

He heard her smile in the darkness. 'I lost my virginity when I was thirteen.'

'Good lord!'

117

'He sang in the church choir. So did I. He was very handsome.'

'And you were very beautiful.'

'He thought so. Do you think I am beautiful?'

'I have told you that I do.'

'And you like to feel my body.'

'Yes,' Tony said.

'But you are betrothed to Elena,' she said. 'The Kostics do not operate a brothel. But they will let a gentleman take a room for the night, and bring a woman with him, no questions asked as to whether she is his wife or not. I spent my first night with Bernhard there.'

She rolled away from him, and a few moments later he heard her begin to snore, very softly and gently, and entirely femininely.

The following morning Tony located the surgeon, and persuaded him to come to the hut and look at Sandrine's feet. The camp was a hum of somewhat depressing energy. More recruits had come in overnight, all with tales of death and destruction, and still very little order was being achieved. Men and women stood around in groups, arguing, discussing, asking after relatives; children played and wailed; dogs growled and occasionally fought over scraps of food. While Elena, not unnaturally, was feeling increasingly depressed.

'When are you going to get me out of here?' she begged.

'We're working on it, believe me,' he said.

At least she seemed to be on quite good terms with her fellow prisoners.

The doctor examined Sandrine's feet. 'These are healing very well,' he said. 'Can you put on your boots?'

'I haven't tried,' Sandrine said.

'Then let us see.' He re-bandaged the flesh – which was now more discoloured than cut or swollen – then eased the first boot over the toes. Sandrine made a face but said nothing. 'There.' He laced the boot. 'Tell me when it is too tight.'

'Now,' Sandrine said.

He tied the laces, then fitted the other boot. 'Stand up.'

Sandrine struggled to her feet.

'Move around. Stamp your feet.'

Biting her lip, she obeyed.

'Is it painful?'

'Yes.'

'That is in the mind. You must try to use them as much as possible.'

'How far would you say she should walk, doctor?' Tony asked.

'Oh, well, one needs to be careful. Anyway, there is nowhere to walk to right this minute, eh? Just make sure she spends as much time as is comfortable on her feet.'

'Thank you. Tell me, doctor, your name wouldn't be Dukic, by any chance?'

'No, no. I am Slivnic. Do you know Dukic? But obviously you do not, or you would not have supposed I could be he.'

'I know his wife.'

Slivnic raised his eyebrows.

'Mrs Dukic helped us to escape from Belgrade,' Tony explained. 'It was she who first tended to Mademoiselle Fouquet's feet. Very successfully, it seems.'

'Oh, yes, Helene would have done that. She was a nurse before she married Josef.'

Tony nodded. 'She told me.'

'And she has survived the Germans?'

'She had survived them, three days ago. But three days ago they had only just arrived. She wanted me to tell her husband this, if I came across him. Do you know where he is?'

Slivnic shook his head. 'He could be anywhere. He could be dead.'

'Well, if you do meet up with him, will you give him his wife's message?'

'Of course. But I will only meet up with him if he comes to

this camp. And if he does that, you can give him the message yourself.'

'That's true.'

Slivnic went off.

'You need to be careful what you say,' Sandrine admonished.

'Point taken. How far is it to your brother's village, Ivkov?'

'From here? Maybe twenty miles.'

'Shit!'

'I can walk twenty miles,' Sandrine said. 'For a hot bath.'

'I will carry you, mademoiselle,' Ivkov said.

'I was sure you would. When do we leave?'

'Tonight,' Tony told her.

But immediately after their midday meal there was an immense stir throughout the camp as an aircraft swept over the hills and along the valley before disappearing round the next peaks.

'Do you think he saw us?' Ivkov asked.

'If he didn't, he must be blind,' Tony replied.

Mihailovic obviously held the same opinion; half an hour later all officers were summoned to the headquarters tent.

'We should disperse our people,' Colonel Zardov said.

'Will we ever get them back together again?' asked someone else.

'What is your opinion, Captain Davis?' the general asked.

'That we should evacuate the valley, certainly, sir. But endeavour to keep in being as an army.'

Mihailovic stroked his beard. 'We will make preparations to move tomorrow morning,' he said.

'Can we delay that long?' Zardov asked.

'Think of the number of valleys that plane has flown over,' the general said. 'So in this valley he saw what he might consider an accumulation of refugees. The Germans know that many people fled Belgrade. They will expect them to congregate. There is no suggestion, from the air, that this is a military encampment.' He gave a sour smile. 'There is not much on the ground to suggest this, either. So that pilot will return to his base and report, and his superiors will decide whether or not to take action. No decision will be made before tomorrow. If we move out at dawn, we will be away before they return.'

'Do you not suppose they will be able to follow our movements from the air, sir?' Matovic asked.

'So we may have to keep moving for a while. I have never supposed we would be able to sit on our asses in relative comfort forever. I think there is a more serious possibility that we have not yet considered: that the Germans may be satisfied with the grip they have taken on the country, and are now intending to attack us here in the mountains. That plane was a reconnaissance, possibly for considerable ground forces. Colonel Zardov, I would like patrols sent out to discover what is happening. They should cover an area of at least twenty miles to the east and north, to ascertain if there are any troop movements towards us.'

'Yes, sir,' Zardov said. 'Now you can earn your keep, Captain Davis. I will give you a platoon of the Fourth Regiment of Foot. They are your friends, eh?'

There was nothing for it, and at least Tony had his revolver returned to him. He hurried back to the hut to put Sandrine and Ivkov in the picture.

'But . . . will you be back by tonight?' Sandrine asked.

'Probably not.'

'Then—'

'We shall have to postpone our departure. But the whole camp is going to move out tomorrow morning. That will be our opportunity to slip away.'

'With Elena?'

'Of course with Elena.' He glanced at Ivkov, who, as usual,

was regarding Sandrine with the expression of a starving man contemplating a large steak. 'Just remember that I am coming back, old friend,' he said.

To his pleasure, his second-in-command was again Matanovic, who also seemed pleased to be reunited with the British officer, although he and his men were obviously aware of the previous day's dispute.

'I hope your lady is well, sir,' Matanovic ventured.

'She is as well as can be expected.'

'I would be happy to vouch for her, sir. For the way she fought against the Germans.'

'Thank you, Sergeant. I may just need to take you up on that.'

He had been given a map of the area they were to reconnoitre, as well as a pair of binoculars and a flashlight for when it grew dark – which it very rapidly did as the afternoon closed in, with heavy black clouds rolling up from the south.

'That is very bad weather,' Matanovic said. 'When it rains in the mountains it can be very bad. There can be flash floods.'

Tony had to assume that Mihailovic was aware of that possibility. On the plus side, heavy cloud cover and rain tomorrow morning would limit the possibility of a Luftwaffe attack.

The patrol – ten men including Matanovic and Tony – made their way through a succession of shallow valleys between the peaks, seeing and hearing nothing until just before dusk. Then one of the soldiers held up his hand. 'Listen!'

He obviously had very sharp ears, but a few moments later they could all hear the noise: the throb of aircraft engines.

'Take cover,' Tony said.

They crouched amongst the heather, and then realised the aircraft were not looking for them. Now they saw a good dozen planes, flying in formation, in the direction of the encampment.

Like so many others before him, Mihailovic had made the mistake of assuming that the Nazi war machine needed time to think before acting.

Chapter Six

Communists

'Where are they going, sir?' Matanovic asked.

'Where do you suppose, Sergeant?'

'Will they be able to find the camp in the dark?'

'Very easily,' Tony said, remembering the total absence of any blackout precautions.

'Should we warn them?'

'Those planes will be there long before we can get back. But we will go back, just as fast as we can.'

The two women were there!

They hurried, although in the darkness it was not always easy to find the way. But they were only some ten miles away from the valley, and fifteen minutes later they heard the sounds of explosions as bombs were dropped. Tony tried not to let himself imagine the scene, but he knew there would be complete pandemonium, sheer terror . . . and a great deal of death and injury.

Once again he found himself thinking of Sandrine rather than Elena, of that pale wisp of utterly beautiful humanity, lying there shattered and broken.

'Get a move on,' he told his men.

It was eleven o'clock before they regained the valley. The planes had only been overhead for a few minutes, but they had left a good deal behind them. As the patrol climbed over the hills and looked down, they saw a mass of fires, and heard a continuing chorus of misery.

'Find your regiment,' Tony told Matanovic, and had to stop himself from adding, *if it still exists.*

He hurried down the slope, tripping over more than one dead body. There were fewer live ones than he had expected. Most of the people had fled, probably irrationally and without orders, to the supposed safety of the surroundings hills. As had most of the animals; even the dogs were gone. There were a few wounded, sitting or lying, groaning and moaning and crying out for help, but no one was giving them any. There were also several officers, roaming through the flickering gloom, shouting commands which were being totally ignored. Of Mihailovic and his staff there was no sign.

He found his way to the hut, shone his torch into the interior . . . and gazed at the faces of Ivkov, Sandrine and Elena. Elena had regained her satchel and thus her pistol, which was pointing at him.

'Holy Hallelujah!' he said.

'Tony!' Elena shouted, getting to her feet and throwing her arms round him.

'How did you get here?'

'The guard ran away when the bombing started. So I and the others forced the door.'

'Where are they?'

'I don't know. They went off. I came here.'

'I made the ladies stay,' Ivkov said proudly. 'I knew you would come back.'

'It was terrible,' Sandrine said. 'The bombs were all around us. I thought we were going to die. How we were not hit is a miracle.'

'It was not as bad as it was in Belgrade,' Elena pointed out.

'I thought we were going to die then, too.'

'Well, let's get out of here while we can,' Tony said.

'Where can we go?' Elena asked.

'To Ivkov's brother. Right?' he asked the bath-keeper.

Ivkov scratched his head. 'If you think that is our best option, sir.'

'I don't think it is our best option,' Tony said. 'But right now it happens to be our only option. You lead us, Ivkov.'

'What is the difficulty?' Elena asked.

'His brother is a Communist,' Sandrine explained. 'And lives in a Communist village.'

Elena made a whistling sound. 'You mean they are outlaws.'

'Perhaps not now,' Sandrine said, always happy to become involved in an argument. 'They were outlawed by the government, but now there is no government, so—'

'For God's sake,' Tony said. 'I don't care if their head man is called Jesse James. They're our only immediate hope of survival. Let's go.'

Ivkov was already outside of the hut, waiting. 'We need to go to the north-west,' he said. 'But . . .'

Tony studied the stars; the clouds had not yet formed overhead. 'That way.'

'How do you know this, sir?'

'Before this damned business started I used to sail boats. One of the things you learn to do as a sailor, even an amateur, is to read the stars.'

'But how can the stars tell you where my brother's village is, sir?'

'They can't. What they do is always point in the same direction. See that big one? That is called the North Star. It points to the north. So if we keep it on our right hand, we are travelling north-west.'

'What a wonderful thing,' Ivkov commented. 'We must cross the stream.'

He led them down the hill.

'Shit!' Sandrine commented as she tripped and fell to her hands and knees. 'What was that?'

'A dead body,' Tony told her. 'There are a lot of them about.' He stooped to help her up, and tripped over something

126

himself, only this was hard. He fumbled in the darkness, and
picked up a rifle. 'Well, glory be.' Another fumble located
the bandolier. He stood up. 'You ever fired one of these,
Ivkov?'

'Oh yes, sir. When I was a young man I served in the army.
Well, I had to.'

'Then here's a present for you.' He held out the rifle and
bandolier.

'Oh, sir!' Ivkov took them as if they were made of gold,
slung them both on his shoulder, and positively strutted down
the hill.

'Now you have made him happy,' Elena said, squeezing
Tony's arm. 'Tell me about this Jesse James.'

'Later,' he promised. 'Mind how you go.'

They had reached the stream. He helped Sandrine down the
bank – Elena had already stepped in – and she gave a squeal
of pleasure.

'Oh, that feels so good. Wait . . .'

They had reached the centre, where the fast-flowing water
was about thigh deep, and she raised her torn skirt to
her waist.

'I could stand here forever. Ooh . . . what . . .'

Tony caught her before she fell over, knocked off balance
by a floating body that had bumped into her.

'Shit!' she commented as he helped her out of the water
on the other side of the stream.

'People,' Ivkov said.

Actually, there was only one person, stumbling through
the darkness, peering at them.

'You!'

'Captain Matovic,' Tony said. 'Bit of a mess, eh? Did the
general survive?'

'The general has evacuated to the hills.'

'I bet he has. Well, give him my regards.'

'He has left me behind to round up stragglers. I will give
you directions.'

'Forget it.'

'If you do not rejoin the general, you will be classified as a deserter.' He waved his arm. 'All of you.'

'I am not a member of the Yugoslav army,' Tony reminded him. 'Neither is Mr Ivkov. Neither are these ladies. So—'

'Ladies?' Matovic came closer to peer at them. He was a sorry sight, for he had lost his cap and his tunic was torn and dirty, presumably from rolling on the ground to shelter from the bombs. But he still had a revolver holster on his belt. 'That woman is under arrest!'

'Now don't start that again,' Tony said. 'She is coming with us.'

'She is under arrest. She—'

'Ivkov,' Tony suggested.

Ivkov licked his lips, then swung his rifle butt. It crashed into the back of Matovic's head. The officer fell to his knees, and then on to his face. He did not utter a sound.

'Shit!' Sandrine commented.

Tony bent over him. 'I hope you didn't kill him.'

'No, no, sir. I did not hit him hard enough. But he will have a headache when he wakes up.'

'And a bad temper,' Elena suggested. 'But I am grateful, Ivkov.'

'I obeyed the captain,' Ivkov said, at once proudly and with some embarrassment.

'Our business,' Tony said, determined not to be irritated by the tendency of his little group to engage in irrelevant conversation at the wrong time, 'is not to be here when he wakes up.'

They made their way through the remainder of the shattered encampment, stepping round fires, stumbling in and out of shallow craters, encountering other people – but no one else attempted to stop them or inquire about them.

The heat of the fires faded as they climbed into the hills to the north.

'When do we eat?' Sandrine asked.

'You mean, *what* do we eat,' Elena corrected.

'I am so hungry.'

'We're only twenty miles from Ivkov's brother's village,' Tony reminded them. 'There we will be fed. Eh, Ivkov?'

Ivkov grunted.

Only twenty miles, Tony reflected. In terms of his own personal fitness and experience this was no great distance, although soon enough his leg began to ache. But none of the others was in the least used to such exertion, and there was also the matter of Sandrine's feet. Soon she was complaining of the pain, and they had to rest regularly; by dawn Tony and Ivkov were again sharing the load of carrying her.

'If you were a horse we'd have shot you by now,' Elena pointed out.

'If I was a horse I would have kicked you by now,' Sandrine retorted.

Again Tony had the impression that he was presiding over the end of a beautiful friendship, although the exchange had been good-humoured enough.

He was glad to be able to call a halt at dawn to survey the situation. He knew they had been descending steadily, and were now in the middle of what appeared to be a series of low hills. Below them was another valley, through which bubbled an especially inviting mountain stream.

'Water!' Sandrine cried. 'Oh, let's get down there. I am so thirsty. And I so want to wash.'

'Be patient.' Tony had retained the binoculars given to him the previous night, and he used these to survey the ground beneath them. The stream certainly looked tempting – he was as thirsty as anyone – but just in front of it he could make out a roughly paved road. He handed the glasses to Ivkov. 'What do you make of that?'

Ivkov focussed. 'It is the road to Divitsar. If we follow that, we will go right into the village.'

'Hoorah!' Elena said.

'How far?' Tony asked.

'Maybe fifteen miles.'

'Fifteen miles?' Sandrine shouted. 'You mean we have walked all night and made only five miles?'

'You haven't walked all night,' Elena pointed out. 'You were carried for most of it.'

'Bitch!' Sandrine snapped, and swung her hand.

Elena caught her wrist and swung her own hand. Sandrine gave one of her shrieks as she was struck across the cheek, but she was full of fight and lashed out with her foot. It was Elena's turn to cry out in pain, as Sandrine had not taken off her boots, but the Croatian had retained her grip on the Frenchwoman's wrist, and the pair of them lost their balance together and went rolling down the hillside, legs kicking.

Ivkov scratched his head.

'Come on,' Tony said, and scrambled down. He was afraid that Elena, so much bigger and stronger, might do the Frenchwoman an injury.

Ivkov followed, dislodging a small avalanche of stones and dust, and they caught up with the women – just in time, Tony estimated, for Elena had Sandrine on her back and was sitting astride her thighs with both hands wrapped round her throat.

'Stop that!' he snapped, and grasped Elena's shoulder to pull her off.

Elena sat down with a bump. 'She is a bitch and a malingerer.'

'She's your best friend,' Tony reminded her. 'And she's one of us. There's to be no more fighting.' He knelt beside Sandrine. 'You all right?'

Sandrine was gasping for breath and stroking her throat. 'She tried to kill me.'

'We're all pretty upset,' he said. 'She just lost her temper.'

'I need something to drink.'

'Over here.' He helped her up and across the road to the stream. 'Mind how you go.'

The bank was lined with thick bushes. Sandrine carefully parted these, lay on the bank on her stomach and immersed her head in the water; he assumed she was drinking at the same time.

She raised her head. 'I would like to go in. Can I go in?' Tony shrugged. 'I have no objection.'

To his amazement she rose to her knees and lifted her dress over her head. Then she dropped her knickers to the ground and sat down to remove her boots and bandages. The rising sun bathed her body in golden splendour. She stepped down the shallow bank and into the water. It only came to her knees, but she waded out until it reached her waist, and there crouched, soaking her hair time and again.

Elena and Ivkov arrived, pushing the bushes aside.

'I told you, you can fuck her if you like,' Elena said to Tony. 'Ram her till she shouts for help.'

Ivkov gave a heavy sigh, clearly contemplating surrogate duties.

'I'm sure she'd shriek for help at the very idea,' Tony said.

'You do not know her. Beneath that china-doll exterior she is a bitch in heat, all the time.'

Tony remembered what Sandrine had told him, of losing her virginity at thirteen. He hadn't altogether believed her.

'Anyway,' he said, determined to lighten the atmosphere, 'I've never been any good on an empty stomach.'

'Well,' Elena said, 'I am going in too.'

She threw her dress and underwear on the ground, pulled off her boots, and entered the water, carefully selecting a spot some yards away from the still soaking Sandrine, who had her eyes closed and was temporarily oblivious to her surroundings.

Ivkov gave another of his sighs.

'Very well, Ivkov,' Tony said. 'You may go in too. But stay away from the women.'

He decided to go in as well; he needed a bath as much as

anyone. He soaked and tried to think. But reality was very hard to grasp. This time last week he had not had a care in the world, only his next meeting with Elena to look forward to. His only problem had been whether he would be allowed to marry the girl . . . and if he really wanted to. He had always been an intensely private person, and the idea of being so intimate with someone scared him.

Now, he did not suppose he had ever been so intimate with anyone before in his life than with these three people. Which added another dimension to his dilemmas: that of responsibility.

He had, as an officer, been trained to accept responsibility. But his responsibility had been that of duty – to responsible men. If, as a section or company commander, he had been responsible for the lives and well-being of his men, there had always been the comforting feeling that those men had been as highly trained as himself, each totally aware of his own skills and his own place in the scheme of things, each requiring only to be pointed in a certain direction by his officer to know what to do next.

These three people, even Elena, had accepted his leadership absolutely, but without the discipline to obey immediately and without question. Yet they were trusting their lives to his judgement, even if they must know that he had as little idea of what might happen next as themselves.

Sandrine waded through the waist-deep water towards him. Now her eyes were open, and water flowed from her pale yellow hair down her cheeks, dripped from her armpits and nipples. 'You are a good man, Tony Davis,' she said.

'You said that once before,' he reminded her. 'I really would wait until we see how this turns out before you make a final judgement.'

She made a moue. 'You are afraid of me. Of my sex. Of what it might do to you.'

'You could very well be right.'

'Listen, I would like to fuck with you.'

132

'With no breakfast?'

'Which is more important to you, sex or food?'

'Well, I hate to sound totally gross, but at this moment . . . Oh, Jesus Christ!'

The roar of engines rose even above the sound of rushing water; the vehicles were quite close.

'On the bank,' he snapped.

He scooped Sandrine from the water and dashed to the bank. He threw her, and then himself, on the ground, pulling their discarded clothes and weapons against them. Elena and Ivkov did likewise, and they huddled beneath the bushes, watching the road, down which there now came four motor-cycle outriders, followed by several trucks filled with soldiers. German soldiers. In the rear of each truck there was mounted a machine-gun; the gunners were glaring at the hills to either side.

Fortunately, their interest was in the hills; they did not even look at the roadside bushes. The convoy passed and continued to descend the hill.

'Is it not strange,' Elena remarked, 'that every time the Germans find us, we are naked.'

'They did not find us,' Sandrine said.

Tony was too preoccupied to notice that his little group was off on a tangent again. 'How many villages lie along this road?' he asked Ivkov.

'Only Divitsar.'

'Then those men must have come from there.'

'I think so.'

Tony looked at his watch; it was just seven. 'Then it was a dawn raid. Do you think the village is still standing?'

'Would we not have heard the firing?' Elena asked.

'Not if it is still more than ten miles away,' Tony said. 'Get dressed.'

They dragged on their clothes.

'What are we going to do?' Sandrine asked.

'Keep going. There is nothing else *to* do.'

133

*   *   *

They walked for five hours, stopping for ten minutes in every hour. They followed the road, keeping a careful lookout for any signs of German activity, but all they saw was the occasional aircraft, too high to be interested in them.

Their stomachs rolled with hunger, and they were again desperately thirsty. Soon Sandrine began to limp, but, stung by Elena's jibes, she refused to ask for help.

And then it began to rain. The sky spent a couple of hours darkening, which was in the first instance a relief as the sun rose higher and became hotter. But by noon the glow was entirely blocked out, a cold wind came down from the mountains, and the rain followed, equally cold.

They looked at Tony.

'We keep going,' he said.

The rain was heavy and made nonsense of their scanty clothing; huge drops thudded on their unprotected heads and shoulders. They walked with bowed heads, and Tony reckoned they could walk right into the middle of a German patrol without even realising it.

And indeed they were in the middle of a group of men before they knew it. The men wore ponchos and waterproof hats, and carried a variety of weapons.

'Identify yourselves,' someone said.

'I am Ivkov the bath-keeper,' Ivkov said. 'I have come to see my brother.'

'Where are you from?'

'We are from Belgrade. These are my friends.'

The spokesman peered at Tony and the two women.

'You are Serbs?'

Tony spoke before anyone else could. 'I am a British officer. This lady is a French journalist. This lady is a Serb.'

Elena snorted, but did not speak.

'Come with us,' the leader said.

Tony walked beside him. 'We had to hide from a German column, down the hill.'

The man nodded. 'They were at our village last night, looking for Yugoslav soldiers.'

'Did they cause much damage?'

He shook his head. 'They found nothing, so they spent the night and went away again this morning.'

That didn't really sound like the Germans who had raped Belgrade, Tony thought, but he decided against saying so. 'Will you give us shelter?'

'That is up to our mayor. You are the sort of people the Germans were looking for.'

'We are fighting on your side.'

'We are not fighting anybody,' the man pointed out. 'You must talk with our mayor.'

'This mayor—'

'His name is Ivkov. He is the brother of the bath-keeper.'

'Thank God for that,' Tony said.

Ivkov did not look convinced. But their immediate hosts seemed happy enough, especially as they found themselves shepherding two extraordinarily attractive young women, even if both Elena and Sandrine resembled drowned rats at the moment.

Half an hour later they came upon the houses, straggling to either side of the road. These were hardly more than huts, but they were solidly built of stone with wood roofs and chimneys, from several of which issued wisps of smoke. Halfway along the single cobbled street on the left there was a larger building, with two storeys, which Tony guessed was the town hall. Opposite was another larger than usual building, although with only one floor; this he reckoned was the tavern. Oddly, there was no church. But then, this was a Communist community.

Just beyond the village there was a stream, tumbling down the hillside from the quite high hill beyond and continuing down the slope behind the houses. The stream obviously kept the community supplied with fresh water, although there could be no doubt, from the smell, that sanitary arrangements were primitive. Above the stream, on the sloping hillside, there was a considerable area under cultivation. This large vegetable garden, taken in conjunction with the numbers of goats on the hills beyond, indicated that these people were totally self-sufficient, at least as regards food.

The rain continued to teem down, but what appeared to be a large proportion of the population turned out to welcome them, including women and children and growling dogs, as well as several goats and a horde of chickens.

They were escorted up the street, surrounded by questions and comments, until they reached the town hall. Here there waited several quite well-dressed men, and one or two women, also clearly a cut above the rest of the inhabitants. One man in particular, tall and stout and wearing a gold medallion on a chain round his neck, was clearly the mayor. He was also clearly Ivkov's brother, and the bath-keeper hurried forward to explain who they were. He had learned his lesson from the past few days, and did not delineate Elena's nationality; Tony could only hope none of these people had ever had any reason to visit the Kostic boarding house.

Petar Ivkov listened carefully to what Boris had to say, the while looking from Tony to the women; disturbingly, he made no effort to embrace his brother as was the Serb way, nor, indeed, did he appear very pleased to see him. But when Boris had finished, the mayor turned to one of his own women. 'Take these ladies and find them some clothes to wear,' he said.

'Do you have a hot bath?' Sandrine asked. 'I am freezing.'

'You can bathe in the stream.'

'But that will be cold.'

'It will have to do.'

'What about food?' Elena said. 'We are starving.'

'And feed them,' the mayor said to the woman who had been instructed to procure them clothing.

'Will we return here?' Elena asked.

'When you have been fed and clothed,' Petar Ivkov said. 'You will come inside,' he told Tony.

Tony and Ivkov followed him into a large warm room; there was a roaring fire in the grate. Petar Ivkov gestured them to the table, where home-made bread and goat's cheese and rough wine was placed in front of them. Then he sat down himself. 'Tell me of Belgrade.'

Tony would have preferred to be offered a change into dry clothing himself, and equally a bed, but the food and wine were most acceptable.

'Did your recent guests not tell you what happened?' he asked as he tore off pieces of bread.

'They said there was some resistance.'

'They have destroyed the city,' Boris said.

'They were fools,' his brother said. 'To attempt to resist.'

'Your people did not attempt to resist,' Tony said, 'until it was forced on them.' He looked around the faces, for several of the men had come into the room with them. 'Do you not resent this?'

The men shuffled their feet and exchanged glances.

'Why did you not surrender?' Petar asked. 'Then you would have been sent to Germany as a prisoner of war. You would have been safe.'

'It is my duty to fight the Germans,' Tony said. 'As it is yours.'

Petar snorted. 'For what?'

It was Boris's turn to snort. 'He takes his orders from Moscow. And Stalin is Hitler's friend.'

'It is not my place, nor that of my people, to fight and die for a corrupt and decrepit regime,' Petar declared. 'I take you in because you are my brother, and I take you in, Englishman, because you are my brother's friend. But there is no war here in Divitsar. Remember this. Now tell me, have you encountered any Cetniks on your way here?'

'Cetniks?' Tony frowned. He had heard the word, of course; in Serbian it actually meant members of an armed company, but it was commonly used to delineate supporters of the royal family, which had suffered in popularity as a result of Prince Paul's subservience to the Nazis.

'He means government soldiers,' Boris explained, waggling his eyebrows.

Tony made a quick decision. He had no idea what the women, and Elena in particular, might be saying to *their* hosts. 'We encountered some troops, yes. Like us, they were trying to escape.'

'Do you know of the bombing raid last night?'

Tony nodded. 'We were there.'

'But you were not hurt,' Petar said thoughtfully. 'And you wish to fight the Germans.'

'As I said—'

'It is your duty. It is my duty to preserve the lives and wealth of my people. The Germans are the enemies of the government of Yugoslavia, which has chosen to defy them. We are also the enemies of the government of Yugoslavia, which has chosen to outlaw us. You understand that?'

'Ah . . . yes,' Tony said. 'I hope you will not blame me for not sympathising with your point of view.'

'Right now, my friend, it is my point of view that matters to you. I have said I will give you shelter – temporary shelter – because you are a friend of my brother. You may remain here while my people see if they can locate others who may be willing to take you in, and who may even wish to fight the Germans with you.'

'But—' Boris began.

Tony silenced him with a quick shake of the head. He was willing to let the future take care of itself; right now they needed rest and recuperation more than anything else. 'Then we are grateful,' he said.

'You should be,' Petar said. 'Now, these women, they belong to you?'

'Ah . . . yes.' Tony couldn't risk them belonging to anyone else.

Petar grinned. 'They are very handsome. But two? I will give you much for the fair one.'

'I'm sorry. She is very special.'

'Ah. Then the dark one?'

'She too is very special.'

Petar frowned, and then grinned again. 'You are a glutton, Captain Davis. A very fortunate glutton. There is an empty house at the end of the street. Its owner recently died. I give it to you for the duration of your stay here. You will be required to earn your keep. You will take your turns on watch in the hills. You have bullets for those guns?'

'Not many.'

'Let me see them.'

Boris handed over his rifle. 'I have a dozen cartridges in this bandolier,' he said.

Petar gave back the weapon. 'Normal army issue. We have bullets. Captain.'

Tony gave him the Webley revolver, and he made a face. 'Point three-eight. I do not think we have these.' He broke the gun. 'Six.'

'And I have six more.'

'They will have to do.' He gave a bellow of laughter. 'Until you meet up with another British officer, eh?'

'We also have a tommy-gun, but no cartridges, and a Luger pistol.'

'Taken from the Germans? Let me see it.'

'It belongs to one of the women.'

'You let a woman have a pistol?'

'I told you, it's hers.'

'And does she know how to use it?'

'Very well.'

'Strange woman,' Petar commented. 'Has she bullets?'

'One magazine in the gun and one spare.'

'Well, if she wants any more, she will have to take them from a German. But a woman, with a gun . . .' He shook his head. 'I should confiscate this gun.'

'We will need it, when we leave here,' Tony reminded him.

'Well, go and rest up.' He gave another bellow of laughter. 'With your two women, eh? Tomorrow you will work.'

One of Petar's men led Tony and Boris along the street to the house they had been allotted. The rain had slackened and it was now growing dark, but the villagers were still out in force, passing comments and asking questions.

Elena and Sandrine were already waiting in the hut. They were both dressed in somewhat heavy gowns, but retained the boots given to them by Mrs Dukic. They had obviously bathed in the stream, which ran quite close to this house; their faces were clear of mud and dust, and in fact they looked more civilised than at any moment since leaving Belgrade, even if quite unlike anything they had ever looked like before.

But they were not in very good humour. 'I thought you were never coming,' Elena complained.

'We had a lot of sorting out to do.' Tony looked around, assisted by the single candle placed in the centre of the table, which occupied the centre of the single room. But at least there was a table, and two chairs. And . . . He peered at the huddle of blankets in the corner.

'There is no bed,' Sandrine pointed out unnecessarily. 'I would have thought there would be a bed. Does your brother not have a bed?' she asked Ivkov.

'He is the mayor,' Ivkov replied. 'He is also the local party secretary,' he added. This was obviously more important.

'They told us tomorrow we must go out with the women to tend the flocks,' Elena said. 'I have never tended a flock in my life. What is a flock, anyway?'

'It's a collection of sheep,' Tony said. 'Well, I suppose in this instance, goats.'

'My God,' Sandrine said. 'I will be butted by a goat.'

'I wouldn't count on it,' Tony said. 'Now, I am pretty damn exhausted. And I imagine you are too. You have been fed?'

'If that was food,' Elena remarked.

'Your stomach is full, isn't it? I think we should all have a good night's sleep, for a change. The situation will look brighter tomorrow. Let's work out how we arrange ourselves.'

'What time is it?' Elena asked.

Tony looked at his watch, which miraculously had so far survived. 'Just gone six.'

'You expect us to go to bed at six?'

'Aren't you exhausted?'

'Well . . .'

'Listen,' Sandrine said.

The plaintive tones of an accordion drifted through the evening.

'That is coming from the tavern,' Elena said. 'Let's go down there.'

'You wish to go to a tavern?' Tony asked.

'Of course. There is music, and there will be people, and laughter, and dancing . . . and liquor. I feel like a drink. I *need* a drink.'

'Me too,' Sandrine said.

They appeared to be friends again.

Tony looked at Ivkov.

'Well, sir . . .'

'What do you intend to do for money?'

'We'll have to owe them,' Elena said. 'They'll trust us.'

'All right,' Tony said. 'Run off and enjoy yourselves. Get drunk. Just don't tell me tomorrow that you are too tired to do anything. Or that your feet hurt, Sandrine.'

'My feet do hurt,' Sandrine said with great dignity. 'But my head hurts more, not with physical pain, but with all the things I have seen, and heard, and suffered. I need to relax.'

'Okay. Have fun.'

'But you will not come?' Elena asked.

'I intend to have a good night's sleep,' Tony said. 'Oh,

by the way, don't get too chummy with the mayor. With respect, Boris.'

'What is the matter with the mayor?' Elena asked.

'He wants to buy you.'

'Me?' It was difficult to determine whether she was shocked or delighted.

'Well, actually, he wanted to buy Sandrine.'

'Me?' Sandrine's squeak was in a higher octave.

'But when I told him that he couldn't have you, he made an offer for Elena instead.'

'Well!' Elena remarked.

'You didn't sell her?' This time it was difficult to determine whether Sandrine was shocked or delighted.

'Of course I did not sell her,' Tony said. 'I told him neither of you were for sale. But that is no guarantee he won't get fresh when he's tanked up and discovers I am not with you.'

'Ha!' Elena commented, by no means mollified. 'I will take my gun.'

'No you will not. You start shooting, and we'll be out on our ears. That's supposing we're not lynched.'

'And suppose he does make advances?'

'Put him off and come back here. That goes for you too, Sandrine. And incidentally, under no circumstances let on that you are a Croat. I'm holding you responsible for your brother's behaviour, Boris.'

Boris pulled his nose, but he followed the women out of the hut.

Tony was actually relieved to be alone, for the first time since the German bombers had appeared over Belgrade, and he wasn't at all sure how long ago that was. The fact was, all his considerable military training had never prepared him for anything like this. Flanders had been chaotic, certainly, but compared with this it had been a very ordered chaos.

The British army had moved forward with the intention of

meeting the Germans along the line of the River Dyle. Having taken up their positions, they had learned that the Germans had broken through to the east, at Sedan, had shattered the French forces opposed to them, and were well on their way to appearing to the south and encircling them. Then it had been a case of getting out while they could; Tony had since learned that GHQ's thoughts had already been turning to Dunkirk and a possible evacuation. That retreat had been chaotic, and had grown more so day by day. But it had always been undertaken by an army in being, with regular and recognised chains of command, and with clear objectives always in view, even if that view had not always been available to the ranker.

In any event, the retreat had only just commenced when his part in the campaign had ended with the bomb which had broken his leg. Before he had properly known what was happening, he had been safely back in an English hospital.

But this . . . He presumed Mihailovic was, or thought he was, the most senior officer to have escaped the invasion. And in the circumstances he could not be blamed for attempting to take over the government, civil and military, as all other authority seemed to have collapsed. But he was also apparently interested in maintaining a *Serbian* government, for the Serbs, and was prepared to treat all Yugoslavia's other nationalities at best as unfriendly aliens and at worst as collaborators. It was as if England were invaded and Whitehall immediately started treating all Irish, Welsh and Scots as hostile.

As for these Communist enclaves . . . Was Communism outlawed in England? He had no idea, but he did know that it was very unlike British jurisprudence to outlaw people simply for their political beliefs. Except in time of war. Such as now.

What a mess.

More important than political and ethical reflections was deciding what to do next. Tony was very unhappy with their situation, and not just in terms of being fugitives. Petar Ivkov's hostility was natural in that he was under orders

– presumably from Moscow but certainly from whoever was the boss of the Communist Party in Yugoslavia – not to oppose the Germans, instructions which would include not to give aid to anyone who *was* intent on opposing the Germans. That meant that their stay here had necessarily to be brief. But where were they going to go after leaving here? Linking up with Mihailovic, or any force under his command, was impossible for Elena. But there did not seem to be anyone else. One thing was certain: the four of them could not survive by themselves in these mountains.

But what was really nagging at the back of his mind were the events of today. The Germans had taken over Belgrade. Thus they had taken over the Yugoslav government, its offices . . . and its files. Thus they would have learned the names and locations of all subversives, as identified by the Yugoslav government. Thus they had come out to Divitsar in the full knowledge that it was a Communist stronghold, had looked around, and driven off again. That just didn't make sense. Hitler might have struck a deal with Stalin, but that did not mean amelioration of the treatment of Communists in Germany, or, so far as Tony knew, in German-occupied territory – which now included Yugoslavia. Yet the people of Divitsar had virtually been patted on the head and told to get on with it.

That could only mean one of two things. The first was that Petar Ivkov had made some kind of a deal with the invaders, in which case a messenger might at this moment be hurrying to the nearest German command to inform them that he had four prizes for them; the only saving grace here was that, were they taken, Petar's brother would also be taken . . . but Tony had gained the impression that Petar was not all that fond of his brother.

The second possibility was that the Germans were following some agenda of their own. In which case this village was doomed. But Petar seemed blissfully unaware of that.

The door suddenly opened and Tony sat up, reaching for

his revolver as he did so. It was now utterly dark, and he had no idea who it was; the door closed again.

'Identify yourself, or die,' he said.

Sandrine dropped to her knees beside him. 'You are so military.'

'It's my business. Where are the others?'

'Getting drunk.'

There was alcohol on her breath as well, and he had no doubt about what she had returned for.

'Won't they miss you?'

'Not for a while. By then I shall be asleep.' There was a considerable rustling noise, and then her fingers plucked at his blanket. 'Will you not make room for me?'

He wished he had the time to consider the situation, to decide whether this was something he really wanted to happen, or dared allow to happen. But oh, how he wanted it to happen. And in any event, she was already beneath his blanket, and when he put his hand down, it encountered naked flesh.

She rippled to his touch. And discovered the reverse of the coin. 'You have clothes on.'

'I thought it might be a good idea.'

'I want you without clothes,' she said, getting to work on some buttons.

He didn't try to stop her. 'I thought you didn't like men,' he said.

'I don't, as a sex. I am very selective.'

She slid his pants down past his thighs.

'What about Bernhard?'

'Fuck Bernhard. No, I shall never see Bernhard again. And if I do, I am going to cut off his balls. Ah!'

She found what she was looking for, and seemed pleased.

'Do you realise that we have never even kissed each other?' he asked.

She had been nuzzling his chest. Now she raised her head, her hair flowing across his face; he thought it remarkable how sweet-smelling it was, after all it had been through over the past week.

She kissed him, still holding him and working her body against his just as she worked her tongue against him.

'Oh,' she said. 'Oh! I am going to have one.'

He had never doubted for a moment that, exhausted as he was, he was going to have one too. Because, no matter how hard he tried to resist it, he had wanted this woman from the moment he had started to rub the ointment on her legs.

She subsided, sighing.

'You are an astonishing woman,' he said.

'Why?'

'Well . . . women aren't usually so . . . well . . .'

'That is my trouble,' she said. 'I am always quick. Men take advantage of me.'

'I am sure they do.'

'But you did not take advantage of me. I wanted you to. I asked you to. But you did not.'

'Well . . .'

'You are a good man.'

'You keep making these unsubstantiated statements. Right now I don't feel like a good man.'

She raised her head to peer at him in the gloom; again her sweet-smelling hair flopped across his face. 'You did not want it?'

'Well, of course I wanted it, Sandrine. But—'

'And you were quick, too. I think we are in love. Can you make it again?'

'No,' he said definitely. 'Not tonight. And we can't be in love. I am in love with Elena.'

She blew a raspberry, and then emitted her favourite expression: 'Shit.'

The door was opening.

'I am asleep,' she whispered, and rolled off him to lie with her back against him.

There were several thumps across the darkness.

'Be careful,' Elena warned in a loud whisper. 'He is asleep.'

Tony hastily pulled up his pants and buttoned his shirt. 'I'm awake.'

'Ah.' More bumps and thumps. 'Stop that!' Elena commanded.

Ivkov gave a high-pitched giggle.

Elena knelt beside Tony. 'Listen. Sandrine has gone off. She just left. I don't know where she is.'

'I am here,' Sandrine said, contradicting her previous decision.

Elena reached across Tony in search of the voice. 'What are you doing there?'

'It is where we happen to be living, remember?'

Elena was moving her hands up and down Sandrine's body. 'I meant, what are you doing next to Tony, with nothing on?'

'I always sleep with nothing on,' Sandrine reminded her. 'And next to Tony is warm.'

Elena's hands moved to Tony. 'But you are fully dressed.'

'I feel safer this way.'

Never had he been so serious.

'Well,' she said, 'I also want to be warm.' There was a rustling sound. 'And I also sleep with nothing on.' She cuddled against him. 'I don't suppose—'

'No,' he said.

'You are too tired,' she said sympathetically. 'I will wait until tomorrow.' She suddenly turned her head. 'What do *you* want?'

'I also wish to get warm,' Ivkov said.

'Well, do it by yourself,' Elena told him. 'And put your pants back on.'

At dawn Tony lay awake thinking, with a naked woman on either side of him – which in the abstract was a very happy position to be in, but which concretely added another problem to those he already had.

He wasn't sure whether or not he should feel guilty, at least partly because he didn't know the truth about Elena, no matter how Sandrine had tried to defend her. The fact was, whether or not she had ever sold her favours, Elena was vastly more sexually experienced than he. He had only ever had one woman before her, and that had been in a French brothel in the autumn of 1939. He had not enjoyed it, having been brought up with a totally different set of manners and mores. Elena's enthusiastic approach to life and love had been a revelation, one he had vastly enjoyed. Being the man he was, and with the upbringing he had had, the mere fact that she had been prepared to share her all had immediately driven him in the direction of 'doing the proper thing', which began with marriage, and then . . . But he had known it could never happen, even if she were not a whore.

While Sandrine . . . Her background, professional status and general outlook on life made her far more suitable to being the wife of an army officer than Elena could ever be. And yet, she was equally representative of an approach to life which was utterly outside his knowledge, or that of his parents and friends at home, or even his brother officers. Most of them, anyway.

So was he meaning to throw Elena over for Sandrine? That he could never do until this crisis was over and she was reunited with her family. And now he was having his doubts as to whether that would ever happen.

Remarkably, he had slept very soundly. Or perhaps it was not remarkable at all, given his exhaustion and his erotically comfortable situation. But, as was so often the case, daylight brought with it a reconsideration of his problems. Overall, they remained immense and very nearly insoluble.

He didn't know how drunk Sandrine had been the previous night, or how affected she had been by the utter intimacy into which they had been thrown over the preceding few days, or how much she had felt she genuinely owed him a favour. But to his great relief she seemed to be utterly sated, and even, he suspected, a little ashamed. In any event, she appeared content to resume her original role as Elena's closest friend, and made no effort to return to his side the following night. She slept on the far side of the hut, having to repel Ivkov to do so; Tony, who could not help but regard her as even more his responsibility after their get-together, would have interfered had he considered it necessary, but Sandrine was more than capable of taking care of herself – certainly as regards someone like the bath-keeper, whose desires were confounded by his anxiety to remain acceptable to them, and particularly to Tony.

Elena seemed entirely to have regained her good humour, now that she was not in any immediate danger of either being shot or raped. As for her own desires, over the next week these were largely submerged by the combination of alarm and amusement. She and Sandrine were indeed required to accompany the women into the hills to watch the goats, and weed or draw the cabbages and carrots from the vegetable patch. This was a totally new experience for both of them.

Elena would probably have been grotesquely out of place on the Champs Élysées, but she was most definitely a city dweller, and even with her physical strength she had found the previous week's unceasing activity exhausting; following a flock of goats up and down hillsides was only slightly less enervating. In addition, despite her deliberately careless attitude towards the possible fate of her family, and even more of her brother, she was clearly very worried about them.

This applied even more to Sandrine, for whom the Champs Élysées was most definitely a natural habitat. Not only had she found their recent adventures even more exhausting than Elena had, but her feet still hurt, and she had not been joking when she said she feared being butted by a goat, a species of animal she had only previously viewed from a distance.

Nor was that her only discomfort. If her feet were soon completely healed, she had her hands to consider. 'Look at them,' she proclaimed, stretching the delicate fingers in front of Tony. 'Look at those nails! They will never be the same again.'

'They're all black and broken,' Elena said helpfully. 'Like mine.'

'And I'm getting a callous. Look.'

'I have one too,' Elena pointed out.

'Why is it the women have to do this,' Sandrine complained, 'when the men just sit on their asses and drink beer and smoke?'

'History,' Tony told her. 'It has always been like this.'

'Then it should be changed,' she said. 'This is exploitation of the weaker sex.'

Tony had no doubt that she also was psychologically damaged by the German invasion. If she had no family involved, the other members of the *Paris Temps* staff in Belgrade had been both her comrades and her friends, and she had had to watch them being snuffed out in seconds. In addition, although Tony had never been there, he understood that she had made her little apartment into the epitome of Paris chic, with every article of furniture, every book, and every painting or framed photograph carefully selected – and now almost certainly gone forever.

On top of all this was her abandonment by Bernhard, even if she knew he had only been obeying orders.

Fortunately the two women had so much to do that they were too occupied to consider the future. All the women were required, as soon as they came in from the fields, to prepare food for their menfolk, as well as do whatever washing was necessary. They grumbled when they were no longer able to take their surplus produce, which included chickens and eggs, into the nearest big town – Uzice – to sell in the weekly market; this had apparently been cancelled because of the invasion. Their visits to Uzice had been the high point of their lives. Now they had nothing to do but work.

'We are slaves,' Sandrine complained. 'This is an affront to natural justice.'

'It could be worse,' Elena pointed out. 'You could be pregnant.'

Women who were pregnant, even when they were within a month of delivery, were still expected to do their share of the work; those with children still at the breast also trooped into the hills every morning.

'Barbaric,' Sandrine grumbled, shooting Tony a quick glance. He presumed that when she had been entertaining Bernhard they had always used a contraceptive, so that if she were pregnant now it could only be his responsibility. Then he reflected that they would be leaving the village long before she would know about that.

Whatever their complaints, however, he was both delighted and relieved that they seemed to be friends again, despite the fact that Elena probably suspected that he and Sandrine had indeed got together on that first night. After all, she had given him permission, even if perhaps she had not meant him to take her up on it. But now, although from time to time she insisted upon what she regarded as her conjugal rights, and took care to make sure Sandrine never had another opportunity to claim *hers*, she seemed willing to share all her other rights with her friend. The two women even fell to arguing as to whether or not Tony should be shaved, Elena being against and Sandrine for. In the event, the idea was dropped, as it would have entailed borrowing a razor – supposing one could even be found in a community where all the men wore beards.

Like the women, Tony and Boris were also expected to fall into the customary behavioural pattern of the village, although in their case it meant a very sedentary, relaxed life. In the morning they went out in squads to look down into the valleys and report back to Petar Ivkov on any movements, whether friendly or hostile. This was repeated, by a different group, at dusk. For the rest, they sat around and drank beer, and gossiped and told dirty stories, while the children played at marbles and chased each other to and fro.

There were some twenty children in the village, counting

all those between four and fifteen in that category. One of the houses was actually a school, operated by a severe-looking woman who, judging by the occasional wails coming from inside the house, believed in corporal punishment. How much she actually taught her charges was a different matter, as she did not appear to have any qualifications beyond the ability to read and write, add and subtract, and carry out limited problems of multiplication and division. She was, however, well steeped in Communist dogma, and instilling this in her charges was her prime responsibility.

Like the adults in the village, the children also attended the daily meeting in the town hall, when the secretary – Petar – would read them some of Lenin's writings and lecture them on Stalin's greatness. Tony and Boris were required to attend these meetings as well, and Tony was happy enough to do so, both because he was anxious to remain on good terms with the mayor, and because Petar regularly sent scouts down to the valley, and even as far as Belgrade itself, to bring him up to date on what was going on. Petar then disseminated such knowledge as he supposed his people should have, while all the time maintaining his attitude of strict neutrality. Tony estimated he was looking beyond the present situation to a future when the monarchy would have been destroyed or discredited, leaving open the possibility of a Communist takeover of the entire country.

Tony could not see that ever happening, at least as long as the Nazis ruled in Berlin.

None of the news they received was good, looked at from the Allied and hopefully true Yugoslav point of view. Moves were being made to separate Croatia from Serbia to form a new, independent state – under Italian auspices – and Serbia itself had been converted into a puppet administration under a General Nedic, who was apparently content to do whatever he was ordered.

At the same time, it did not appear as if the Germans were taking the occupation very seriously. According to Petar's scouts, while they were using the river valleys as corridors to move men and matériel south to Greece – obviously with the intention of assisting their Italian allies – they had also withdrawn a good many units, and especially panzers, back to the north, as if they regarded the Yugoslav question as being settled. Tony could not help but consider that a strategically timed attack on the thin line of communication might well cut off the German forces in Greece and give the Allies a much-needed victory. But the only man, as far as he knew, who commanded sufficient men and weaponry to undertake such an attack was Mihailovic, and nothing he had seen or heard in the general's camp had suggested that he was capable, either physically or mentally, of carrying out such a coup.

Meanwhile his own future, and that of the two women, remained dangerously obscure. Petar had not again raised the question of their moving on, but Tony suspected that this was less because he valued the services of Boris and himself – or even that he felt he should help his brother as much as possible – than that he liked having the women in the village, and probably even still had designs on them. This raised the even more unpleasant question of when Petar might choose to forward these ambitions. Tony realised he was in a most invidious position: as their self-appointed protector, he would have to be disposed of. He did not suppose this would be very difficult for Petar to achieve, as Tony's only friends in the village were the women and Boris, and there was no guarantee that Boris would back him against his own brother.

He doubted that Petar, who took himself very seriously as both mayor and party secretary, would descend to plain murder, and there was also the reassuring presence of his wife, a large and formidable woman who Tony could not see allowing her husband to engage in any open high-jinks. But there was always the possibility of an accident or fatally dangerous mission.

Yet he had no alternative but to remain in the village, at least for the time being. There were only two possible havens he could seek. One was to return to Mihailovic, but that was impossible as long as he had Elena in tow. The other was to try to get north into Croatia, but he did not like the idea of that if the Croats were indeed allying themselves with the Axis power.

What a fuck-up, he thought, to quote Sandrine.

And there was no one he could discuss the situation with. The only member of his little group who had either the intellectual capacity or the lack of prejudice to consider their situation dispassionately was Sandrine, but ever since virtually raping him – and quite apart from Elena's constant and protective presence – the Frenchwoman seemed determined not to find herself alone with him again. He wondered if that was from embarrassment, or if she was afraid of Elena's reaction, or if he had not turned her on sufficiently – or if she feared that she might find herself irresistibly having another go at him . . .

So he reckoned his only course was to watch his back and wait for something to turn up. When it did, it was not what he had expected.

He was out in the hills on afternoon patrol, with several other men including Ivkov, just over a fortnight after their arrival in Divitsar. Suddenly they saw dust in the distance. Tony still had his binoculars, and these he levelled, soon identifying several cars and trucks on their way up the road that led to the village.

'Are they Germans, do you suppose?' Boris asked.

It was difficult to imagine who else they could be. In which case Tony had to suppose that Petar had after all decided to turn them in. In *which* case . . . He frowned as he refocussed the glasses. The approaching vehicles lacked the smartness he associated with the Germans, and they were not accompanied by the motorcycle outriders he associated with German patrols. And now that they were closer he could make out that the men in the open cars were not wearing German caps or helmets, or any uniforms at all, although they certainly appeared to be well armed. But that such a group – he estimated them to be about a hundred strong – should be moving about the hill country, openly and in broad daylight, raised all manner of possibilities.

'Let's get back to the village,' he said, and led the group down the hillside.

The women were just returning from the hills, and they and the children clustered round them, asking questions. Tony went directly to the town hall.

'Not Germans?' Petar was as surprised as Tony had been. 'What can it mean?'

'That the Germans have withdrawn?' Tony asked. They had seen no troop movement, not even an aircraft overhead, for the past week.

'If that could be so . . .' Petar said. He waved his arms. 'Prepare to greet our visitors,' he shouted.

Now they could hear the growl of the engines as the motorcade drove up the road, and a few minutes later it came into view around the bend. Tony noted that in the time since last he had seen it, it had changed its formation. Now one of the trucks was in the lead, and this vehicle swept through the street – which was lined with cheering villagers – until it reached the far end, just beyond the last house, which was, in fact, that occupied by Tony, Boris and the women. Here it stopped, and disgorged its load of some twenty men armed with tommy-guns, who took up their positions as if on parade, but with guns levelled.

Tony was the only one who noticed this development, or the fact that the last truck had also stopped away from the main body, at the other end of the street, and its twenty occupants had also got down with tommy-guns levelled.

The villagers' attention was taken by the two cars and the third truck, which had pulled to a halt in the centre of the village immediately before the town hall. Here again armed men debouched, and one of them – a heavy-set man with a thick moustache and a revolver on each hip – walked across the street. He exuded such an atmosphere of menace that even the dogs slunk away from him.

Petar Ivkov hurried down the steps to greet him. 'Welcome,' he said. 'You are from Belgrade?'

'I am today from Uzice,' the commander replied. 'But my home is Zagreb.'

'Zagreb?' Petar frowned in bewilderment. 'But that is—'

'In Croatia,' the commander said. 'My name is Ante Pavelic, and these are my men.'

'Well . . .' Petar was still totally confused, but Tony had a sudden understanding of who these men had to be . . . and why they were here.

He grasped Sandrine's arm and thrust her towards the hut. 'Inside,' he snapped. 'Elena . . .'

Both women gaped at him in amazement. Everyone else was looking at Pavelic.

'If you will tell me how we may help you,' Petar was saying.

'You can help me by lining up against those walls,' Pavelic said. 'You are going to be shot.'

PART THREE

RESISTANCE

Phoebus, arise:
And paint the sable skies,
With azure, white and red.

William Drummond

Chapter Seven

Massacre

For a moment neither Petar nor his companions moved; they even attempted to laugh, assuming that what they had just been told had to be a joke. Then it slowly dawned on them that it wás not a joke.

'Haste,' Pavelic said. 'We have not got all night.'

The villagers exchanged glances. In their eagerness to greet people they had assumed to be friends, they had left their firearms in their houses.

'Get in there,' Tony muttered, pushing the two women into their hut. Ivkov followed him.

'What is happening?' Sandrine asked. 'He can't be serious.'

'I'm afraid he is serious.' Tony looked at Elena. These were her people. But for the moment even Elena looked utterly confounded.

'You too, ladies,' Pavelic was saying. 'Be sure you have your brats with you. Captain Grosnic, make a selection.'

Tony watched through the slightly open door of the hut as the Croatian captain walked up and down the still shocked line of women.

'You,' he said, pointing. 'And you. And you. Step out.'

The three girls – they were only teenagers – looked at each other, then left the ranks.

'Marina!' one of the older women screamed.

The youngest of the girls stopped to look over her shoulder, and had her arm seized by one of the Croat militiamen, who jerked her, and her companions, into their midst. Captain Grosnic selected three more women, these slightly older, and all married; the six women were the most attractive of the villagers.

'What do they want with them?' Sandrine whispered at Tony's elbow.

'What do you think? For God's sake, keep out of sight.'

Petar Ivkov had at last regained some of his composure. 'You cannot be serious,' he protested.

'I am always serious,' Pavelic told him. 'Now, all of you, turn round and face the wall.'

'Why are you doing this?' Petar shouted. 'You are Yugoslav. We are Yugoslav. We should be fighting the Germans, together.'

'But you are Communists,' Pavelic said. 'You are the enemies of mankind. Your fate is to be exterminated. Besides, the Germans are our friends. Commence.'

The tommy-guns began to chatter, and the evening dissolved into horror. Several men, women, and children fell in the initial bursts. Too late, some of the men turned and ran at their assassins, but were cut down before they could cross the street. Mrs Ivkov ran to her husband's side, and died on her knees before she could reach him. Petar himself just stared at his murderers, his right hand clutching his medal of office, then he joined his wife on the ground. Some of the villagers tried to run up the street, and were met by the bullets of the men posted to block the road. Others tried to regain their houses, but were followed by the chattering tommy-guns. A few tried to get between the houses, but suffered the same fate. The machine-guns were turned even on the dogs, but only a few of these were hit; the rest scampered off into the gloom.

The initial slaughter was over in a few minutes; the gunshots, and the shrieks of pain and terror, were swallowed up in the echoes from the hills to either side. Now there were single shots, as the murderers slung their tommy-guns and drew their pistols, to despatch anyone lying amidst the corpses who revealed the slightest sign of life.

Tony's fingers curled round the butt of his revolver, but there was nothing he could do against a hundred armed men. At the same time, he realised he was going to have to do something, and very soon; the militiamen were starting to go through the houses, kicking the doors open, and dragging those who had had the time to seek shelter out into the open to be despatched. The fugitives were nearly all women and children, which made the already sickening evening worse.

Tony realised that he did feel sick. This was certainly not warfare; it was genocide. Not a single person in the village had had the time to arm himself. Now they lay scattered against the wall while their blood flowed down the sloping street.

Elena stood at his shoulder beside Sandrine, and they heard the scream of the first girl being raped.

'These are your people,' he reminded Elena.

'My people? These are Ustase. I have heard of this man Pavelic. He has been to our house in Belgrade. Even then I knew him for a thug. Why do you not shoot him? He is right there.'

She drew her Luger from her satchel.

'Because if either of us shoots him, we are dead,' Tony said.

'Do you not think we are going to die, anyway?'

'That is up to you.'

She regarded him for several seconds, then faced the door as it was pulled open.

'Well, hey,' said the militiaman, looking from Elena to Sandrine. 'Here's a couple of beauties. Outside! And you,' he told Tony and Ivkov.

'I am a Croat,' Elena said, very loudly.

'Out!' the man repeated, reaching for her arm while keeping his tommy-gun pointed at Tony.

'My name is Elena Kostic,' Elena said, more loudly yet.

'My father is Benjamin Kostic, who owns the Kostic boarding house in Belgrade. Tell your commander this.'

Pavelic had heard the argument, and now himself came over to them. 'Elena Kostic,' he said. 'I remember you. But . . . are you a Communist?'

'Of course I am not a Communist,' Elena snapped.

'Then what are you doing here?'

'I am a refugee from Belgrade. With my friends.'

'Tell them to come outside.'

'To be shot?'

'If they are truly your friends, and can explain what they are doing here, they will not be shot.'

Elena made a face at Tony, but there was no alternative, so he nodded. She stepped through the doorway into the midst of some twenty men, whose expressions reminded Tony of wolves.

'Us too,' he said. 'But leave the talking to Elena and me.'

He went outside.

'This man is armed,' Pavelic said.

'Of course he is armed,' Elena said. 'Captain Davis is an officer in the British army.'

'British army officers do not wear beards,' Pavelic said.

'And I wouldn't, if I had a razor,' Tony said.

Pavelic looked him up and down. It was obvious that Serbo-Croat was not Tony's native tongue. 'What are you doing here?' he asked.

'I was a military attaché at the embassy in Belgrade,' Tony said. 'When the embassy was evacuated following the invasion, I was separated from my comrades, so I decided to get out of Belgrade – with Miss Kostic.'

'He is my betrothed,' Elena said proudly.

'You, and a British officer?' Pavelic looked from one to the other, clearly amazed. Tony could only hope he was not going to say something stupid. But his attention had been caught by Sandrine. 'And this one?'

'I am a French journalist,' Sandrine said. 'Sandrine Fouquet.'

162

'You are Vichy?'

'Yes, I am Vichy.'

'Then what are you doing here? You are a neutral. There was no reason for you to leave Belgrade.'

'She is my friend,' Elena said. 'And the Germans tried to rape her.'

Pavelic stroked his moustache, then looked at Ivkov. 'And who are you claiming to be?'

'I am Ivkov, the bath-keeper.'

Pavelic frowned. 'Ivkov. That is the name of the mayor.'

'He was my brother.'

Pavelic gave a cold smile. 'Then you had better join him.' He snapped his fingers, and his men hurried to surround the bath-keeper.

'You'll not touch this man,' Tony said.

Pavelic turned to him. 'Do you suppose you can give me orders?'

Tony thought quickly, and decided that only arrogance – of which Elena had once accused him – would carry the day here. 'I am your superior officer.'

'You? A captain?'

'Elena was mistaken. My rank is colonel.' With his tunic and all his papers gone, there was no way of disproving his claim. 'What is *your* rank, *Mr* Pavelic?'

'Me? I am a commander in the Ustase. I am *the* commander of the Ustase.'

'As I understand it,' Tony said, 'the Ustase is not a military body. It is a secret society devoted to murder and mayhem.' He looked around at the scattered corpses, now slowly being concealed by the gathering darkness. 'As you have demonstrated here today. You, Mr Pavelic, have no military standing, and no right to be here, other than as a condemned criminal.'

Everyone stared at him, including Pavelic himself. The two women were obviously holding their breaths. Well, he was only breathing himself by an act of will.

Pavelic pulled himself together. 'My military standing is the hundred men I have at my back, Colonel Davis. As for my right to be here, orders were given to me by the German commander in Belgrade to seek out and destroy all Communist nests that can be discovered.'

'You admit to being a collaborationist?'

'A collaborationist? My people have no quarrel with the Germans. Rather, we see them as allies, who will free Croatia from Serbian rule and restore its former glory.'

'If you believe that, then you are as stupid as you look,' Tony said.

Pavelic flushed. 'I can shoot you now,' he said. 'And no one would be any the wiser.'

'Are you going to shoot Miss Kostic too? She is a fellow Croat.'

The two men glared at each other. Then Pavelic said, 'You still have not explained what you are doing here, in a Communist enclave.'

'When we left Belgrade,' Elena said, 'we made our way into these hills. Our intention was to make our way north, into Croatia. But we needed food, and some shelter. So when Ivkov told us his brother was mayor of a village in this vicinity, we decided to come here.'

'There are elements of the Yugoslav army in these hills. Did you not seek shelter with them?'

'We saw no Yugoslav soldiers,' Elena said. Her ability to lie with complete conviction was amazing.

'So you sought shelter with the Communists. Because you are Communists yourselves.'

'That is nonsense. How can a British colonel be a Communist?'

She had made a telling point; Pavelic scratched his ear.

'We did not know these people were Communists,' Elena added.

Pavelic turned to Ivkov. 'You did not know your brother was a Communist?'

'I did not know this. I have not seen my brother in years.'

Pavelic turned back to Tony. 'And what were you hoping to do in Croatia?'

'In the first instance, marry Elena.'

Elena gave a happy giggle.

'And in the second, get out of the country. With my wife.'

'And her?' Pavelic jerked his head at Sandrine, who was being uncharacteristically quiet.

'She must stay with us.'

'Because she was raped?'

'I was not raped,' Sandrine said with dignity. 'He *tried* to rape me.'

'And you kept your legs pressed together,' Pavelic sneered.

'I shot him,' Sandrine said quietly.

Well, Tony reflected, the one burst she had fired from her tommy-gun might have hit one of the men who had been assaulting her.

Pavelic gazed at her in consternation.

'So if the Germans catch her, they will hang her,' Elena pointed out.

'They will tear her apart,' Pavelic suggested. 'And you say she is a journalist.' For the first time he looked at the massacre he had commanded.

'Quite,' Tony said. 'I think we need to discuss this.'

'Discuss what?'

'At the very least, Mr Pavelic, you have committed a horrendous crime, for which you may well be indicted after the War.'

'After the War, I shall rule Croatia.'

'I have an idea that the British and French governments, not to mention the reconstituted Yugoslav one, may have something to say about that.'

Pavelic snorted. 'They are defeated, yesterday's men. The only people with whom I shall have to deal are the Nazis.'

'Who commissioned you to carry out this slaughter, so that they would not be embroiled with their Russian allies.'

Pavelic frowned at him.

'However,' Tony said, 'I have no doubt that you have written orders from the German commander in Belgrade authorising this business, or perhaps instructing it.'

'Of course I do not. Orders such as these are never written down.'

'Hm. Then I strongly advise that you consider what your position will be when the Soviets inquire as to what happened here. They will learn of it, you know, if only when one of their other cells inquires after their comrades and discovers they are all dead. I think you need to determine which will be considered the more important to the Nazis – supporting you, or maintaining their alliance with Russia?'

Pavelic continued to stare at him, his expression indicating that these were aspects of his situation he had not previously considered.

'However,' Tony went on, 'if you were to possess some mitigating evidence, for example if you were to say that you were fired upon as you approached the village . . .'

'Of course we will say that.'

'But who is going to believe you, Mr Pavelic? You will need corroboration, and that can only come from a neutral or even potentially hostile source, such as Mademoiselle Fouquet, and myself, and Ivkov here, who has just watched his brother being murdered.'

'You expect me to trust you?'

'In exchange for our lives, we would give our words. We will give you written statements, if you wish.'

Pavelic considered for a few minutes longer, but Tony had no doubt he had gained a victory, or at least a respite.

'I will consider your offer,' the Ustase commander said at last. He turned to his men. 'Prepare to evacuate this place.' Already the stench of death was driving away the fresh mountain air. 'We will make camp for the night further down the valley.'

'You mean we are free to go?' Elena asked optimistically.

'You will accompany us,' Pavelic said. 'Until I decide what to do with you.' Again his gaze drifted over to Sandrine. 'Until I have talked with you some more.'

They were crammed into the back of one of the trucks, together with its complement of Ustase gunmen and also three of the girls. They were virtually sitting on top of one another, and were jostled against each other as the truck bumped and bounced over the uneven surface. The Serb girls moaned and groaned as their captors continued to play with them; they had been stripped of their clothing.

'Those bastards,' Elena said, speaking French. 'What are they going to do with them when they are finished?'

'That's not something to be thought about,' Tony said. His entire brain seemed to be consumed by a white-hot fury, made worse because it was an impotent fury. Even if he might be tempted to sell his own life dearly while taking as many of these murdering fiends with him as he could, he couldn't contemplate what would happen to his own women were he not here to protect them.

But was it not going to happen anyway?

'Are we going to get away?' Elena asked.

'It's something we need to work on.'

'It has to be done quickly,' Elena said. 'That arch-bastard Pavelic has designs on Sandrine.'

'Yes,' Tony said grimly.

'Don't bother about me,' Sandrine said. 'I will survive. Even him.'

Tony tried to look at her – the sentiment was not one he would ever have expected to hear from her lips – but her face was indistinct in the darkness. Yet there could be no doubt that Pavelic did intend to get his hands on her . . . and again, there was nothing he could do about it.

The trucks stopped, remaining in the centre of the road, and there was well-disciplined activity as the men disembarked, tents were pitched and sentries were posted. Within minutes a fire was blazing and goat meat – the gunmen had taken the opportunity to kill several of the animals – was roasting over it, while jugs of rough but drinkable wine were being passed around. The Ustase were certainly capable of relaxing.

Pavelic sat with them to eat. He seemed in a high good humour. 'I have been considering the situation,' he said, 'and I think my best course is to take you into Belgrade and hand you over to the Germans. Do not be alarmed. They will send you to Germany as a prisoner of war.'

'How exciting,' Tony commented. 'And my wife?'

'Your fiancée, you mean? Well, she will have to remain in Yugoslavia for the duration of the war. I think her best bet is to continue into Croatia. She may accompany me when I return there.'

'Her parents live in Belgrade.'

'Her parents have disappeared. I was in that area of the city only a few days ago. Their house is relatively undamaged, but is shuttered up. No one knows where they have gone, but it is most likely that they also have gone to Zagreb. Elena will be able to link up with them there.'

'There was also a brother.'

'Svetovar. Yes. A somewhat erratic young man.'

'He was in the Yugoslav army.'

'Well, if he has any sense, which I doubt, he will have deserted by now and made his way up to Zagreb as well. That is where all true Croats should go. Anyway, I have said that I will see your fiancée to safety.'

'And Ivkov?'

Pavelic shrugged. 'He can go back to being the bath-keeper. Now, will you write this paper stating that we were fired upon by the Divitsar people, and were forced to respond?'

'No,' Tony said.

Pavelic raised his eyebrows.

'I said I would give you that paper in return for the freedom of my people and myself. I don't regard being sent to Colditz as being set free. However, I do intend to inform the world of the massacre you have just perpetrated.'

'I am trying to help you. Can you not understand that?'

'Your help would leave me feeling dirty for the rest of my life.'

'But if I set you free—'

'Some things are worth being dirty for.'

Pavelic pointed. 'Because you are a cheat and a liar. If I were to set you free, you would still denounce me and claim your paper was a falsehood.'

Tony grinned at him. 'We have a saying in England, that all is fair in love and war.'

Pavelic snorted and stood up. 'And do you not realise that if I did set you free, you would die very rapidly? In these mountains, with every man's hand against you, you would not survive twenty-four hours.'

'That's surely my problem. Our problem.'

'Bah. Give me your gun.'

Tony hesitated, but he was surrounded by watching men. At least the Ustase had not thought to search Elena's satchel, he reflected. He drew his revolver and handed it over.

'Good,' Pavelic said. 'Now you will not be tempted to do anything stupid, eh? Now, you . . .' He pointed at Sandrine, seated a few feet away. 'Come with me.'

'Now wait a moment,' Tony said. 'She was part of the deal.'

'But now we have no deal, Englishman.'

Sandrine got up. 'Do not concern yourself, Tony. He only means to fuck me.' She gave a twisted smile. 'Have I not been fucked before?'

Tony felt Elena's hand on his arm. She wasn't prepared to risk his life to save Sandrine some discomfort. He nearly shrugged her away and went for Pavelic anyway as the Ustase commander gave a contemptuous smile and led Sandrine away into the darkness, but then common sense came to his rescue.

Was it common sense, or cowardice? He did not think he was a coward. He had never been aware of fear before, of either death or serious injury. And throughout this disastrous period of his life, and the life of Yugoslavia, he had endeavoured to keep his sense of perspective, his sense of responsibility to the three people who had entrusted themselves to his care . . . It would certainly be irresponsible to get himself killed in a dispute over a woman.

What was clouding his mind was the fact that the woman was Sandrine, that the thought of her lying naked in the arms of another man was like a knife twisting in his gut . . . and that he was not sure he would have felt this deeply had Pavelic chosen Elena to be his bedmate.

Elena continued to squeeze his arm. 'She will survive,' she assured him. 'As I would survive.'

He wasn't sure whether or not she could read his thoughts, and was grateful for the darkness.

The sentries were changed, and the camp settled for the night.

'You come in here, eh?' invited one of the Ustase gunmen, gesturing at the flap of the nearest tent. From the sounds within at least one of the captured Serb women was already inside.

'We'll bivouac,' Tony told him. It was a fine night, moonless but clear of cloud.

The man shrugged, and went into the tent. Most of the other men were also in tents, although some chose to sleep in the open. Ivkov curled himself into a ball and appeared to go immediately to sleep. More and more he made Tony think of a large, helpless dog.

Elena snuggled against Tony, resting her head on his shoulder. 'What is going to happen?' she asked in a whisper.

'You heard the man.' He could not stop himself from thinking about Sandrine.

'I do not wish you to be sent to prison.'

'Join the club.'

'I do not wish us to be separated.'

'Snap. But—'

'Listen. I am sure, when everyone is asleep, we could sneak out of here.'

'We'd never get past the sentries.'

'I still have my pistol.'

'I don't think one pistol and a dozen rounds of ammunition is going to work very well against a hundred men armed with tommy-guns. Anyway, we can't possibly abandon Sandrine.'

She digested this for some minutes. 'You fucked her, didn't you.'

'You told me I could,' he countered.

'And now you do not wish her to be fucked by anyone else.'

'Well . . . I regard her as my responsibility. All of you,' he added hastily.

'She is very beautiful,' Elena said.

'Well . . .'

'Far more beautiful than I am.'

'I wouldn't say that.'

There was another short silence. Then she asked, 'Are you really going to marry me?'

'Of course,' he said fiercely.

She seemed reassured, and a few moments later he heard her snoring gently. How ambivalent could you be? he wondered. But it really was irrelevant, at least until he could think of some way of getting out of this mess – together – and at the moment he couldn't think of any. Tomorrow they would return to Belgrade, and then . . . There *had* to be a way, but right now . . .

He realised he was too tired to think straight, and, although he had been a soldier all of his adult life, he was still shocked by the cold-blooded murder of over a hundred people, of whom a good twenty had been small children. When he thought of that his blood started to boil all over again, and even more at the way he had been forced to stand by and watch it happen, simply to protect the women . . . who were now beyond protecting.

He slept, without meaning to, and awoke with a start from a nightmare as a hand touched his arm. He gazed right into Sandrine's eyes.

Her face was as calm as always. He recalled that even when weeping or moaning in pain, her face had remained essentially composed.

He sat up, and she touched her lips with her finger.

He held her close. 'Are you all right?'

'I am all right. Listen, let us leave this place.'

'Leave? But . . .' He looked down at Elena, and then at Ivkov.

'Oh, bring her,' Sandrine said. 'And him, if you wish.'

'They will come after us, and kill us.'

'Not if we kill them first.'

'Sandrine . . .'

'Give me your hand.'

He obeyed, and realised she had a large bag with her. Now she put his hand into the bag, and he gasped as he fingered a tommy-gun, and more than one spare box of ammunition. And another Luger pistol, with several clips. And . . . his fingers caressed a string of grenades.

'Where, in the name of God . . . ?'

'They are Pavelic's.' She gave a little giggle. '*Were* Pavelic's.'

Elena woke up. 'Sandrine? What has happened to you?'

'Nothing that matters. We are leaving now. Will you come?'

'But how? We'll be killed.'

172

'We'll have company.'

Tony drew the tommy-gun from the bag, made sure it was functional. Then he handed Elena two spare magazines for her pistol.

'Will you take the other pistol?' he asked Sandrine.

'No,' she said. 'I will take the tommy-gun. I wish to kill people. Lots and lots of people. These people.'

'Let's be logical,' Tony said. 'We can't do it all at once.' But he handed her the tommy-gun, taking the second Luger for himself. Then he nudged Ivkov. 'Don't make a sound,' he said. 'But prepare to move out.'

Ivkov scratched his head, looked left and right.

'That way.' Tony pointed up the hill. The way lay past the parked trucks, where he reckoned the Ustase were most vulnerable. 'On all fours, now, until I say so.'

They crawled away from the tents. The entire camp seemed to be asleep, save for the sentries.

'How many?' Elena whispered.

Tony had checked that out before it had grown dark. 'Six.'

'I do not see any.'

'They're widely spaced. There's the first.'

They had reached the first of the trucks, which were parked side by side in an ideally neat row; the two open cars were just beyond them. The sentry was leaning against the bonnet of the first truck, smoking a cigarette.

'I wish I had a knife,' Tony said.

'Here.' Sandrine pressed a long-bladed knife into his hand.

'You are a bloody marvel,' he remarked. 'Now, all of you, when I say move, move, at your best speed, straight up the hill. Until then, don't move a muscle.'

He had already slung the grenades round his neck. Now he inched forward, still on his hands and knees. He had done this often enough in training, but never in real life. Also, creeping up on an enemy sentry presupposed that one's army was advancing, and all his combat experience had been in retreat. In any event, the idea of what he was about to do turned his stomach. He had to force himself to think of the women, of what they had already suffered, and of how much more they would have to suffer if he failed them.

Predictably, Sandrine loomed largest.

He also reminded himself that this man, like all of his comrades, was guilty of the most cold-blooded murders imaginable.

He crawled beside the truck until he reached the bonnet. There he stood up. As he did so, the sentry took a final drag on his cigarette, dropped it on the ground and stamped on it, then turned.

Tony had intended to cut his throat, but, taken by surprise, he opted to thrust the knife straight forward. The sentry reacted instinctively, closing one hand on Tony's wrist while trying to bring his rifle round with the other. Tony drove on with all his strength, and they fell together, the Croat underneath. As he fell, he fired his rifle. It sounded like a cannon in the stillness. Then Tony stabbed him twice. Neither one was fatal, but the man was left gasping and shrieking.

'Move!' Tony shouted. 'Move, move, move.'

He plucked a grenade from the string, and pulled the pin. The others ran past him while the camp awoke to a roar of bewildered sound. Tony rolled the grenade under the truck, scrambled to his feet, and chased behind the others, but was overtaken by the roar of the exploding truck; the blast threw him headlong and left him for a moment senseless.

His arms were grasped by Ivkov to pull him up, and they staggered up to the women, who were crouching in the shelter of some rocks. Behind them the other two trucks and then the command cars also exploded. The noise was tremendous, the shock waves deafening, and the blazing petrol turned the night into day.

For the moment the Ustase were entirely concerned with the destruction of their transport. Quite a few were firing their tommy-guns, under the impression that they were being attacked; from the shouts and curses, they seemed to be hitting each other. And they lacked command, at least for the moment.

'Let's go,' Tony said, and led his little band further up the slope. Soon they ran out of breath, and had to pause and look back down the hill. The flames were dying down, and the encampment was again plunged into darkness; there was a great deal of activity, but still, so far as Tony could make out, entirely uncoordinated.

'Come on,' he urged them on again, and they climbed, panting and gasping – as much, he reckoned, from the emotion of the escape as from exertion. Tony kept them going, with only brief pauses for rest, until the first light. Then they collapsed on their bellies for several minutes.

He was first up, and surveyed their situation. The encampment was out of sight; there was not even any smoke to be seen.

Sandrine stood beside him. 'You are all bloody,' she said. 'Where is the pain?'

'There is no pain. The blood is that sentry's.'

Elena joined them. 'Why are they not following?'

'Maybe they have too much on their minds.'

'Yes,' Sandrine said. 'Pavelic.'

'What happened to him?' Elena asked. 'What did you do to him?'

'I hit him on the head while he slept.'

Tony licked his lips. 'After . . .'

'After. I had to wait for him to go to sleep. Then I bundled up all his weapons, put them in that bag, and left. I should have killed him, I know. But . . . I could not.' She looked up at Tony. 'Did I do wrong?'

Tony put his arm round her shoulders to hug her. 'Sweetheart, you did everything just as right as was possible.'

Chapter Eight

Death

'Will they come after us, when Pavelic has recovered?' Elena asked.

'I don't think they will, right this minute,' Tony said. 'They know we have a head start, and they know that we're pretty well armed. They also know they are in hostile country – which will become more hostile when the facts of what happened at Divitsar become known, as they will, soon enough – and without transport they could be in a dangerous situation. My bet is they'll head back to Belgrade, or Uzice, and aim to deal with us later. However, the one thing we need to do is never get caught up with them again. What Pavelic would like to do to us, and to you in particular, Sandrine, doesn't bear thinking about.'

'I should have killed him,' Sandrine said. 'Oh, what a fool I was.'

'Yes,' Elena said.

Sandrine glared at her.

Tony sighed, and looked at Ivkov. But the bath-keeper merely looked at him ingratiatingly. He had developed a supreme faith in the English captain's ability to sustain them.

As had the women. 'What are we going to do now?' Elena asked.

'Needs consideration,' he said. 'There appear to be four forces operating in this vicinity, all of whom hate each other,

176

and all of whom hate us. So, we have the Germans, who will shoot us on sight. If we're lucky. Then there's the Ustase, ditto. Then there's Mihailovic's lot, about whom we can also say ditto – at least regarding you, Elena. Then there are the Communists . . . Are there any other Communist enclaves in these hills, Boris?'

'I think so. But—'

'Oh, quite. As the only survivors of Divitsar they're not likely to love us either.'

'There is another group,' Sandrine said.

'Such as?'

'The Muslims.'

'Muslims?'

'There is a large Muslim minority in Yugoslavia. We did a feature on them last year.'

Tony recalled that he had seen quite a few obvious Muslims in Belgrade from time to time, without paying them much attention. 'And you think there may be some in these hills?'

'I know there are Muslim villages in these hills.'

'But whose side will they be on?' Elena asked.

'I think mainly they do not like the Serbs, or the government, because they are treated as inferiors.'

'In other words they will be supporting the Germans.'

'I suppose so,' Sandrine said.

'So that is another of your shitty ideas,' Elena remarked.

'Now look here, you two,' Tony said. 'This bickering has got to stop, now. Whoever starts the next one is going to be put across my knee and have her backside tanned.'

The women exchanged glances, and he realised he might have made a mistake.

But there were more important things on Sandrine's mind than being spanked by a lover. 'When do we eat?' she asked.

'You mean, again, *what* do we eat?' Elena corrected.

Tony knew that was the most pressing problem. Food and shelter. Otherwise they would die, or at least become very weak and vulnerable from exposure and malnutrition. The solution to the problem was utterly simple, but it was a solution which made his stomach roll with distaste.

He looked from face to face. 'We go back to Divitsar.'

'There?' Elena was aghast. 'But—'

'I know. It's not going to be nice. But there is food there. And shelter. And it is extremely unlikely that either the Nazis or the Ustase are going to return.'

'But . . .' Sandrine was looking sick. 'The smell—'

'Will be bad. But only for the next twenty-four hours or so. And we have no alternative, if we are to survive.'

There was no real argument, if only because they were all extremely hungry. It was now mid-morning, and there was still no sign of pursuit. As Tony had estimated, Pavelic was probably accepting the realities of his situation. He would also be supposing that his escaped captives were hardly going to survive, and that if they did, they could easily be rounded up on his next marauding expedition, when he would again have transport.

They picked their way down the hillside and back towards the road. The going was slow, both because they were all exhausted and because the women continued to be hampered by their heavy skirts.

'We would do better if we took these off,' Elena suggested.

But at that moment it began to rain, which made the idea less attractive, even if the now soaked skirts became heavier yet.

'What do you think happened to those girls?' Sandrine asked, moving up to walk beside Tony while Elena and Ivkov trailed behind.

'It's not something I really wish to think about.'

'I would like you to tell me what is likely to happen to them.'

'Are you that ghoulish?'

'You do not understand. When the war is over – or this part
of the war – I will need to re-establish myself as a journalist.
So I must write about the war in Yugoslavia. About what
happened here.'

'You can think about that, now?'

'Would you prefer that I went mad?'

'No,' he said. 'I would not prefer that. There are only two
possible fates for those girls. One is that they will be taken
into Belgrade and put into army brothels. The other is that
they will be shot out of hand as unnecessary baggage. If that
was going to happen, it probably already has.'

'How can men be such brutes?'

'Because, when the chips are down, men are only beasts
in the field, like any other animal. So are women, you know.
And their bestiality is enhanced by two other factors. One is
the ability they have developed over the centuries of being
able to think, to reason, to analyse, which leads them to
plan and develop ever more atrocious ways of treating their
fellows. The other is that streak of sadism which demands
that we should dominate, or attempt to dominate, our fellows,
whether mentally or physically.'

'You are a very thoughtful man,' Sandrine remarked. 'I
would like you to collaborate on my book.'

'Let's get to the end of the War, first,' he suggested.

'And then you will marry Elena.'

'We are betrothed,' he reminded her carefully.

It rained for the rest of the day, sometimes quite heavily.
This was chilling and uncomfortable, even though it meant
that they need only open their mouths to slake their thirsts.
But Tony reckoned the weather was a fortunate development,
as it virtually prohibited pursuit, washed out their tracks, and
might make things slightly more salubrious where they were
going. But not that much.

It was noon when they regained the road; they stopped to
rest, and saw several goats peering at them.

'There is food,' Ivkov said.

'Not immediately,' Tony pointed out. He wasn't sure he was in the mood for shooting an inoffensive goat, and even less cutting its throat. In any event, lacking matches and in the pouring rain there was no means of lighting a fire, and he certainly wasn't in the mood for eating raw goat meat.

The weather didn't tempt them to rest for more than was absolutely necessary. Tony was intent on regaining the village before nightfall, and he reckoned they still had several miles to go. They plodded on through the afternoon, and stopped in their tracks at about four.

'Jesus!' Sandrine fell to her knees.

The smell of decaying flesh was all around them.

'You two stay here,' Tony said. 'Boris, you'll come with me.'

'What are you going to do?' Elena asked.

'See what needs to be done, first.'

'But you will come back?'

'I'll fire a shot when I want you to come in.'

'But you will be careful.'

'Sweetheart, there are only dead bodies in there. I have never been able to believe in ghosts.'

She crossed herself. 'These will be vengeful ghosts.'

'If they blame me for what happened, they're not as bright as ghosts are supposed to be. Now remember, wait for my shot. But just in case you need us back, for any reason, fire your own gun.'

'I think you should take the tommy-gun.'

Sandrine hugged the weapon to her breast; Tony reckoned that at that moment it was her most precious possession.

'Ghosts,' he said. 'I'm not aiming to shoot any of them. Come on, Boris.'

Ivkov crossed himself, but, like Sandrine with regards to food, he had a one-track mind. 'I should have a weapon,' he complained. 'It is not right for the women to be armed, and not me.'

'You have no one to shoot, Boris. The women may need to defend themselves.'

'No one to shoot? All of those people—'

'Are already dead. Pull yourself together.'

The houses came into sight. It was now just twenty-four hours since the massacre, and quite a few of the bodies were still in rigor mortis. But enough had begun to disintegrate, and the stench was appalling. The rain had helped, in that much of the blood had been washed away, but the long row of corpses was still an acutely depressing sight, especially as the dogs had returned and were tearing at the bodies, only stopping to snarl at the intruders who they suspected would interrupt their feast.

'My God, sir,' Ivkov whispered. 'We cannot use this place.'

'We must,' Tony told him. 'There is nowhere else.'

'But these people . . . we cannot bury them all.'

'No, we can't. But we can get them off the street.'

'Where, sir?'

Tony had been considering that, and had already made a decision. 'We put them in the tavern.'

'The tavern, sir?'

'It's the only place that's big enough, apart from the town hall, and that has steps. The tavern is on ground level. We drag the bodies in there.'

Ivkov was holding his hand across his face. 'One hundred people, sir?'

'Let's get started. That way we'll finish sooner.'

He drew his pistol and fired several shots in the air. The dogs growled and barked, but slunk off. Then Tony led the way, beginning with Mrs Ivkov, holding her wrists and dragging her across the cobbles and then across the floor of the tavern to rest against the counter. Ivkov did the same for his brother. After putting Petar beside his wife, he went behind the bar, took down a bottle of brandy, and drank from the neck. Before long, Tony was doing the same.

Back and forth they went, while the last light faded, and their empty stomachs rolled. Suddenly Tony's heart nearly jumped straight out of his throat when he looked back along the road and saw someone standing there. Then her hair fluttered in the breeze and he realised that it was Sandrine.

'I told you to wait for my signal.'

'You did signal. Was it not you who fired those shots?'

'Damnation.' He had forgotten that. 'Well, you had better go off again for an hour or so.'

'I have come to help you.'

'This isn't woman's work.'

'Are there not women here? And children?'

Soon they were joined by Elena, and it wasn't long before the women were also drinking brandy. When the tavern's stock was finished, they switched to wine. None of them got drunk, or even tight. By nine o'clock the last body had been dragged in. Ivkov carried several bottles of wine out on to the street, while Tony hunted in the larder and found some bread and some smoked meat, which he also carried outside.

'You cannot possibly mean to eat that,' Elena protested. Although slightly cleaner now, the air still smelled heavily of death.

'We may have to.' He made sure all the tavern's windows were shut, then closed and locked the door. 'Now,' he said, 'shall we see what else we can find in the way of food?' It was twenty-four hours since they had last eaten.

'No,' Elena said. 'For God's sake, no. The very thought makes me feel sick.'

She was actually speaking for all of them, himself included, but he also knew that by the next day they would be ravenous, so he stored the food in the town hall.

Then they returned to the hut they had shared before. Their blankets were still there; they stripped off their wet clothes and all four of them huddled together for warmth and comfort, sinking almost immediately into a deep sleep composed as much of emotional as physical exhaustion.

When Tony awoke it was just past dawn; the others were still sleeping. His hunger – as well as his thirst, after all the brandy and wine he had consumed – had induced several dreams during the night. One had been an erotic dream, no doubt brought about by the naked woman on either side of him. In an earlier nightmare, he had kept opening doors only to have dead bodies tumbling out on him.

He eased himself out from the blankets. His clothes were still damp, so he left them and went outside. The rain had stopped, and it was a crisp and clear morning, with nothing but blue sky above. The air was almost clean now; nothing was escaping from the sealed-up tavern, although he dared not think what conditions might be like inside it.

There were so many things to think about.

He left the village and went to the stream to bathe. Inquisitive goats peered at him while uninquisitive hens clucked around him, searching the ground for food as a cock crowed in their midst. He found it amazing that, having witnessed so much human death over the past few weeks, and having contributed himself to the mortality rate in no small way, he could yet feel an extreme repugnance at the thought of having to kill any of these essentially harmless and innocent creatures. Yet here was an almost inexhaustible source of food.

He heard splashes, turned round, and found Elena behind him; she also had not bothered to dress. Now she put her arms round him for a long kiss while she rubbed her breasts against his chest.

'Is it not wonderful to be alive, when . . .' She gave a little shudder.

'Snap.'

'I wish to have sex.'

'Now?'

'You always say that. Did you say that when Sandrine came to you?'

'As a matter of fact, I think I probably did.'

'And then you fucked her anyway. Come.' She held his hand and they crawled out of the water and lay on the bank. 'This is necessary.'

'I am sure it is.' In fact, he was anxious for it too, coming as it did on top of his dream.

'It is necessary,' she said, 'here and now and in the open air, to remind us, remind the world, remind the universe, that we have survived, and that we will survive. Now, now, now.'

He had hardly had the time to caress her, but yet they were both ready. It was, as she had said, necessary.

They were still gasping their climaxes when Sandrine joined them. She did not say a word, just got into the water and bathed herself, as usual paying special attention to her hair, which she rinsed again and again.

Elena sat up. 'I suppose you want your turn.'

'I am never going to have sex again,' Sandrine said. 'I could not bear the thought of it.'

Tony wondered whether she was referring to Pavelic or the dead bodies.

Elena snorted. 'That I have heard before. I am starving. And I want something clean to wear.'

'We'll find you some clothes,' Tony said. 'Although you will probably have to wash them. As for food . . .'

'Not that stuff you took from the tavern after we put the bodies in,' she said.

'All right,' he said. 'We'll look in the other houses. There'll be food.'

Ivkov appeared. 'Why do we not kill a goat?' he asked.

'We might come to that,' Tony agreed. 'Once we have worked out how to do it.'

'Before I became the bath-keeper,' Ivkov said, 'I was a butcher.'

'Ivkov,' Tony said, 'you're a man of hidden depths.'

'I shall never eat meat again,' Sandrine declared. 'I could not.'

'Wait till she has a goat chop put in front of her,' Elena said.

Suddenly they all worked with a will. Tony supposed there were several reasons for this. It was just sinking in that they were alive, and that over the past three weeks they had survived just about everything the war had been able to throw at them.

They had established an intimacy he would never have imagined before, although he was still anxious to find them some clothes as rapidly as possible. Looking at the two extremely attractive female bodies was keeping Ivkov in a state of continuous arousal, and although this did not appear to embarrass either of the women, it bothered him; unlike Tony, Ivkov had not had access to any relief since they had got together.

Finding clothes turned out to be a relatively simple business; there were some in every house. Soon Elena and Sandrine were both dressed in skirts and blouses, and had tied their hair up in bandannas; as the boots they had been given by Mrs Dukic were still usable, they looked almost decent, even if they had not found any underwear which either fitted or they were willing to wear next to their skin.

Ivkov quickly found pants and a shirt and even a jacket to fit. Tony gave him the knife and let him go off in search of food. They had found a considerable amount of bread and goat's cheese for breakfast, as well as several boxes of matches, and when Ivkov returned with a dead goat slung across his shoulders, they lit a fire and roasted the meat while the women went into the field to cut cabbages. They had an excellent lunch; the food was even washed down with some wine.

'We could live here forever,' Elena said.

'If it wasn't for *that*,' Sandrine said, looking at the tavern even as she munched on a piece of goat. Her refusal to eat meat, as Elena had suggested, had been very temporary.

'They are not troubling you,' Elena pointed out.

Sandrine made a face.

After the meal, Tony let them spend the rest of the day lounging. He had no doubt they needed it, as they had been through a great deal. Moreover, he was the only one who had been the least trained for this kind of life. Besides, he needed to think.

It was very tempting to take Elena's suggestion seriously. Because, apart from this village, their situation was absolutely desperate. As he had outlined to them the previous day, there was simply nowhere for them to go, no haven for which they could aim – at least as a group. Of the four of them, only Sandrine, being neither Serb nor Croat, Fascist nor Communist, and possessing a neutral nationality, was outside the immediate political situation. But she had managed to create quite a few enemies, and as a most attractive woman was perhaps the most vulnerable of them all.

But just staying put and hoping that the tide of war would pass them by was not really an option either. Someone, some time – and probably quite soon – was going to come to the village; it had not been cut off from the rest of the country. Were any visitors to be killed, to preserve their secrecy? That would have to depend on how many came at once, and whose side they were on. It was still a pretty devastating thought.

There was also the constant nagging reminder that he was a British officer, that his erstwhile comrades were fighting a war for survival against the Nazi threat, and that for him to sit on his backside doing nothing was at the very least a dereliction of duty. Against which was the reflection that anything he did try to do would necessarily put at risk the lives of Elena and Sandrine, who had become the two human beings he most valued in the world.

He wished he could be certain which one was the more important to him.

Besides, what *could* he do? Divitsar was miles from

anywhere, and he had no transport – and limited arms. That was the most insidious reflection of all.

They very rapidly settled into a peaceful, relaxing routine, which consisted mainly of doing what they had done while living with the Communists; Elena and Sandrine did the housework, the vegetable-gathering and the cooking, and Tony did the watch-keeping. He relieved Ivkov of this duty, as the bath-keeper was now the butcher as well as the handyman.

Even socially they adopted a pragmatic routine. The only fire Tony would permit them was in the town-hall kitchen, and this he would allow only at night, so that the smoke from the chimney would not be visible. They gathered here in the evenings, both for their meals and for company, although conversation was limited; they all had pasts that were too different to be easily acceptable to the others – and in more than one case, Tony suspected, contained secrets that were worth keeping – and they all had visions of the future which were equally individual and mutually unacceptable.

Elena had now fully accepted that she and Tony would marry, but she had no wish to try to fill in the details of when and where and how, and even less wish to consider where and how they might live. Her view of the future of Yugoslavia was equally vague. Tony had more than a suspicion that she supported the idea of an independent Croatia, even if this had to be achieved under the Fascist, Italian aegis. Yet she was wholeheartedly against the Nazis, and she certainly appeared totally to condemn the Ustase.

He came to the conclusion that her future – and by extension, his – might depend very much on whether any of her family had survived, or would survive . . . and what their situation and political outlook might be when the shooting stopped.

Emotionally she was a far more serious problem. He was sure she claimed her rights as his woman – which she did with great regularity – more because she needed constant reassurance that she *was* his woman than from any great sexual urge. The tragedy was that, however necessary he felt it was to do his duty, he no longer had any great sexual urge for her. He had fallen in love with Sandrine. And, as with every other aspect of his situation, there was damn all he could do about that either, for several reasons. One was that sense of duty. He was well aware that being betrothed to a woman in Yugoslavia was the same thing as being married to her, and even if the mould of conventional behaviour, whether British or Yugoslav, had been shattered by the War, he still felt it necessary not to let her down: as regards their relationship, she was blameless.

He also knew that to change partners now – were he that kind of man – would be to split their fragile unity, and leave him with a yet more insoluble problem.

And finally he was faced with the fact that he was quite uncertain of Sandrine's feelings towards him. If he was sure she found him attractive, and, like the others, was relying entirely on him to get her out of this mess, that was a long way from the sort of love he wanted. And if she had come to him, so hungrily, on their first night in this very village, he still didn't know whether that had been alcohol or just a hunger, for any man.

There was so much he didn't know about Sandrine. She never spoke of her background. He estimated that she had been born and brought up in some French provincial town, her childhood as distorted as that of any other contemporary French child by the Great War – he reckoned she was about the same age as himself. If she had attended church regularly enough to have been seduced by a choirboy, he could presume that her upbringing had been both gentile and perhaps even bourgeois, judging by her care for her clothes and her appearance, her constant desire to be clean. No doubt she had attended college of some sort, graduated as a journalist, and got herself on the staff of *Paris Temps*. That, at the age of twenty-five or so, she had got herself posted to Belgrade as an editor, even if a junior one, indicated that she had both talent and ambition.

He could not fault her behaviour under the kind of stress she could never have expected to experience; even her somewhat over-feminine reactions to the various physical misfortunes she had been forced to undergo were attractive. But the woman herself was wrapped up in a shroud of mystery, which he doubted even Elena knew anything about. Were her parents still living? Did she have any siblings? And what of her abrupt changes of mood and intention? She had revealed enough – as in her reaction to her rape by Pavelic – to indicate that she could be quite ruthless, and yet not ruthless enough to kill . . . at least in cold blood.

Perhaps it was her mystery, apart from her looks, that made her so attractive. But it was that attractiveness, when combined with the easy sense of intimacy she allowed to the three of them, that was the big problem. Tony had an idea that all of them – Elena included – from time to time had the urge to sweep the Frenchwoman into their arms for a few moments of desperate passion. That they did not was because of the presence of the other two. He and Elena had each other when they needed to let off steam; Ivkov, large and slow and brooding, had no one. His passions were kept in check only by his anxiety to please Tony, a man he clearly both admired and feared.

All matters that required continuous consideration. But the Germans came first.

Tony was sitting up on the hilltop overlooking both the village and the slopes down to the valley when he heard the drone of the aircraft engine. It was mid-morning and he quickly sighted the machine, glinting in the sunlight and flying quite low. They had now been living in the village for some two months, and in all that time had neither seen nor heard any enemy activity. It seemed very unlikely that the plane was specifically looking for them after so much time, but even if it was on a routine patrol it represented a threat.

There was no time to get back down to the houses, but he had issued positive orders that in the event of the approach of any possibly hostile units, and in his absence, they were to conceal themselves immediately and allow no sign of life to be revealed. He had to believe that his orders were now being carried out.

He concealed himself behind a couple of boulders. The aircraft did not pass immediately overhead, and gave no indication of having seen him, and although it circled the village twice, it did so from its maintained height; had it seen any movement he would have expected it to sweep lower.

He remained where he was until the plane was out of sight, then returned down the slope to the village.

'Did you see it?' Elena asked.

'Of course I saw it. The important thing is, did it see you?'

'I don't think so. The moment we heard it, we went inside.'

'Hm.' He inspected the village, and suddenly realised where they had made a potentially fatal mistake.

'What is bothering you?' Sandrine asked.

'We must assume that Pavelic and his men returned to Belgrade, or some point of civilisation, and that Pavelic reported what he had done to some German command.'

'Would he dare do that?' Elena asked. 'It was an act of genocide.'

'In which he had been encouraged, if not directed, by the Germans. The point is, if he reported what had happened here – that the entire village had been wiped out and then left exactly as it was – that aircraft would have expected to find the corpses still lying on the street.'

Sandrine cast a glance at the still sealed tavern. 'Those people will be nothing but bones by now.'

'They are all still dressed.'

'That plane did not come low enough to see,' Elena argued.

'They certainly would have had binoculars.'

'So what are we going to do?' Sandrine asked.

'Sit tight, I suppose. And keep our fingers crossed.'

That evening Elena walked with him when he went a little way down the road. 'Do you think that plane suspected something?'

'As I said, we must hope not.'

'But if they did . . .'

'We may have to clear out in a hurry.'

'And go where?'

'I wish I knew.'

'If we went to Zagreb . . .'

'That's Pavelic's home town. And the headquarters of the Ustase.'

'But if we could link up with my parents . . .'

'Do you seriously suppose that your parents could protect us from the Ustase?'

She sighed. 'I suppose not.' Her head jerked. 'What was that?'

'That was a scream.' He began running back up the road to the village. It had· actually been less of a scream than a shriek of outrage and anger, and he knew it had come from Sandrine . . . just as he knew what had caused it.

With Elena at his heels, he pounded along the cobbles between the houses, and saw Sandrine running towards them. She was naked, her hair streaming behind her, and had clearly been having her evening bath. Now she ignored them, and instead ran into the house.

'Shit!' Tony muttered.

But the catastrophe had been waiting to happen.

They reached the door of the house as Sandrine re-emerged. She had not dressed, but was carrying her tommy-gun.

'Sandrine!' Tony tried to hold her arm, but she wriggled past him, his fingers slipping on her still wet skin.

'Don't try to stop me,' she said. 'I am going to shoot that bastard.'

'Sandrine!' Elena had caught them up and now she threw both arms round Sandrine's waist. Sandrine tried to wriggle free, but Elena was the stronger woman by far.

Tony took the tommy-gun from Sandrine's fingers. 'What happened?'

'What do you think happened?' She spat the words at him. 'That bastard—'

'It's your own fault,' Elena said. 'Wandering around naked.'

'You bathe in front of him. He's never tried it on *you*. Give me back my gun.'

'Not until you simmer down,' Tony said. 'Did he, er . . .'

'No, he did not,' Sandrine said. 'I kicked him in the balls.'

'Ah.' Tony looked up the street and saw Ivkov coming down. The bath-keeper was fully dressed. He waited until the big man was close to them, then he asked, 'Why did you have to do that?'

Ivkov licked his lips. He looked apprehensive, but not repentant. 'I need a woman,' he said. 'I have to have a woman. You have a woman, Captain, sir. Why can I not have a woman?'

'He has a point,' Elena muttered. 'Ow!'

Sandrine had kicked her on the ankle.

'And this woman,' Ivkov said, 'she is so lovely. And did I not save her life? Did I not carry her, mile after mile? Did I not bring you here, to shelter? Did I—'

'You've made your point, old fellow,' Tony said, and looked at Sandrine.

'If you let this man have me,' she said, speaking quietly but with great intensity, 'I will kill you all before I kill myself.'

Elena snorted. 'Pavelic had you, and you did not kill him.'

'I will kill *him!*' Sandrine said again.

Tony sighed. But he had always known it would come to this. Perhaps they were fortunate that it had not happened sooner, when they had been more vulnerable.

'Well, there it is,' he said. 'I'm sure you will agree with me, Ivkov, that it would be a waste of time to ask for your word that this will not happen again.'

'Well . . .' Ivkov lifted his head. 'Are you going to shoot me?'

'Yes,' Sandrine said.

'No,' Tony said. 'You have been a good comrade. But you cannot stay with us. You will leave now. I would say it is about a week's walk to Belgrade. Take as much of the food as you think you will need and can carry, and go.'

'I do not know where to go.'

'I showed you the North Star, remember? Keep it on your left hand, and when the sun rises, keep that on your right hand, and you will be travelling north-east. That will bring you to the Sava in only a couple of days, and then you can follow the river into the city. Who knows, you may even find a bus working, or get a ride on a riverboat.'

'You are sending me out, without money?'

'We have no money.'

'Then at least give me a gun.'

'We need our guns. We are sending you out with your life, Ivkov. Be grateful.'

'The Germans will shoot me.'

'There is no reason for them to do that, although they might if they found any weapons on you. You are a civilian, and your home is in Belgrade. Tell them that we kidnapped you to guide us out of the city, but that you escaped from us. Now it is time for you to go.'

Ivkov hesitated, then went to the town hall to collect his food.

'You are too soft-hearted,' Sandrine said. 'All you men

193

are alike. It is because you have never had anyone crawling all over you, trying to put their fingers into you . . . ugh!'

'Listen,' Elena said. 'Go inside and put some clothes on. Men are men and there is an end to it.' She pushed Sandrine into the house, and closed the door. 'But I agree with her,' she told Tony.

'About having men crawling all over you?'

She grinned. 'I should be so lucky. No, that Ivkov should have been shot. He is very resentful. Don't you think he will tell the Germans we are here?'

'I have an idea they already know . . . that *someone* is here, in any event.'

'Then what are we going to do?'

'We are going to have to leave. Tomorrow morning. Can you kill a goat?'

'I can shoot one. And then skin it, I suppose. You will have to help me.'

'You can teach Sandrine. It might help her to work off some of her angst.'

Ivkov reappeared, a sack slung over his shoulder. 'I am sorry it has come to this, Captain, sir,' he said. 'I have enjoyed serving you. How can we let a woman come between us?'

'You go on like that and I will shoot you myself,' Elena said.

'It's a fact,' Tony said. 'Women are just as human as men, Ivkov. If you could get that through your head, you'd probably be a happier man.'

Ivkov gazed at him for several seconds, then turned and set off down the street.

They ate their supper in silence. Then Sandrine said, 'I suppose you think I am to blame for this.'

'Yes,' Elena said.

'No,' Tony said.

Elena glared at him.

194

'It had to happen,' Tony said. 'I knew it had to happen. I should have done something about it earlier.'

'You should have left him behind in the Serb camp,' Sandrine said.

'Then we would not have found this place,' Elena pointed out.

'Would we have been any worse off?'

'How can you say that? We have lived in comfort for two months.'

'Comfort? The Ustase—'

'Were a hiccup, I agree. But for the rest, we have had food to eat and clothes to wear and a roof over our heads. We are well armed—'

'And a hundred people are dead.'

'They would have died whether we were here or not.'

Sandrine looked at Tony.

'She is right about that,' Tony said. 'Listen, both of you, as I said, it was bound to happen. It was a situation about which I had not been taught, and I just did not know how to handle it. The fault is mine. Now we must put it out of our minds and think about what we are going to do next.'

'But you are angry with me,' Sandrine said.

'Yes,' Elena said.

'No,' Tony said.

Another glare.

Sandrine got up. 'I will sleep in another house tonight.' She left the room.

'What do you reckon?' Tony asked Elena.

'About her? Do not worry about her. She is not the type to do anything stupid. But you do worry about her, eh?'

'I worry about all of us.'

'Ha! You know what I think? I think it would have made more sense to expel Sandrine rather than Ivkov. She'd be perfectly safe, with her Vichy-French neutrality. The Germans would probably set her up with her own newspaper.'

'Do you have any idea how many times she would be raped before she reached Belgrade?'

'That is important? Think how many times she has been raped already, in the past couple of months. And she's still smiling.'

'Not very often. And she was raped precisely once.'

'Ha! You are not including yourself, then?'

'Oh, for God's sake. Go to bed.' He stood up.

'You are not coming with me?'

'Not just now. I must see Sandrine first.'

'Ha! You are going to make it three, eh? Or have I lost count?'

'You are going to make me very angry in a moment. I am going to see Sandrine to tell her to lock her door and keep her weapon handy; Ivkov might come back.'

'And what about me?'

'You will be sleeping beside me,' he told her.

It was completely dark outside, and Tony had no idea where Sandrine had gone. So he followed his instincts, and tried the cottage next to theirs. He knocked, and then opened the door, trying to peer into the darkness. 'Are you there?' he asked.

There was no reply. Mentally cursing, he stepped outside again, and then had another idea. He walked away from the houses, and saw her sitting on the edge of the stream, her legs drawn up; at least she was fully clothed.

She did not turn her head, but she knew who it was. 'I'm sorry,' she said. 'Truly sorry.'

'And I have told you that you must not be.'

'It was just that after Pavelic,' she said as if he had not spoken. 'Pavelic . . . do you know what he did to me?'

'Do you really want to tell me?'

'I am telling you. He made me lie on my face, with my ass in the air. I thought he was going to come in the back way, you know . . . Some men like that.'

'Some women too,' Tony said, thinking of Elena.

'Oh, I like it too, with the right man. But Pavelic, he buggered me.'

'Shit!'

'He hurt me. Oh, he hurt me. I bled. I bled for a couple of days. And I felt so ashamed. And then, Ivkov—'

'Don't tell me . . .'

'No. I don't think so. I don't know what he wanted to do.' She gave a little giggle. 'I kicked him first.' The giggle was followed by a sigh. 'I could have kicked Pavelic too. But I knew that if I did, he would have killed me, and then perhaps killed you all as well. Besides, I had already seen all the weapons he had in his tent, and I knew that if I could just wait until he went to sleep, I could perhaps get us all free.'

'As you did, by gritting your teeth and submitting. I think you are all kinds of a heroine, Sandrine.'

'Do you? Do you really, Tony? Then you mean you don't hate me?'

'Hate you?' He held her face between his hands and kissed her on the mouth. 'I love you, you adorable little girl.'

'Oh. Tony!' She clung to him. 'But—'

'I know. I am going to see what I can sort out. But for the time being, I must go along with Elena.' He didn't doubt that she would kill to defend what she regarded as her property. 'You will have to be patient for a while longer.'

'But . . . you will come to me, when you can?'

'When I can.'

'You are here now.'

'She is waiting for me. Now you must go to bed. But listen. Lock the door of your hut, and sleep with your tommy-gun beside you. Ivkov may come back.'

'I will do that. But . . . tomorrow . . .'

'As I said, I'll see what I can work out.' He kissed her again, then walked with her back to the houses. 'Remember, lock your door.'

Elena was already beneath the blanket. 'Don't tell me she was bathing again.'

197

'She was thinking.'
'What has she got to think about?'
'Everything *we* have to think about.'
'We could still leave her here when we go tomorrow.'
'We are not going to do that, Elena. Now go to sleep.'

He locked their door as well, and slept with his pistol by his head. But he half expected Ivkov to come back, and only dozed from time to time. He could only hope the big man had more sense. Because if he did come back, both women would undoubtedly vote for his execution; their experiences of the past few weeks had entirely robbed them of what might have been called feminine charity.

He wondered if Sandrine would ever again be able to sit at a table on the Champs Élysées, elegantly dressed, knees crossed, sipping a cup of coffee. More to the point, he supposed, he wondered if she would ever be able to get there.

Suddenly he was awake. There had been a noise, rising above the whine of the wind. It had not disturbed Elena, who was snoring gently; he stretched out his hands to wrap his fingers around the Luger.

Yet it had been a distant sound, certainly not anyone trying to get into the house. Then Sandrine . . . He sat up. But Ivkov could not possibly know which house she was using. Still, if he was out there . . . Tony eased himself out from beneath the blanket.

Elena woke up. 'Where are you going?'
'To have a look outside.'
'Someone is there?'
'I don't know.' He pulled on his pants.
'I will come with you.'
'You stay here. But have your gun ready, and if anyone comes through that door, except Sandrine or me, shoot to kill.'

She snorted, and he guessed she might have excluded Sandrine from the safe conduct.

Cautiously he opened the door, right hand holding the gun against his shoulder. There was a lot of cloud, but there was also a full moon. A hunter's moon, he thought, and reminded himself that he was the hunter.

He went outside, back against the wall of the house, and looked up and down the street. It appeared deserted, and the door of Sandrine's house was closed. It must have been a dream, he supposed, and turned to go back inside, then checked as he saw Ivkov.

Even in the gloom the bath-keeper was instantly recognisable, at once from his size and his movements; he was making no effort at concealment, but was running straight up the centre of the street, panting and staggering.

Tony stepped away from the shelter of the wall, even as he realised that it could not possibly have been Ivkov's movements that had awakened him, since the bath-keeper was only just entering the village. He levelled the pistol. 'Stop right there.'

Ivkov kept on coming. 'Germans!' he panted. 'Coming up the hill! They will be here in seconds.'

Chapter Nine

Partisans

The door behind Tony opened and Elena stepped out. She had dressed herself, and was carrying her pistol, which she now also levelled. 'Bastard!' she said. 'Betrayer!'

'No,' Ivkov gasped, reaching them and falling to his knees. 'No. I was resting, down the road, and I heard the noise of their engines.'

That must be the noise that woke me up, Tony thought. But . . .

'They stopped, half a mile away,' Ivkov said. 'And came on foot. When I saw them I returned here as fast as I could. They are right behind me.'

Tony listened, but there was no sound above the wail of the wind. 'How many?'

Ivkov panted. 'A truckload. A command car. Two motorcycles.'

Tony made a hasty calculation. Possibly thirty men.

'He betrayed us,' Elena insisted. 'Let me shoot him.'

'He would hardly have come to warn us after betraying us,' Tony pointed out. 'It was that plane.'

Sandrine's door opened, and she stepped out. Predictably she was naked, although she was carrying her tommy-gun. 'What is happening?'

'Germans. Get some clothes on.'

'What can we do,' Elena asked.

'Get up the hill.'

He ran back into the house, gathered up the string of grenades, the spare magazines for the pistols and the spare box for the tommy-gun. He stepped outside again. Elena and Ivkov were still there.

'I told you to get out.'

'I have no gun,' Ivkov protested.

'So keep your head down. Go, go, go.'

He could hear voices snapping commands from the other end of the street; the Germans were realising their approach had been discovered.

Elena ran towards the stream. Ivkov hesitated for a moment, then followed her.

Tony opened the door of Sandrine's house; she was just coming out, dressed and still carrying her tommy-gun.

'Quick,' he said.

But as he spoke there was a burst of firing . . . from the stream.

'Shit!' he muttered. The village was surrounded.

Now he heard the bark of Elena's Luger, and then a scream. It was high-pitched and terminal, but Tony was sure it had not been Elena.

'Oh, God,' Sandrine whispered. 'Oh, God.'

Boots clattered on the cobbles as men ran up the street towards the sound of the firing. But *they* were not firing yet; miraculously, they had not yet seen the two people still in the village.

Tony grabbed Sandrine's arm and pushed her round the building into the alley at the back of the house. His every instinct was to go towards the sound of the firing, but that would be to die instantly. In any event, the firing had now stopped. Whatever had happened, had happened.

Sandrine was panting, and tugging against him. 'Let me go,' she whispered. 'I want to shoot them.'

'Don't you think they'd shoot you back?' he asked.

'But . . . Elena . . .'

'I know. But getting ourselves killed won't help her.'

He held her close. The village was now filled with Germans, but they were only interested in what had happened at the stream. Now an officer spoke, 'Report!'

Both Sandrine and Tony spoke fluent German, but it wouldn't have mattered if they had not: they both recognised the voice. Sandrine made a convulsive effort to get free; Tony had to hug her so hard she gasped with pain.

'We have lost a man, Herr Hauptmann,' someone said. 'Shot by this woman.'

They listened to scrabbling feet and some gasping. Tony gave a sigh of relief. At least Elena appeared to be alive.

'There was also a man, Herr Hauptmann,' the sergeant said. 'But he is dead.'

Poor Ivkov, Tony thought. After all, he had died a hero, trying to warn them. But Elena . . . Yet surely, Bernhard was a friend . . . or had been a friend.

He sounded like one now. 'Elena!'

'You?'

'Well, certainly it is I.' He had switched to speaking French. 'Where is Sandrine?'

Tony felt Sandrine move in his arms.

'She is not here,' Elena said.

'Well, I can see that. So where is she?'

'She left, yesterday. With Tony. They went to get help.'

'I see. Where did they go?'

'There is a guerilla group, not far from here. Tony and Sandrine went to see if they would take us in.'

'Why should they not take you in? You are all on the run.'

'Because I am a Croat,' Elena said. 'The Serbs will not help us.'

'That is true. Did you not know those were Croats you attacked last month?'

'We did not attack Pavelic. He took us prisoner, after killing all the people in this village. We escaped.'

'Killing several of his men in return. You realise that makes you guilty of subversive activities.'

'They were murderers.'

'They were executioners, Elena. And now you have shot one of my men. You understand that that is a capital crime?'

'Your people were shooting at me, so I shot back.'

'That also is a capital crime. Even if you had not hit anyone, it would still have been a capital crime.'

'Then shoot me,' Elena said.

'I would hate to have to do that. We are old friends, are we not? I would like to be able to help you. I *will* be able to help you. If you are prepared to help yourself.'

'How am I supposed to do that?'

'By cooperating with us in every way. You will still be guilty of a capital crime, but I can have the death sentence commuted to imprisonment.'

Elena snorted. 'How can I cooperate with you?'

'There are many ways,' Bernhard said. 'But you can begin by answering a few very simple questions.'

'Well?'

'Firstly, who is the dead man?'

'Ivkov, the bath-keeper from Belgrade.'

'Ah, yes. He escaped with you, and brought you here, to his Communist brother.'

'Yes. He said we would be sheltered here. And we were, until Pavelic and his people came along.'

'Very good. You just keep on being cooperative, and you will do very well. Now, you say Sandrine went off with Tony. Why did you not go with him instead?'

'He wanted to take her. He did not wish to leave her alone here with Ivkov. Ivkov fancied her. And besides, he had to be sure that the Serbs would take me in.'

'It was not because he and Sandrine have become lovers?'

'Well of course they are lovers,' Elena said. 'He is a virile man, and she is a virile woman – also a beautiful one.'

'Is he not betrothed to you?'

'I am very broad-minded.'

'And her betrothal to me?' Bernhard continued to speak quietly, but there was a good deal of suppressed emotion in his voice.

'She hates you,' Elena said. 'If she were here now, she would shoot you, even if she died for it.'

Undoubtedly she felt sure they were within earshot. Tony had to suppress another convulsive wriggle. His big fear was that Sandrine would say something, or squeeze the trigger of her tommy-gun.

'Well, then,' Bernhard said. 'It seems that I must hate her back. And Tony, to be sure. Now there is one other question. Where is this guerilla camp they have gone to?'

'I do not know.'

'Elena, be logical. These mountains cover a great area. You cannot possibly pretend that Tony and Sandrine just set off into the blue, in the hopes of encountering some of these people. They must have known where to go. That means you must also know. I wish you to tell me. Or if you cannot name the place, show me on the map.'

'I do not know where they went,' Elena said.

'Elena, you are not cooperating. Well, then, tell me the direction in which they went.'

'They climbed the hill over there. I do not know which direction they took after that.'

'Elena,' Bernhard said. 'I wish you to concentrate, and listen to me very carefully. Like every other civilised person, I was appalled when Pavelic reported what you and Tony – and my fiancée – had done.'

'What *we* had done? Do you know what *he* did, right here?'

'He was carrying out a necessary duty. Your attack on his camp was an act of war.'

Elena snorted.

'Thus we were ordered to find you, and punish you. I will confess that it never occurred to us that you might have returned here. It was not until our search aircraft reported that there was life in this village, and that the dead bodies had disappeared . . . Where are they, by the way? The dead bodies.'

Elena must have pointed. 'There.'

'In the tavern?' Bernhard's tone was incredulous. 'How many?'

'All of them.'

There was a moment's silence, and Tony could envisage them staring at each other.

Then Elena said, 'Why don't you look?'

'Sergeant!' Bernhard snapped.

Boots clumped on the cobbles.

'As I was saying,' Bernhard went on. 'When it was determined to check the village out, as it was supposed that it had been reoccupied by your group, I volunteered to lead the squad; I still hoped to be able, shall I say, to save you from yourselves. My request was granted, but as it is well known that Sandrine Fouquet is – or *was* – my fiancée, I was reminded that my duty as a German officer came before any other consideration, even that of love. And now, you see, even the consideration of love for that bitch no longer exists.'

Tony felt another flurry of activity against his chest.

'However,' Bernhard said, 'I am still prepared to help you, if you will help us. But if you will not, as it is important that we find and destroy these guerilla groups as quickly and completely as possible, I am going to have to hand you over to the Gestapo for interrogation. There is a Gestapo headquarters established in Uzice. That is not far from here, and I will take you there now. I do not know if you have ever heard of the Gestapo, but in this situation they function as the military police for the Wehrmacht. Their methods are entirely their own, and are quite unspeakable. If I hand you to them, you will tell them the location of this guerilla camp in a few minutes, simply because you will be in such pain you will not know what you are saying. What is more, when they have finished with you, they will either lock you up or execute you, but in neither case will that mean anything to you, because once you have been interrogated by the Gestapo you can never again function as a normal human being. Please understand this. Listen, tell me where this camp can be found, and I give you my word, firstly, that Tony will be treated as a prisoner of war, and secondly, that Sandrine will be deported back to France.'

There was a peculiar sound, and then the sound of a slap. Tony estimated that she had spat at him, and that he had hit her.

'That was extremely uncooperative of you,' Bernhard said. 'Very well.' He switched back to German. 'Call up the transport,' he shouted, and then demanded, 'Well?'

The sergeant's voice was trembling. 'They're in there, Herr Hauptmann. Skeletons. Hundreds of skeletons. Grinning at us.'

'Pull yourself together,' Bernhard snapped. 'Are you a soldier, or a frightened little girl? There cannot be hundreds, Sergeant: there were only a hundred people in the village in the first place. Set fire to the tavern. And have the village searched.'

They heard the sergeant's heels click as he saluted, then all other sounds were drowned out by the noise of the vehicles coming up the hill. Tony pushed Sandrine in front of him, and they sidled along the alley until they reached the rear of the buildings.

'What are we to do?' she whispered.

'Not get caught, for starters. Down there.'

He pushed her towards the slope, and a moment later they were sliding down the hillside, the noise of their descent shrouded in that of the engines. Their tracks would be clearly visible come daylight, but Tony did not think the Germans were going to hang around until then, shaken as they were by the discovery of the corpses in the tavern. This was now erupting into flames above his head.

They reached the bottom of the slope, panting and bruised. 'Can we not kill them all?' Sandrine asked.

'You reckon?'

'There are only thirty of them. We have your grenades, and my tommy-gun. And we would take them by surprise.'

'The odds on the two of us, even taking them by surprise, being able to kill thirty armed men before they kill us are too great to be contemplated. And in any event, the first person to be killed would probably be Elena.'

'And if she is not killed, what will they do to her? Do you *know* what they will do to her? The Gestapo? I have read about the Gestapo.'

'Our dying will not help Elena,' he said. He had to keep repeating this, over and over again, in the hopes that he would come to believe it.

'That bastard was *there*,' Sandrine said. 'I could have killed him with a single shot!'

'Maybe you'll have another chance, some time.'

'Shit,' she said. 'Shit, shit, shit.'

'Snap,' Tony said.

As Tony had estimated, the German search of the village was perfunctory; their sole desire was to get away from the mound of dead bodies as quickly as they could. But before they left they fired some of the houses, and the night sky above the village became quite bright.

Tony and Sandrine remained huddled in the shelter of the bushes at the foot of the slope until the little cavalcade had driven back down the road. Then they slowly climbed the hill again, and stood by the stream to look at the leaping flames. Sandrine's knees seemed to give way, and she sat on the ground. Tony sat beside her.

There was nothing for them to say; they had too much to think about. *Should* he have dashed into the midst of the enemy, firing his pistol and hurling his grenades, waiting for the thuds as bullets tore into his own body? What purpose would it have served? In fact, the Germans would probably not even have considered it necessary to kill Elena before killing him.

And Sandrine? She would have followed him without hesitation, tommy-gun blazing, until she too had been cut down, that exquisite body a bleeding, shattered, hideous mess. But worse yet was the possibility that she might have been taken alive, handed over to the Gestapo, and suspended naked from the ceiling while electrodes were attached to her nipples and between her legs, to leave her, once the current was switched on, screaming and writhing in agony.

That was what was going to happen to Elena!

Almost without thinking he stretched out his hand to squeeze Sandrine's. It was a long moment before she responded.

'Did we cause this?' she asked.

'By coming back to the village? I don't think so. Once they started looking, they'd have found us even more quickly in the open. Supposing we would have been able to survive, in the open.'

'I meant, by loving where we should not have loved.'

'Love is where you find it,' he said. 'It seldom is where it should be.'

'You were engaged to Elena. She thinks you still are. That is why she has sacrificed herself for us. It was for you.'

'I know that. It doesn't make me feel very good.'

'It makes me feel like a lump of shit,' she said. 'And Bernhard . . . I know if I had shot him, I would have died. We both would have died. I didn't want to die, Tony. I don't want to die, now. But I swear to you, if I survive this war, I am going to find Bernhard, and I am going to shoot him in the balls, and then stand on them while he dies.'

Tony gulped. He could never escape the feeling that Sandrine was in fact capable of doing the things she threatened, however often she changed her mind. And with every catastrophe that happened to her or around her, that streak of hardness, of ruthlessness, was growing.

And him? His trouble was that he was a professional soldier. He had wanted to be a soldier ever since he was a small boy. The proudest moment of his life was the day he had been accepted for Sandhurst. He loved everything about the army, and accepted its tenets as the basis for all life. One was not supposed to hate the enemy; rather, one was encouraged to respect him, both for his skill and his humanity. Certainly one did intend to kill him, but there remained the assumption that once one side understood that it was defeated, and surrendered, it had to be treated with every courtesy and respect. Personal feelings, personal prejudices, personal likes and dislikes – even personal loves – could not be allowed in any way to interfere with cold-blooded judgement. Hatred had no place in any of the above considerations.

That was why he did not hate Bernhard. To be sure, he had Elena. But he, personally, was not going to harm her. He was merely obeying orders in what had become, almost overnight, a very dirty war, the dirt inspired as much by Yugoslav internecine hatred as by Nazi ideology.

His fingers had gone limp as he brooded. Now Sandrine squeezed them. 'What are we going to do?'

The summer sky was lightening, and the flames were dying down.

'Let's see what's left, for a start,' he suggested.

They stood up; Sandrine glanced to their left, and shuddered. Ivkov's body lay where it had fallen. 'Can we bury him?'

'If we can find a spade. I don't think they'll be coming back in a hurry.'

'Am I guilty of his death as well?'

He held her shoulders. 'Sandrine, you are guilty of no one's death.'

'I had him driven from the village.'

'If he had not been driven from the village, we would all

be dead, or certainly prisoners, because we would still have been asleep when the Germans came.'

He led her into the village, both of them carrying their firearms at the ready. But it was utterly deserted. Even the dogs had abandoned it, probably because of the heat. Presumably they would be back, but they would have no reason to stay; the tavern was a collapsed and burned-out shell. No doubt there was still a mass of bones in there, but they were lost beneath the smoking timbers. The town hall had also been burned to the ground, and the houses to either side were at least partially destroyed.

Tony returned to the house he had shared with Elena. No doubt the Germans had looked inside, but only to ensure there was no one hiding there. He found his shirt and his shoes. Sandrine returned to her house as well, and found her boots. Then they hunted around, eventually finding a spade which was cool enough to touch. Tony returned to the stream and buried Ivkov in the soft earth beyond, while Sandrine knelt and watched him. It was now quite late in the morning. Neither of them felt like eating, but Tony knew that they had to, so they went into the fields and drew some carrots, which they ate raw; their food supplies as well as their matches had been in the town hall.

Then they moved back to the stream, drank some water, and sat beside each other. It was symptomatic of both their moods that Sandrine had no desire to bathe, and although she put her arms round him to hold herself against him, there was no sexual desire in her embrace.

'Now what are we going to do?' she asked.

The question he had dreaded.

'I'm working on it.'

'What *can* we do?'

There had to be something. Any plan, however hopeless, had to be better than just sitting here, waiting to die.

'We find Mihailovic's people,' he said. 'That is our best bet. He has no quarrel with us now that Elena is gone.'

She shuddered.

'We may even be able to persuade him to lend us some people to mount a raid on Uzice, and perhaps get her out.'

'Why should he want to get her out? She is a Croat.'

'Well, maybe the past couple of months have taught him that they really are all one people.'

'So, when do we leave?'

'I would say as soon as possible.'

She released him and stretched on the grass. 'I would like to lie right here, forever.'

Temptation. 'We can't do that, Sandrine. We'd starve.'

'Can we not shoot a goat? Or kill a chicken?'

Amazingly, they were still there, clucking and pecking.

'I'm sure we can. But how can we cook the meat?'

'Do you have to have matches? Were you not a Boy Scout?'

'I'm afraid not.'

'Well, I was a Girl Guide. I know how to make a fire by rubbing two sticks together.'

'When did you do this last?'

'Oh . . . twelve years ago.'

'And then, I imagine, using appropriately carved and selected sticks, not the branches of a few stunted bushes. I think our best bet is to fill our pockets with carrots. That should keep us going for a day or two. In that time we should come across somebody.'

She gave one of her little shrieks, but this was of laughter. 'What an inane conversation, at such a time.'

He lay beside her, on his elbow. 'It made you laugh.'

'Is that important?'

'Very.'

She pushed herself up. 'Then let us gather the carrots. Oh, shit!'

Tony sat up in turn, and saw five men standing on the other side of the stream. They had come up through the burned-out village, unseen.

Sandrine reached for her tommy-gun, but Tony grasped her arm. Not only did the men have their guns levelled, but they wore Yugoslav army uniforms. And one of them . . . He scrambled to his feet. 'Svetovar!?'

'Tony? What happened here?'

'The Germans were here. They burned the village,' Tony said.

'They killed Elena?'

'No, they took her prisoner.'

Svetovar's face twisted. 'Is that not the same thing? When did this happen?'

'Last night.'

'But you survived.'

'Yes,' Tony said, looking him in the eye. 'We were lucky. They did not find us.'

'You let them take my sister. Your fiancée!' He glanced at Sandrine, who had moved closer to Tony.

'Yes,' Tony said. 'I thought it best to stay alive. That way we may be able to rescue Elena. With your help,' he added.

'Rescue her,' Svetovar said contemptuously. 'That is a dream.'

'Nonetheless, it is something I wish to discuss with General Mihailovic. Will you take us to him?'

'Mihailovic?' Svetovar's tone was more contemptuous yet, and Tony realised that as he was a Croat he would hardly be any more welcome in the Serb camp than his sister had been.

'You mean you are on your own?' He looked from Svetovar to the other four men; they were all armed with rifles and bandoliers.

'We serve the secretary-general,' Svetovar said.

'The . . .' Tony frowned. 'That sounds like a Communist official.'

'That is correct. He sent us to find out what happened here, but we heard from the last village we were in how the people were wiped out by the Ustase, and how you fought them, and destroyed them.'

'Not quite efficiently enough,' Tony confessed. He had had no idea their conflict with the Ustase was so widely known; presumably Pavelic's men had revealed what had happened.

'Nevertheless, our general wishes to speak with you.' Again his face twisted. 'He had hoped to speak with Elena as well.'

'We will certainly come with you,' Tony said. 'But let me get this straight: you are now a member of a Communist group?'

'I belong to a group dedicated to ridding Yugoslavia of the Germans. We call ourselves Partisans.'

'But your leader is a Communist.'

'Yes.'

'The Communists we met here would not fight against the Germans.'

'That is all changed now.'

'What caused this change?'

'Haven't you heard?' Svetovar was amazed. 'Germany has invaded Russia. It is our business to defeat them.'

Not for the first time in this so rapidly changing situation was Tony left utterly dumbfounded. Sandrine clapped her hands. 'Then your general will help us to free Elena.'

'We will have to see,' Svetovar said. 'Let us move out. Our camp is two days' march from here. Have you any gear?'

'What you see.'

Svetovar inspected Sandrine's tommy-gun. 'I didn't know you knew anything about guns,' he remarked.

'I have been practising.'

He looked at Tony, who waggled his eyebrows. He then turned back to Sandrine. 'This is a German weapon.'

'I took it from Pavelic.'

'The Ustase commander?'

'Yes.'

'Just like that? He did not object?'

'At the time, no. Have you any food?'

Predictably she had regained her appetite.

'Only our rations.'

'But you can kill a goat,' she said. 'You have matches?'

'Of course.'

'Then we can make a fire and cook it and have a feast. I am very hungry.'

Svetovar scratched his head, but one of his men said, 'I will do it,' and set off up the hill.

Svetovar returned to what he felt was the more important subject. 'We have heard a rumour that Bernhard has returned.'

'Yes,' Sandrine said. 'He was here last night. His men burned the village. And took Elena.'

'Bernhard? Well, then, she should be all right. They are friends.'

'Not any more,' Tony said. 'He is turning her over to the Gestapo.'

'But why?'

'In his eyes, she is guilty of murder, for killing German soldiers.'

'Then they will certainly execute her.'

'I don't think they will, immediately. They also think she knows the whereabouts of a guerilla headquarters. Probably yours. I have an idea they will interrogate her for a while.'

If only he could get Bernhard's warning out of his head – that anyone who had been interrogated by the Gestapo would never again be quite human.

'He said he was going to take her into Uzice. So we may be able to get her back,' he went on. 'If we act quickly enough. If your general will help.'

Svetovar nodded. 'I think he may well do so. We have received orders from Moscow that we must do everything we can to hurt the German war effort, and he was looking for something big to start off with. If we could mount a raid on Uzice, and take one of our people out of the hands of the

Gestapo, it would be tremendous.' He looked at Sandrine. 'And you? Is Bernhard not your fiancé?'

'Not any more,' Sandrine said. 'I am Tony's woman now.'

Svetovar looked at Tony.

'It's a long story,' Tony said. 'I think we should concentrate on getting Elena back. There is a problem. Will your general do it if he knows that Elena is a Croat?' He frowned. 'But you are a Croat yourself.'

'Of course. In our group, there are no Serbs and no Croats, no Slovenes and no Bosnians, only Yugoslavs.'

'Now there is something I have been hoping to hear since this war started,' Tony said.

'But they are all Communists,' Sandrine suggested. 'We are not Communists.'

'Our business is to beat the Germans first, and worry about our politics afterwards,' Svetovar said grandly. 'That is what Tito says. Anyway, he is a Croatian himself.'

'Tito?' Tony asked. 'His name is Tito?'

'No, no. His name is Broz. Josip Broz. But we call him Tito.'

It was mid-morning two days later before they reached the Partisan encampment. As with Mihailovic's camp, this was situated in a narrow valley, but was far better protected from the air by overhanging cliffs. It was also better guarded, by sentries who looked down on them from various vantage points, and was clearly more disciplined; the tents had been pitched in orderly rows, there was a complete absence of women or children, and although there was a flock of goats, these were under guard and prevented from straying by several obviously well-trained dogs.

Josip Broz sat outside his tent, drinking coffee. He was a big, heavy-shouldered man, ruggedly handsome in a square-jawed fashion. He exuded charisma; everything about him suggested that he was a leader of men, in a manner Mihailovic had so sadly lacked. 'An English officer!' he declared, shaking Tony's hand in a powerful grip. 'I have heard of you, Captain Davis. All Yugoslavia has heard of you.'

'That's very complimentary,' Tony said. 'I can't imagine why.' He felt distinctly inferior at that moment. His beard now stretched down to his chest, and his clothes were in tatters. Tito was both clean-shaven and well-dressed.

'Because of your attack upon Pavelic's thugs.'

'You know Pavelic?'

'We have met. The next time we do, I will kill him.'

'Me too,' Sandrine said.

She stood beside Tony, looking hardly less bedraggled.

'You are the French journalist,' Tito said.

'Yes. Am I famous too?'

Tito grinned. 'Indeed. How do you know Pavelic?'

'He raped me.'

'I see. Well, we will have to find somewhere for you to live for the time being.'

'I will stay here.'

'There are no women in this camp.'

'Then I will be unique. I *am* unique.'

Tito looked at Tony.

'She can fight as well as any man,' Tony said.

'Perhaps. But a woman—'

'I am not *a* woman,' Sandrine pointed out. 'I am *his* woman.'

Again Tito looked at Tony.

'I will be responsible for her,' Tony said. 'She has suffered a great deal, and she has killed Germans. I cannot let her go off by herself.'

Tito considered, then shrugged. 'If she stays, she is, as you say, Captain, your responsibility. But also, if she stays, she will be regarded as a man. If we suffer, she suffers. If we are overrun, she fights or dies like the rest of us. I cannot, and will not, spare one man to protect her.'

'I do not need protecting,' Sandrine said. 'Just leave me my tommy-gun.'

Tito gave a brief smile. 'You are welcome to it. Captain Dravic, will you issue Mademoiselle Fouquet with a tent.' He glanced at Tony. 'For two. And a ration card. Captain Davis, I wish to talk with you.'

Sandrine looked at Tony, who gave her a quick nod and a reassuring smile. She followed the captain out of the tent, and Tito gestured Tony to one of the folding camp chairs, then seated himself. An orderly poured them both coffee, while Tony took in his surroundings: secretaries were seated at desks within the tent, apparently busy; orderlies hurried to and fro; there was even a small hand-operated printing press, clacking away as it turned out reams of paper. Tony had to suppose this was mostly Communist propaganda.

'You are from the embassy in Belgrade,' Tito said.

'That is correct. Unfortunately, I was not at the embassy when they received orders to pull out.'

'So you have been operating on your own. Carrying on a one-man war against the Germans.'

'That's a bit of an exaggeration, Colonel Broz. I did take on Pavelic and his thugs, but that was to save my own skin. And those of my companions.'

'Have you been able to contact your erstwhile comrades?'

'I haven't had the means. I imagine I'm on the "missing, presumed dead" list.'

'We must try to remind them that you are still alive.'

'Can you do this?'

'I think so. We are in radio contact with Alexandria. I will inform them that we have found you.'

Tony remembered how Mihailovic had refused to use his radio for fear of giving away his position. But obviously a great deal had happened in the two and a half months since he had last seen Mihailovic. 'Is it important? To you?'

'Yes, Captain. It is important to me, and my people. I understand that it is impossible for us to receive any physical help from your people at this moment, at least not until Greece has been regained—'

'Say again?' Tony interrupted. 'Are you telling me that Greece has been lost?'

'Did you not know? Your British troops have been driven out and Greece has surrendered. The entire Balkans are now under Nazi control. You have also been defeated in North Africa, and there is even talk that Cairo may be indefensible. Things are very bad.'

'So it seems,' Tony agreed. 'But surely the Russians—'

'According to the German reports, the Soviet army lost well over a million men in the first week of the campaign, and casualties are continuing at a frightening rate. The Germans are confidently predicting that they will have Moscow well before the coming of winter.'

'Surely that is all propaganda.'

'It may be. However, the German claims are not at this time being denied by the Soviet government, at least as regards casualties. The only good thing that has come out of it is that your government seems prepared to help the Soviets.'

'Yes,' Tony said drily.

Tito grinned. 'You do not approve of them. Of Communism.'

'It is not my idea of what's best for the world, Colonel Broz. But, like my government, I am prepared to help anybody who will fight the Nazis.'

'Then there is no cause for a quarrel between us. I can use a man like you, Captain Davis. Svetovar Kostic tells me that you served in France.'

'Briefly. I was wounded in May last year.'

'Still, you have served. Too many of our people have not seen combat. And your credentials are enhanced by the way you took on Pavelic. I will put you on my staff. But more importantly, when we contact your people, you will tell them that we need their help. As I was saying just now, I understand that they cannot help us with men, but they can fly in munitions and arms, surely.'

'If they have any to spare,' Tony said. 'Their first business must be to defend Egypt and the Canal. After England, of course. And it appears that any surplus will be needed in Russia.'

'We will not ask for very much. We have a good opportunity here, to strike some hard blows at the Axis. The Germans attacked us with overwhelming force, and we were not well led—'

'And not all of your people were prepared to fight,' Tony could not help interjecting.

'That is true,' Tito agreed equably. 'This is not yet a nation, Captain. Perhaps this war will help to make it so. But as I was saying, having overwhelmed us with the greatest ease, the Germans now seem to regard us as a cowed and beaten people. And of course, they need most of their strength to deal with Russia. Thus the great majority of the army that invaded us has been withdrawn. We have a splendid opportunity for doing them much harm. But to do that, we need modern weapons, and ammunition. Will you help us to obtain these things?'

'Certainly,' Tony said. 'But there are a couple of points to be taken into consideration.'

'Yes?'

'Firstly, it would be more correct, and more likely to be responded to by London, if the appeal were made on the instructions of General Mihailovic.'

Tito frowned. 'Why?'

'Well . . . he is the ranking Yugoslav officer still in the field, is he not? In fact, he regards himself as the de facto government of Yugoslavia at the moment. Or has that too changed? What has happened to King Peter?'

'He escaped the country, and I believe is in England.'

'Then no doubt he has formed some sort of government-in-exile.'

'I imagine he has,' Tito said without great interest. 'It can have little effect on us here.'

'Then Mihailovic is right when he claims to be the state, here in Yugoslavia.'

'There are many people who would dispute that,' Tito said. 'It all depends on how he intends to lead. Thus far he has done very little.'

Tony nodded. 'I assume he is trying to maximise his forces.'

Tito snorted. 'That is nonsense. A guerilla war, which is what we must fight, is best carried out by small but dedicated groups. They attract less attention, can coalesce and then separate at will, and if they meet with disaster, it does not involve the whole movement. Believe me, Captain, I have experience of this.'

Tony raised his eyebrows. 'You have fought in a war?'

Tito gave a shout of laughter. 'Hasn't everyone? I began my military career in the Austrian army, in 1914. Croatia was governed by Austria then. I fought against the Russians, would you believe it? But that was Tsarist Russia. They were even worse led than were we. But by their very numbers they gained some victories. In one of those I was taken prisoner. I spent some years in a Russian prison camp. That, my friend, is not an experience you ever wish to suffer. I was still there in November 1917. The Bolsheviks let us out, but there was nowhere to go. So I joined the Revolution. It was that or starve, eh? Besides, I had read some of Lenin's work – it was freely distributed in our camp – and I understood that his was the way of the future. The only way.'

'It's a point of view,' Tony murmured.

Tito did not take offence. Instead he grinned. 'One with which you do not agree. It is something we must argue, when we have the time.'

'And that was your war.'

'That was only the beginning. I fought in the Great Civil War – now that *was* a war. I must have pleased my employers, because then I was sent back here to organise the Yugoslav Communist Party.'

'And got yourself outlawed.'

'That would have happened anyway, given the characters of men like King Alexander and Prince Paul.'

'You approve of Alexander's assassination?'

Tito shrugged. 'Perhaps that too was inevitable. I do not approve of the men who did it, who would have us submit to rule by Fascist Italy. But there was nothing I could do about it, save keep the party in being as best I could, and wait. I knew my time would come. So did Moscow. But they wanted me to keep my hand in. So they sent me off to another war. I fought for the Republicans in Spain.'

'And got beaten.'

'The odds were too great on Franco's side. He had half a million Italian soldiers fighting for him. We had the International Brigade. Do not misunderstand me. They were brave men. Many of them were British. They fought well. But they were idealists, not professional soldiers. And they were too few. So we were beaten. Now I am being given the opportunity to fight Fascism again. This time we will not be beaten.'

'Despite German claims?'

Tito grinned. 'Despite.'

'And you will begin with an attack on Uzice? It is important to act very quickly.'

'In the hopes that the Kostic woman may still be alive? If she is not, we can at least avenge her.'

Tony swallowed. However well known she might have become, Elena was obviously just a name, and a statistic, to this man. It was even possible that he might welcome her death, as providing him with a martyr.

'She is a very close friend,' he said.

Tito raised his eyebrows.

'We were engaged to be married,' Tony explained.

'You said the Frenchwoman was your woman,' Tito pointed out.

'Situations change. Especially when you are a group on the run, seeking what shelter you can find.'

Tito stroked his chin.

'The point is,' Tony went on, 'Elena sacrificed herself because she believes she is still my fiancée. I cannot let her down.'

'I wonder if you are not something of a scoundrel, Captain Davis,' Tito mused. 'But also a brave man. And, I suspect, a ruthless one. Those are all qualities I can use. I would like you to fight with us.' He gave Tony a quick grin. 'I will not even thrust Communism down your throat. But there are rules you must obey. Only two.'

Tony waited.

'The first is that if you join my command, you place yourself under my orders, totally and without exception.' Another quick grin. 'I promise you that I will accept your advice, where it is relevant, and even bow to your superior military training . . . where it is relevant.'

'I accept that,' Tony said.

'The second rule is that your relationship with these women you have accumulated must be an entirely personal matter. I am already breaking one of my own rules by permitting the Frenchwoman to remain and to share your tent. I am doing this because I am beginning to realise that it is not possible to keep a force like this in being without some access to feminine companionship. Your Frenchwoman will be a test case, eh? You tell me this woman can fight with men. I look forward to seeing her do this. Women, if they can fight, may well prove to be a valuable recruiting base. But as I have said, they must take their chances and share the hardships. However, in this test case, I must warn you: should your friend reveal the slightest indication of promiscuity, she will be expelled. Do you understand this?'

'Yes,' Tony said. 'And if she is subjected to promiscuity she does not wish?'

'You will report any such incident to me, and I will deal with it.'

'That is fair enough.'

'Equally, however, supposing we manage to regain Miss Kostic, it will be your business to arrange your private life in an acceptable manner. By that I mean that it will not be acceptable for you to share your tent with two women. One of them will have to go, either away from my group, or into the tent of another man in my group. Do you understand *this*?'

Tony swallowed. But that was a bridge he would have to cross when he came to it. 'I understand.'

'Very good. Now, I understand how anxious you are to attack Uzice. I am equally anxious. However, Uzice is a sizeable town and is strongly occupied by the Germans, not to mention units of the Ustase – and of course, that Gestapo detachment you overheard mentioned. It is not a place we can simply walk into, shoot up, extract Miss Kostic, and leave again. It will take careful planning, and as many men as we can muster. I will send some of my people to infiltrate the town and bring us back some positive information as to the situation there.'

'That is brilliant,' Tony said. 'But isn't it very dangerous?'

'So is fighting a war. I have also sent a message to General Mihailovic, inviting him to a meeting so that we may unite our forces for this operation.'

'Will he come? My impression was that he is hostile to both Croats and Communists.'

'He will come. Only about half of my people are Croats, and only about half are Communists. But I command several hundred men.' A grin. 'And one woman, to be sure. This is a sizeable force. United with Mihailovic's command, we can call ourselves an army. This is an opportunity for success, and glory, and international recognition; he will be unable to resist.'

'He will require you to serve under him.'

'I will accept that. At least for this operation. As I have said, much will depend on how well he leads. Now, I know you have had a tiring few days. Take the rest of today off. I have requested the meeting for noon tomorrow.'

'Tomorrow? But . . . by then Elena will have been in the hands of the Gestapo for four days.'

Tito nodded. 'That is regrettable. On the other hand, if they were going to kill her, they would probably have done so within twenty-four hours – in which case we would be too late anyway. If they did not do so, well, then, an extra day or so will not matter. She will still be alive.'

'Because she will still be being tortured.'

'Sadly, that is probably correct. But . . . she is, or was, your fiancée. If she was worthy of that honour, do you not suppose she will be able to withstand torture?'

'Does anyone truly withstand torture?' Tony asked. 'Even if they survive?'

Tito regarded him for several seconds. Then he said, 'You are tired, and dispirited. I am giving you an order. Go to your tent and rest, with your other woman. And then spruce yourself up. Apply to Captain Dravic, my adjutant, for some clean clothes and a razor. Get rid of that beard. I want you looking your best when we meet Mihailovic.'

'If you think it is a good idea to take me along. I imagine General Mihailovic considers me to be a deserter.'

'You are now a member of my staff, Captain.'

One of the sentries showed Tony to the tent he had been allocated. On his walk through the camp he was again impressed, by several factors. In addition to the obviously carefully chosen overhanging cliffs which made it difficult to be found by aircraft, such fires as there were were carefully controlled, so that any smoke was confined to wisps which dissipated long before they rose above the level of the surrounding hills. A further indication of Tito's caution was

his decision not to invite Milhailovic into his headquarters –
where he would be able to see just what he commanded and
how – but to meet some distance away.

Then the camp itself was clearly a military establishment
rather than an accumulation of refugees. The absence of
women and children helped to create this impression, and
the animals were strictly controlled; the only dogs were
those on shepherd duty. The men, if not all uniformed,
were all well armed, and appeared to be spending most
of their time cleaning their weapons instead of aimlessly
sitting around. Some were gathered in groups being lectured
by officers; there was no way of knowing whether these
were attempts to instil military knowledge and discipline
or merely Communist ideology, but they created a strong
sense of purpose which had been entirely lacking in his first
contacts with the resistance. Of course, Tony understood
that he had seen Mihailovic's people at their worst, in the
immediate aftermath of the invasion and their hasty flight,
but he wondered if things had improved over the past couple
of months.

Sandrine was already at work making the interior of the
tent habitable. 'Well?' she asked.

'We are welcome. So long as we obey certain rules.'

'You mean we are not allowed to sleep together?'

He hugged her. 'Oh, we may sleep together. But if you so
much as wink at another man, you're out.'

'As if I would do such a thing. What about if he winks
at me?'

'He gets his come-uppance. That's official.'

'And the other rules?'

'Just one. I can only have one of you. So, when Elena is
rescued . . .'

'Yes?' Her tone was watchful.

'I am going to have to sort something out.'

'Such as?'

'Well . . . like telling her it's over between us. I didn't

want to have to do that until I could at least reunite her with her family . . .'

'She will be reunited with Svetovar.'

'Thank God for Svetovar. Now, how would you like to get cleaned up?'

She gave one of her shrieks. 'A hot bath?'

'Ah . . . I'm not sure that's on. But we can obtain clean clothing and' – he stroked his beard – 'I'm required to shave. I was getting used to the fungus.'

They went in search of Captain Dravic. The only clothes he had were blouses and shirts and pants, but these came in all sizes, and some were even small enough to fit Sandrine. She was also given a sidecap, which sat neatly on her yellow hair.

'I have never worn pants before,' she said, walking up and down in front of him. 'How do I look?'

'Magnificent.'

Tony was also equipped, and shaved, and then they joined Tito and the officers for lunch. In the strongest contrast to the general air of gloom and despondency that had pervaded Mihailovic's camp, this was a very jolly affair, and the officers treated Sandrine with the utmost gallantry.

After the meal they lay in each other's arms in the privacy of their tent.

'I am happy,' Sandrine said. 'I did not think I would ever be happy again. But you are not happy, Tony.'

'I will be.'

'After we have attacked Uzice?'

'Yes.'

'Because you love her still.'

'Oh . . . shit. Do you not think it is possible for a man to love two women at the same time?'

'Of course. I have always wanted to belong to a *ménage à trois*.'

'But Tito wouldn't permit it.'

'We shall have to work something out.' She was silent

for a few moments, then she said, 'I love Elena too, you know.'

'I know,' he said.

'We should have died with her. At least we would have taken that bastard Bernhard with us.'

'Would you really like to be dead?'

She nestled against him. 'No.' She was silent for a little while, then she asked, 'Am I coming with you to see Mihailovic?'

'That's not Tito's idea.'

'You will leave me here, alone, with all of these men?'

'They are not going to touch you.'

'I hope you are right,' she remarked. 'Well . . . hurry back.'

'I shall.'

She hugged him. 'Do you trust this man Tito?'

'Right this moment, we don't have any option other than to trust him. Keep your fingers crossed.'

Waiting for them in a small grove of trees a few miles from the Partisan camp were Mihailovic, Zardov and Vidmar, and several other officers Tony remembered, but not, he was relieved to discover, Matovic. Yet their greeting was frosty enough.

'That man,' Mihailovic said, 'is a deserter.'

'He did that to fight the Ustase,' Tito pointed out, 'which is more than any of us have managed to achieve thus far.'

'The Ustase are acting only against Communist elements,' Vidmar remarked.

Tito surveyed him with a cool gaze. 'They are acting against Yugoslavia, Colonel. However, it is time for us all to commence hostilities. I have called this meeting so that we may coordinate our forces to attack Uzice.'

'To do *what*?' Mihailovic was aghast.

'One of my people is being held in Uzice,' Tito explained. 'But that is not the real reason for the attack. It is an important town, a rail centre, and a German headquarters. If we can carry out a successful raid, it will be an enormous propaganda coup.'

'There is a German garrison in Uzice,' Zardov pointed out quietly.

'If there was not, there would be no point in attacking it.'

'The idea is madness,' Mihailovic said. 'You are asking me to use my men on some kind of suicide assault on a strongly held German position—'

'They would be acting in concert with *my* men,' Tito reminded him.

'Your men?' Mihailovic looked past him. Tito had brought only four aides to the meeting, one of whom was Tony.

'I have nine hundred men at my call,' Tito said.

'And where are these nine hundred men?'

'Some of them are overlooking you at this minute.'

The Serbs looked left and right at the surrounding hills.

'Just what do you mean by that?' Zardov inquired.

'I am a man who takes precautions,' Tito said. 'Now, I understand that you command two thousand men, General. Between us we have an army.'

'Which you propose to sacrifice. Do you have any idea of the casualties we would suffer?'

'Casualties are an inescapable concomitant of warfare, General. It must be our business to inflict more serious losses on the Germans, in matériel as well as men.'

'And what about when the Germans retaliate? Have you considered the number of innocent people they will shoot?'

'Those are actions – crimes – for which they will have to answer after we have won the War.'

'And if we do not win the War?'

'That, General Mihailovic, is very close to treason.'

The two men glared at each other, and Tony was rather glad that they were being overlooked by Tito's men.

Then Mihailovic said, 'As I am commanding general of the Yugoslav forces still in the field, and as such am de facto ruler of Yugoslavia, I will decide, Colonel Broz, what is treason and what is not. I consider your plan to be ill-advised, hare-brained, of no value to our cause, likely to incur unacceptable casualties to our forces, and certain to bring disastrous results to our people. Nor do I see how an attack upon a single town can in any way help the general war against the Nazis.'

Tito was obviously keeping his temper with considerable difficulty. 'Even if our attack upon Uzice is unsuccessful, General, if as a result of it the Germans bring one division back from the Russian front to bolster their hold on Yugoslavia, we will have won a signal victory.'

'Oh, yes,' Mihailovic sneered. 'Now we are at the truth of the matter. The Russian front. You are acting on orders from Moscow. Well, I will tell you this, Colonel Broz: I will not sacrifice a single man of my command to help the Russians. Your friend Stalin has made his own bed by murder and treachery. He must now lie on it.'

'You refuse to commit any of your forces to an attack upon Uzice,' Tito said, appearing to wish to get his facts completely straight.

'That is correct. What is more, as your commanding officer, I forbid you to undertake such a senseless plan.'

Tito stood up, and bowed. 'Then I will bid you good day, General.'

He led his men away from the trees.

Tony walked at his shoulder. 'There's a put-down. What do we do now?'

Tito glanced at him. 'Do you think I would accept orders from a traitor like that? We will carry out the attack on our own.'

Chapter Ten

Counter-Stroke

Tony looked at Tito in a mixture of admiration and consternation. 'You said we did not have enough men to go in on our own.'

Tito grinned. 'I have never met an army commander who did not wish for more men. The Germans are saying they have invaded Russia with three million men. Let us suppose they are telling the truth. I will still bet you anything that Rundstedt, or whoever is in overall command, is telling his aides he wishes he had another million.'

'But have we sufficient to do the job?'

'We will have to make sure of it.'

'And when will you mount the assault?'

'Tonight. At least, we will move out tonight to take up our positions.'

Again Tony glanced at him in amazement.

'This is necessary,' Tito said. 'Now that Mihailovic knows that I and my people are in this neighbourhood, he will make every effort to find out where we are. He may even warn the Germans of our presence.'

'You think he is that much of a traitor?'

'Whether one goes down in history as a traitor depends on whether one wins the war. Besides, did he not himself say that he would decide what was treachery and what was not?'

'If you carry out a successful raid on Uzice, will this not cause a split between you?'

Tito grinned. 'There already is a split between us, Captain Davis. We have different aims. Mihailovic dreams of a restoration of the status quo ante: the monarch on the throne, Yugoslavia once again ruled by the bureaucrats in Belgrade.'

'And what do you dream of, Colonel?'

Tito gave a shout of laughter. 'Not that, to be sure. A restoration of the status quo ante would mean that I and my people would again be outlaws. As to what we would like to see . . . Let us win the War first, eh?'

The spies had returned from Uzice. They spread a plan of the town and a map of its surrounding area on the table in Tito's tent. 'The garrison headquarters is here, the barracks behind. You will see that there is a wall, Colonel, and an iron gate. This is guarded.'

'How many men?'

'Officially, one regiment. But there are absentees, men on leave, sick, and so on. I do not think they muster more than five hundred fit for combat.'

'Panzers?'

'No panzers, sir.'

'What of the Ustase people?'

'There is a Ustase headquarters – here – but as far as we were able to ascertain, it is only occupied by half a dozen people at this time.'

'Pavelic?'

'He is not there.'

'That is a pity. As I said, gentlemen,' Tito observed, 'they regard us as beaten. But I assume there are patrols?'

'Only occasional. They are relying upon the local police to keep order in the town.'

'You mean the town's approaches are not guarded?' Tony could not believe his ears.

'Not by patrols. But there is an outpost, here' – the man stabbed the map – 'on this hillock. It is, you see, half a mile from the town itself. It is manned by a dozen men with two heavy machine-guns. It has a telephone connection to the town.'

Tito nodded. 'And the Gestapo headquarters? This is inside the barracks?'

'No, sir. The Gestapo headquarters is here.' He prodded the street plan. 'You will see it is two blocks from the barracks. It is a private house which has been taken over.'

'How many personnel?'

'A dozen men and four women. But the house is guarded by men from the garrison.'

Tony drew a deep breath. 'And have they any prisoners in the house?'

'Oh yes, sir. Several people have been arrested and taken into the house.'

'And have they been seen again?'

'Three people were hanged in the square, the day before yesterday.'

Tony felt quite sick. 'Was any of them a woman?'

'Yes, sir. One was a woman.'

The sickness grew. 'A tall, dark-haired woman, very pretty?'

The man frowned. 'No, sir. The woman was fair-haired.'

Tony's breath came out in a gush of relief. Tito slapped him on the shoulder. 'We will get her out.'

'Unless she has already been executed in secret.'

'The Gestapo do not execute people in secret,' Tito said. 'They do it with the maximum publicity, because they believe that this spreads terror, and that terror breeds obedience. Now here is what we are going to do. Timing is the essence of this operation. We will move out tonight, and reach our positions within five miles of Uzice by dawn tomorrow. We will lie up for the day, and carry out the assault tomorrow night. Our forlorn hope, commanded by you, Captain Maric, will be in position by ten thirty, here.' He indicated the map. 'The rest of us will be in position by eleven thirty. At eleven forty-five,

Maric, you will cut the telephone line to the outpost. At eleven fifty, Captain Asztalos, you will assault and destroy the outpost on the hill. You will have a hundred men. If it is practical for you to remove the machine-guns, you will do so. If not, you will destroy them.'

Asztalos nodded.

'At this same time,' Tito said, 'I will lead the main body into the town. Once we are in the town, you, Captain Fuderer will take your sixty men and destroy the railway station. You will also destroy any trains you find there and tear up as much track as you can. After half an hour you will withdraw. You, Captain Milic, will take your twenty men to assault and destroy the Ustase headquarters. You will take no prisoners. You, Captain Davis, will take your forty men and attack the Gestapo headquarters. You will free and remove any prisoners you find there, and kill all the inmates, without exception. Again, there are to be no prisoners. You will then withdraw. Understood?'

The officers nodded; Tony swallowed. According to the spies, there were four women on the Gestapo staff. He had never killed a woman in his life. He had never even fired at one. But probably they did not sleep at the headquarters, he reflected, and would be in their own billets or out on the town when the assault took place.

'Very good, gentlemen,' Tito said. 'Join your men. Tell them what they have to do, and prepare them to move out. Synchronise. The time is fourteen minutes past six.'

The officers checked and, where necessary, adjusted their watches.

'Take your maps and street plans,' Tito said. He had had his printing press run off sufficient copies of each. 'Move out at eight o'clock. When the operation is completed, we will rendezvous here, but as we must expect German retaliation, we shall then withdraw further into the hills. However, we shall retreat across country, and this is something the Nazis cannot do. It is only their aircraft that concern us. In any event, I shall not see you again until we return here in three days' time. So I shall wish you good fortune now.'

He shook hands with each of them in turn.

'Tony!'

Tony, on his way back to his tent, turned to look at Svetovar Kostic.

'I have been given permission to accompany your force,' Svetovar said. 'If you will have me.'

'It will be a pleasure. But . . . you know I am to assault the Gestapo headquarters?'

'That is why I wish to come with you.'

'You understand . . . well . . . what we find there may not be acceptable.'

'I understand. I wish to be there. Can *you* understand?'

'Yes.' Tony clasped his hand. 'Welcome aboard. We leave in an hour and a half.'

'I am so excited,' Sandrine confessed as they watched the dawn rising out of the east.

They had walked all night to reach the position allotted to them, and now, forty strong, were crouched in a hollow. In front of them low hills continued to undulate; they could not yet see Uzice. Immediately beneath them a road wound its way through the valleys, but this early in the morning there was no traffic. The men sprawled on the ground, content to rest after their long march, and content too to leave their fates in the hands of their officer, who, however foreign, was one of the very few of them who had actually seen action in this war; the story of how he had broken out of the Ustase camp, and virtually destroyed it in doing so, had been passed from man to man through the Partisan force.

Sandrine squeezed his hand.

'You know that some of us are going to be killed,' he reminded her.

'Is there a better way to die than fighting, shoulder to shoulder?'

'No, I don't think there is.'

She kissed him. 'But *we* are not going to be killed. We are going to survive, and live forever. With Elena.'

'Tito might have something to say about that.'

'Fuck Tito. Actually, that might be rather fun. But let him make his rules. We shall obey them until the War is over, and then . . . Do you know what? I shall take up wearing trousers permanently. I like the feel of them against my legs.'

Tony thought she might do very well. In the strangest way, in her pants and blouse and sidecap she was even more feminine than in a dress, and certainly much more attractive than in one of those shapeless ankle-length Serb gowns.

'You'd better get some sleep,' he recommended. 'It's going to be a long night.'

He even dozed himself, but awoke regularly, his nerves taut; once he saw a German convoy on the road beneath their position. In real terms, this was a weakness in the German situation. Their army was heavily mechanised, as Tito had said, and while this gave them tremendous power of speed and movement, without their panzers this movement could only be along roads, and thus in clearly calculable directions.

But they still represented the most formidable fighting force the world had yet seen. And they were about to be defied by a relative handful of men, and one woman, armed only with rifles, tommy-guns and hand grenades.

Tony was not aware of fear, except of what he might find in the Gestapo headquarters. He knew they would have the advantage of complete surprise, in that the enemy would not have the slightest suspicion that there was an armed force so close to them, virtually surrounding them. Rather, Tony felt a sense of exhilaration because they would be going into battle aggressively instead of defensively, even if it would be only a raid followed by a precipitate retreat. If they could carry out their several objectives they would nonetheless have scored a victory.

Sandrine woke up. 'Do you think Bernhard will be there?' she asked. 'I hope he is. I want to kill him.'

Tony squeezed her hand.

The group became tense as the evening drew in. Weapons were checked again and again, and there was much chaff, not all of it good-natured. At nine o'clock it was still quite bright, certainly too bright for any large body of men to approach the town. The men grew restless. Most were standing up and walking to and fro, looking anxiously at their commanding officer; although nearly all of them wore watches, they knew it was his which mattered. Tony felt just as eager as his men; the hands of his watch barely seemed to be moving. But at last it was five minutes to ten.

'Prepare to move out,' he said quietly, and waited for them to form up, going on sound, as it was now quite dark. 'Move out.'

He had spent some of the day memorising his map as well as the town plan, and struck out confidently across the rolling countryside. This presented no great difficulty, but he needed to bear in mind that they had only an hour and a half to cross five miles, and could not afford to slow down.

At twenty to midnight they descended the last hillside and looked down on the lights of Uzice, only half a mile away. The only glow was that of streetlights and the occasional building. Still there was no suggestion that anyone in the town had the slightest idea of what was about to descend on them. There was little wind, and almost no sound. It was equally impossible to believe that there were 900 men crouching in these hills, with murder and mayhem in their hearts.

Again the hands of his watch seemed to move with interminable slowness. But finally they reached five to midnight.

'Check your weapons,' Tony said.

He was surrounded by clicks, and Sandrine gave a last squeeze of his arm.

'Thirty seconds!'

The night was split apart by a huge outburst of firing to their right. Asztalos was attacking the outpost.

Tony stood up. 'Let's go. At the double, but keep it steady.'

They trotted down the hill, and reached the road. They crossed this and approached the houses from the appointed side. Before they gained them they heard more gunfire from in front of them, and the wail of a siren. Dogs began barking, and people began shouting and screaming. Heads poked out of windows as they ran up their chosen alley.

'Get inside,' Tony shouted at them. 'Take cover!'

They reached a main street, and were confronted by a policeman riding a bicycle. He dismounted. 'Who are you?' he demanded. 'What are you doing?'

'We are Partisans,' Tony told him. 'Take cover.'

The policeman gaped at them, and reached for the pistol on his belt. One of the squad cut him down with a single shot, then they were all leaping over him and the fallen bicycle and running along the street.

Now the firing was all around them, and general. The alarm was still wailing, and various whistles were being blown. Shutters banged as people began taking shelter.

They heard the deeper thuds of grenades, and a moment later crossed the head of the street at the far end of which was the German barracks and headquarters. There was a considerable battle going on down there, men shouting, grenades exploding, rifles and tommy-guns firing; as far as Tony could judge, Tito had not yet broken through the gates. But that was not his immediate concern. He pointed, and his men followed him down a side street; they emerged in front of the Gestapo headquarters.

As he had been warned, there were four guards outside the building. Their presence helped him to identify it; as it was after dark, there was no flag. The sentries were obviously very agitated by what they could hear happening to every side, but were maintaining their position with commendable discipline. Now they stared through the darkness at the approaching people, able to make out that there was a considerable number but not that they were armed.

One stepped forward. 'Halt there!' he shouted. 'Or we will fire into you.'

In reply, and without waiting for the command, the Partisans opened fire. The soldiers were scattered across the ground; only one or two managed to fire their own weapons, and the shots went wild.

Tony led the rush across the small square and up the steps of the building, aware that Sandrine and Svetovar were immediately behind him. Someone opened the front door to look out, saw the armed people charging at him, and hastily closed the door again. Tony fired a burst from his tommy-gun into the panelling before any bolts could be shut, and then hurled the door open, jumping over the dying man inside.

He had turned on the hall light, and Tony looked down a corridor with several doors opening off it; on the right-hand wall there was a staircase going up. This had a landing, and on the landing there now appeared a woman, still pulling her dressing gown over her nightgown. She was in her thirties, Tony estimated, and wore her blonde hair in two plaits.

'Shit!' he muttered, but before he could make up his mind what to do there was a burst from the tommy-gun beside him. The front of the woman's nightdress exploded into red, and she came tumbling down the stairs, arms and legs flailing.

He looked at Svetovar.

'No prisoners,' Svetovar reminded him.

A shot rang out, and one of the men behind him gave a gasp and fell to his knees. The man who had fired the shot appeared briefly on the landing and then disappeared again, followed by a hail of bullets.

Tony pulled himself together. 'Sergeant Pilnic,' he snapped, 'take half your men and clear out the top. Use grenades.'

'Sir!' Pilnic waved his hand and his men followed him up the stairs.

'Clear each room down here,' Tony told the rest of his people, himself kicking in the first door. This room was empty, but there were two men and a woman in the next, behind a locked door. This was knocked in, and the people inside backed against the wall, hands held high.

'Hold your fire!' Tony shouted.

The three of them gasped in relief.

'You!' He pointed at the woman. Like the men, she wore what he presumed was a uniform: white skirt and black blouse, with black tie, stockings and low-heeled shoes. She was a small, neat woman with dark hair, and she actually looked less afraid than her two companions. 'You have prisoners here.'

She hesitated, and Svetovar stepped up to her and jammed his tommy-gun into her stomach. 'Speak, or die.'

The woman gasped. Now she glanced left and right at her companions, and licked her lips. 'Yes, there are prisoners here,' she said in Serbo-Croat.

'Where?' Tony asked.

Another quick glance at her companions, but Svetovar was again driving his gun muzzle into her stomach, and her face twisted with pain. 'Downstairs.'

'Right,' Tony said. 'Show us.'

Svetovar grasped her shoulder and thrust her into the hall. Firing continued all around them; upstairs was a mass of explosions, and Tony could now smell smoke. The Partisans had broken into the room next door, and two dead bodies lay on the floor. When Tony saw them he remembered the two living bodies he had just left behind.

'Dispose of those men,' Tony snapped over his shoulder.

'No,' the woman gasped. 'Please!'

'Shut up,' Svetovar told her, and thrust her at the stairs

239

leading down. She stumbled on to them, but it was dark, and she tripped and landed on her hands and knees at the bottom. Following her down, Tony swept his hand over the wall and found the light switch; the upstairs lights were still on. Now the naked bulb glowed, and he looked past the woman. They were in a small lobby, off which opened three doors.

She raised her head to point, then buried it in her arms again. Tony kicked the door she had indicated, sent it swinging in, and followed it, tommy-gun thrust forward. There were three men in the room. They were naked, and were suspended from hooks in the ceiling by ropes round their wrists. Their bodies were a mass of red weals. But they were alive, their eyes opening and their muscles twitching as they tried to understand what was going on around them.

'Take them down,' Tony commanded. 'Get them out of here.' He turned back to the woman. 'There was a woman,' he snapped. 'Tell me where she is.'

The woman raised her head again, and encountered the muzzle of Sandrine's tommy-gun. She gasped again at the pain. 'Upstairs,' she said.

'Where upstairs?'

She drew a deep breath. 'In the commandant's bed.'

'Shit!' he said. From both the noise and the smell there could be no doubt that the upper floors of the building were well alight.

'She goes there?' Sandrine asked.

'He makes her,' the woman panted. 'He makes her every night.'

'Bitch,' Sandrine said, and shot her through the head.

Blood flew, but Tony was already pushing past her and through his men to run back up the stairs, where he saw the rest of his men. Sergeant Pilnic was holding Elena in his arms. She was naked, but did not appear to be seriously harmed.

'Elena!' Sandrine shrieked, running forward to throw both

240

arms round her friend and the sergeant, tommy-gun and
all.

'Sandrine!' Elena kissed her and looked past her at Tony.
'I knew you would come.'

Tony replaced Sandrine to embrace her and remove her
from the sergeant's grasp. 'Are you all right?'

'Now that you are here.'

'Elena!' It was Svetovar's turn to embrace his sister. 'What
did they do to you?'

'This is not the time,' Elena said.

'Sir,' Pilnic said to Tony, 'we must get out. This house is
burning.'

The heat was intense, and smoke was starting to drift
down the staircase; they could hear the crashes of collapsing
timbers.

Tony looked at the cellar staircase, where the three other
prisoners were being brought up; they could barely stand.
'Find something for these people to wear,' he said.

'Here,' called one of the Partisans.

Just inside the front door, and swept aside by the initial
rush, there was a stand, on which there were several caps and
greatcoats. The coats were handed out, and wrapped around
Elena and the three other prisoners.

'A weapon,' Elena said. 'I must have a weapon.'

One of the Partisans gave her a pistol he had taken from
a dead German.

Tony opened the front door and stepped outside. They
had not been inside the Gestapo headquarters for more
than fifteen minutes, but the sounds of conflict had deep-
ened, with heavy firing coming from the barracks on their
right. Some people were now on the streets, either unable
to suppress their curiosity or determined to get into the
fight.

It was, however, obvious that Tito and the main body were
having a harder time of it than they had expected.

'Sergeant Pilnic,' Tony said, 'take six men and the captives and get out of town. Make for the rendezvous. You go with them, Sandrine.'

'No,' Sandrine said. 'I came here to kill Germans.'

'You've already done that.'

'Not enough. I am staying with you.'

Tony looked above her at Elena.

'I am staying too,' Elena said. 'I have not killed anyone yet.'

'The commandant . . .'

'The sergeant shot him.'

Tony looked at Pilnic, who waggled his eyebrows.

'Very well, Sergeant, take four men and those three and get out of town. The rest of you—'

A shot rang out, followed by a fusillade. Three men fell. The others thrust their way back inside the burning building, coughing in the smoke.

'What the shit . . . ?' Elena gasped.

'You in there!' a voice shouted.

'Bernhard!' Sandrine breathed.

'We have this street blocked,' Bernhard shouted. 'You cannot escape. Throw down your weapons and come out.'

'Where did he come from?' Svetovar asked.

'The important thing is that he is here,' Tony said. He tried to think. The German force could only have broken out of the barracks, which meant that things were really not going well. But what sort of a force was it? He still commanded nearly forty men . . . and two women.

And they could not stay where they were. Everyone was now coughing, including himself.

'We must charge those men,' he said.

'But . . . if they have machine-guns . . .' Pilnic said.

'If they had a machine-gun, Sergeant, they would be using it. Our business is to get through them before they can bring one up. Everyone ready?'

The men looked anxious, but determined enough. The two women merely looked determined.

'Right. As you come out, move out of the line of fire, but keep shooting.'

'Those civilians . . .' someone said.

'If they have any sense, they'll get out of sight as soon as the shooting starts. If they don't, they'll have to take their chances. Now remember, get out of the direct line of fire, but keep shooting and keep advancing as fast as you can. There can't be more than a dozen of them. Once we are through, rally on my whistle.' He turned to the women. 'Can you manage in bare feet?' he asked Elena.

'I can manage.'

'Then both of you stay behind me.'

'You in there!' Bernhard shouted again. 'I will give you ten seconds to surrender, then I will open fire.'

Tony drew a deep breath. 'Let's go.'

He threw the front door open and ran down the steps, immediately moving to his left, as he did so firing at the cluster of figures he could see occupying the centre of the street about a hundred yards away; he could only pray that they were Germans and not innocent bystanders.

They were Germans, and they immediately returned fire. But they were scattering themselves, as they had obviously not realised just how large a force had been inside the headquarters. Several fell, but then Tony knew some of his own people had been hit as well. He went down himself, but felt no immediate pain, and thought he must have slipped on the cobbles.

Elena held his arm and helped him back up. Sandrine had also fallen, but from the stream of 'shits' Tony reckoned she was not badly hurt either. Now she shouted, 'Bernhard! Where are you, you bastard?'

They reached the German position, stumbling over dead and dying bodies. There was still firing all around them, and Tony went down again. This time he had felt the impact, and knew he had been hit. And suddenly Bernhard was standing above him, uniform as resplendent as ever.

'You,' he said. 'I might have known it would be you.' His gaze moved to Sandrine, who was being helped up by Elena. 'And you. What a jolly reunion. You are under arrest.'

Tony tried to assess the situation. Bernhard had several men at his back, and his own people seemed to have dissipated to either side, into the flickering light and dark of the flames which were now all around them. And he was hit; he could feel the blood dribbling down his leg, and now the pain had started. But to surrender . . . His hand, still holding his pistol, twitched.

'Move, and I will kill you,' Bernhard said, and waved his men forward.

'Bastard!' Sandrine yelled at him.

Bernhard looked at her. 'I am going to make you scream,' he said.

'In hell,' Sandrine told him, and brought up her tommy-gun, which he had not previously noticed in the gloom.

Bernhard squeezed his trigger, but Elena threw herself forward in front of her friend, giving a gasp as the bullet struck her. Then Sandrine was firing past her and over her as she fell. Her bullets seared into Bernhard's body, and then into the men behind him. Tony got his gun up and resumed firing, and now they were joined by Svetovar, who had returned to see what had happened to them.

'The road is clear,' Svetovar said.

'Elena!' Sandrine cried.

They both knelt beside her.

'Shit!' Sandrine commented.

Tony pushed himself up and crawled to where Elena lay. Her eyes were shut, but now they opened; even in the darkness he could make out the huge red stain on her chest.

'Get out,' she whispered. 'Get out.'

'We will take you with us,' Sandrine said.

'I'm dying,' Elena said. 'Get out.'

'You saved my life,' Sandrine told her.

'So what's new?' Elena asked. 'Listen, take care of Tony.'
Her eyes flopped shut again.

Tears streamed down Sandrine's face, and she lowered her
head to kiss Elena on the forehead.

Tony could do nothing but bite his lip against the pain
in his leg.

'She's right,' Svetovar said. 'We should go while we
can.'

'You'd better leave me too,' Tony said.

'Leave you?' Sandrine asked. 'You are mine. We go
together or we stay together.' She put her arm round him
to help him to his good leg.

At that moment Bernhard tried to sit up. His tunic was
a tattered, blood-stained mess, but he still held his pistol.
'Whore!' he muttered, and levelled the gun.

'Bastard!' Sandrine replied, and shot him in the groin.
And again.

'I thought we had lost you,' Tito said, sitting beside Tony,
who lay in an improvised stretcher put together by his men.

'We were delayed,' Tony said. 'But you . . . the assault?'
A large number of their men had made the assembly point,
and were grouped around.

'It was a triumph,' Tito said. 'Heavier than we expected,
certainly, but the better for that. The railway line was
destroyed, several engines wrecked, both the Gestapo and
the Ustase headquarters burned, the army headquarters damaged, and at least a hundred of the enemy dead. We lost
twenty men.'

'And one woman,' Sandrine said.

Tito looked across the stretcher at her. 'I am sorry about
that. But she died well, I understand.'

'She died saving my life.'

He nodded. 'She will be remembered. And she took part
in a great and glorious operation, one which will resound our
fame around the world.' He grinned. 'And it is one in the

eye for Mihailovic, eh? Now, we must move out, into the mountains. The Germans are temporarily stunned, but they will recover quickly, and seek vengeance. I'm afraid we have an arduous time ahead of us, Captain Davis. But we will take you to safety.'

'I will care for him,' Sandrine said.

Tito looked at her again. 'Yes,' he said. 'I believe you will. And when we get to a safe position . . . Why, do you know, Captain, we have been in touch with Alexandria, and they are prepared to send a light aircraft to take you out.'

Tony gazed at him for a moment, and then looked at Sandrine.

Sandrine licked her lips.

'Will you tell me something, Colonel?' Tony asked.

'If I can.'

'Am I going to recover from this wound?'

'Oh, yes. Now that our surgeon has got the bullet out, he says you will make a full recovery.'

'Then, with your permission, sir, I would like to stay and fight with you. If you will have me. I can be your liaison officer with the British, as you wanted.'

'If I will have you? There is no one I would rather have. But . . . this war is only just beginning. And we have had it relatively easy here. The time ahead is going to be very rough. You must be sure you wish to stay.'

'I am sure, Colonel.'

'Well . . .' Tito looked at Sandrine.

'I am to look after him,' Sandrine said.